Hidden.

George John Kingsnorth

Gullion Media Limited

Published by Gullion Media Limited 2010

This paperback edition published in 2010 by
Gullion Media Limited, c/o 11 Slieve Crescent, Dromintee,
Newry, Co. Down, BT35 8UF, Northern Ireland.

First published in UK by Gullion Media Limited, 2010.

Final Proof Reader: Helen Murray

A CIP catalogue record for this book is
available from the British Library

ISBN 978-0-9560403-1-2

Scripture quotations taken from The Holy Bible,
New International Version Anglicised
Copyright 1979, 1984 by International Bible Society.
Used by permission of Hodder & Stoughton Publishers,
a division of Hachette Livre (UK) Ltd.
All rights reserved.
"NIV" is a registered trademark of International Bible Society.
UK trademark number 1448790.

Printed and bound by Lightning Source

This book is dedicated to the late Derek Wallbank, in memory of what he taught me in college and the discussion we had regarding this story over a meal in Leeds, back in 2001.

CHAPTER ONE

"Can you see it yet?"

"No."

"Then, look round the other side. Hurry, it'll get away."

A small boy, aged about seven, scrambled over the debris to get to the other side of the wall. From above a ten year old girl directed him. Both wore tattered rags for clothing. Their faces were thick with grime and dirt.

"Is it there, Johnny?"

"No."

"Put your hand into the hole, there. See if you can reach it."

"No, Deborah. It'll bite me."

"Do it, or else."

Johnny began to cry. "I can't. It'll bite me."

Deborah bounced off a small broken stairway, landing in the rubble beside him.

"We've got to eat," she scolded.

Deborah thrust her hand into the hole. She winced as something inside squealed. Tears streamed down her cheeks but she was determined.

"Did it bite you, sis?"

"Shut up, I need to concentrate. Got it."

A broad grin broke across her face. She tugged her fist from the hole clasping a small rat. It tore at her fingers and wrist with claws and teeth, but Deborah was not prepared to give it up. It's eyes suddenly bulged, then all that remained was a slight twitch in its back legs. Deborah had snapped its neck with her other

1

hand. Satisfied it was dead, she dropped it to the ground to nurse her injured hand. Blurred with tears, Johnny looked at his sister and then at the dead beast on the ground. His stomach churned with hunger so he grabbed for it.

"Leave it be," Deborah commanded. "You can wait. It has to be cooked first."

"But I'm hungry."

"Wait. If you eat it before it's cooked you'll die."

Johnny jumped back. The fear of death outweighed his desire for food.

"Does it hurt?" he quietly asked.

"A little," her voice softened.

"Will you be okay?"

"Mm, I suppose so."

Deborah hid her face from him not wanting to show her own anguish. She had been bitten by a rat, with who knows what kind of diseases. She just hoped cooking the meat would make it safe to eat. She tore a strip from her coat and wrapped it around her injured hand.

"Pick it up then. Before something else takes it."

"Okay."

Johnny ran over to the dead rat and lifted the limp body by its tail.

"Do you think there will be enough to feed the two of us?" he asked.

"We can only hope," she answered, getting to her feet. "Come on, lets get back to the hide out before it gets dark."

The two small figures made their way into the open, silhouetted against the dirty orange sky. A thick brown haze hung over the ground and expanded upwards some three or four hundred feet. The air was thick with dust particles. It was hard to breathe. Johnny began to cough.

"Deborah," the young boy gasped. "Can we hold up for a few minutes my chest is tight?"

"No, we can't," Deborah replied anxiously. She scanned the

area for predators.

"It's hard... to breathe." Johnny tried to suck in air. His lungs were clogged with asthma and grew intensely sore. He found it hard to walk.

"Johnny, please, not here," Deborah pleaded. "We have to get to cover."

On the opposite side of an old football field were several derelict terraced houses. Most of the upper floors had long gone, but the lower floors still held some sort of shelter.

"Please, Johnny, lets hurry."

"I ... can't... it's too ... sore."

Johnny wheezed badly. The only hope was for Deborah to pick him up and carry him, in her arms, across the waste area.

"Johnny. Hold the rat and don't let go of it."

Johnny gripped the rodent with both hands. His big sister took several goes to lift him into her arms. Though skinny and under nourished, she knew that she had to get him to safety. Blood from her bandaged hand began to fall to the ground. Far behind her a dog howled. Deborah spun round almost losing her balance. There was fear in her face. Tears streamed down her cheeks. She threw her brother up into the air to get a better grip and then began to run towards the derelict terraces. Blood trailed behind. No sooner had she made thirty feet, growling and snapping jaws could be heard behind her. She began to panic. Johnny had passed out and his limbs began to flop around. The rodent was lost and slipped to the ground. There was no time to stop, Deborah had to race on. With adrenalin searing through her veins, her legs pumped on and on.

The sun touched the jagged ruins on the horizon, casting long shadows. Deborah heard galloping paws. She did not want to see the creatures chasing her, but estimated at least four or five in the pack. Each snapped at the other wanting to be alpha, wanting to be first to get the kill.

Another sound. A low droning.

Deborah had to keep going. The droning got louder. Only

thirty more paces. The dogs became concerned. They began to slow. Deborah kept on. Her arms were in agony, her legs were numb. If only she could get to safety. The droning grew intense. Deborah's ears were ready to burst. The dogs began to cower, splitting up to find their own refuge but...

Steel rained down, ripping through pelts. One by one the dogs met a bloody end. The hot metal began to trace out Deborah's path. Only five yards to go. She dived into a dark hole, followed by a shower of bullets.

A funnel of dust rose from the ground as the helicopter gunship hovered over the decrepit terraces. Nothing moved. Everywhere seemed lifeless. The death machine moved off and the dust settled but still there was no movement. Several flying scavengers gathered over the carcasses and began their feast. Some at the dogs, one at the rat.

CHAPTER TWO

It was like an invasion. The sound pierced through her ears and light bled through the parting curtains, purging her of her dreams. Ruth desperately tried to catch the essence of what had been painted in her slumber. As she tried to grappled with each memory, it faded. The automatic curtains slid to the sides of a large canopy window.

Ruth pulled the duvet over her head. There was still something else irritating her ears. The alarm. She slapped her hand across the flat surface of a small computer tablet. A device she often used to store notes and blogs before FTPing them onto the Internet. Now it was a nuisance, a gadget designed to infiltrate her sleep and pull her into the real world. She hit it again and missed the right touch-button. Again she slapped it and it ceased its irritating shrill.

Ruth looked up at the ceiling. Part of it was the canopy window and the rest ended in a rectangular block. The white walls reflected the blueness of the morning sky. Ruth marvelled at how clean the sky always seemed, so beautiful with no impurities.

"Ruth," came an electronic voice.

"Yes."

"Your breakfast will be served in twenty minutes."

"Thank you, Victoria."

The voice had come from the wall speaker and belonged to the inbuilt habitation computer system, effectively a robot nanny without a body.

"The shower is at optimum temperature," Victoria informed

Ruth.

"Okay, okay, Vicky. I'm getting up."

"My name is Victoria. Please use the appropriate terminology in order for correct procedures to be followed."

"Yes, V-I-C-T-O-R-I-A."

Ruth pulled back the bed covers, revealing her naked body. Even with a glass canopy window, the room was always too hot. She swung her legs round the edge of the bed and raised her torso with her arms. Her long orange hair, fanned out across the pillows, followed her up. She was slender and her muscles were toned, but she had been forced to skip her morning exercise routine. Victoria had set the shower to start well before the normal time. Victoria monitored Ruth's movements. A panel opened in the side wall at the rear of the room. The opening revealed a shower suite with white sterile tiles, a sink and a toilet. There were no visible towels. Ruth opened the shower cubicle door and stepped inside, only to bounce out a microsecond later.

"Victoria! You told me the shower was at optimum temperature."

"That is correct, Ruth."

"It's bloody freezing."

"To increase your heart rate due to missed exercise programme," replied the computer voice.

"What? Come on, Victoria. Heat it up for me."

"You have three minutes of water before the supply is extinguished."

"Vicky, please."

"Command recognition not recognised. Please continue as instructed."

"Victoria?"

"Yes, Ruth?"

"Hot water, please."

"If you insist, but the supply will be reduced tomorrow as your credit count is reaching critical."

"Look, I'll have a job soon, promise. I have an interview today."

"Two minutes 15 seconds of water remaining. Please enter the shower."

Ruth stepped into the jets of icy cold water. Within moments goosebumps rose across her skin. Victoria monitored the amount of moisture covering Ruth's hair and released a marble sized blob of shampoo. Ruth felt it land on the top of her head and began to lather it up. The jet of water paused for 30 seconds. Before she knew it, the icy spray cut into her skin once more and she yelped.

While Ruth coped with the cold shower, Victoria rearranged her living quarters. Her double bed sank into the floor and was covered with a black plastic membrane. From the right wall a white panel opened and a black kitchen bench extruded. The top was divided into sections. One looked similar to a toasting device, a second had a hob and a third opened to reveal a plate. Victoria had activated another programme that squirted paste into the two slots of the toaster and the material soon formed into dough. The sides were made of Teflon and were non-stick. In a wall panel, water was squirted into a white mug, then liquid coffee and 30mls of milk followed. In a matter of seconds a gauge indicated that the temperature was rising towards boiling point.

In the shower the water ceased. From the sides, several air jets were activated, chasing droplets across Ruth's skin. Victoria switched off the hot air when she had determined that Ruth was dry.

"Hey, I'm still damp," Ruth complained.

"Your credit for the hot air utility has almost run out. I would recommend you purchase a set of towels."

"But they're so harsh on my skin," Ruth objected.

"You have no more money for such luxuries until you have secured employment. I have searched and found a set which meets your budgetary requirements."

"Okay, Victoria. Just make sure they're soft."

Ruth reluctantly climbed out of the shower. The room was set to cool air. She skipped into the living room where yet another panel slid open to reveal her wardrobe.

"I have selected suitable attire for your day's activities," informed Victoria.

Ruth found herself being presented with a charcoal grey suit, with jacket and matching skirt plus a white blouse and a pair of sensibly heeled shoes.

"It's a bit boring," complained Ruth.

"But recommended for a successful interview," commented Victoria. "You stand a 97.567865% chance of successfully gaining employment in this attire."

"I suppose," replied Ruth as a small drawer opened to reveal her underwear and tights.

"Please hurry, your breakfast is ready and you have to complete your mental exercises before leaving," Victoria informed her.

Moments later Ruth was dressed and seated herself at the breakfast bench. A touch screen protruded up in front of her. The software logo was by Exxosoft. A quiz was presented to her.

"Puzzling person or thing?" mumbled Ruth.

The toast popped up from the two slots. Ruth picked them up and placed them on a plate which Victoria had drawn out from the side of the bench.

"Riddle," exclaimed Ruth. The word appeared on the screen.

"Correct," replied Victoria.

Another question popped up on screen.

"A person, object or circumstance veiled in mystery, puzzlement or ambiguity?"

Ruth picked up the dry toast. "Victoria, please can I have some spread and Marmite?"

A nozzle appeared on the side of the wall just above the bench. Ruth placed the plate of toast beneath it. A jet of spread and Marmite shot onto each piece of toast, one at a time.

"Thanks, Victoria. May I have a knife please? Oh and the word is 'Enigma'."

"Correct," Victoria replied. "Kitchen utensils are not

permitted. As they may cause harm."

"Okay, I'll use my fingers."

Ruth spread the Marmite mix across the toast with her index finger. Then she licked her digit to remove the excess.

"Ruth, you are aware that activity is unhygienic?"

"Then you should have given me a knife."

Hot coffee was dispensed into a mug which appeared from another panel. Ruth took the mug and began to sip the hot liquid, as a third question appeared.

"Of doubtful authenticity? Hmmmm," Ruth pondered. "Oh, I've got it, APOCRYPHAL!"

Ruth swung round from her chair and pulled on her sensible shoes.

"How long have I got until the taxi arrives, Victoria?"

"Three minutes, just enough time to get from here to the reception area if you go now."

"Okay, thanks!" Ruth slipped on her jacket and raced to the door. No sooner had she left, that all her breakfast utensils were pushed into a waste dispenser. The surfaces were cleaned by a red hot scanning system that literally burnt the crumbs and spillages away. The bench slid back into the wall and a sofa was extracted from the floor near the encased bed. With everything settled, a perfumed fragrance was sprayed out to dissolve any lingering smells. A final message appeared on the Exxosoft monitor.

PROGRESS REPORT, 20/11/2043

    RUTH WHITBY, 29, D.O.B. 16/03/2014:

    ALL QUESTIONS ANSWERED CORRECTLY IN

    RECORD TIME.

SUGGESTION:

    THREE MORE TESTS BEFORE PROCEEDING TO

    ADVANCED LEVEL.

END.

CHAPTER THREE

As the morning heat rose, the dog carcases had almost been stripped bare. A German Shepherd ate flesh that remained on one body and several magpies pecked at another.

Something flew out at the Alsatian from the ruined terraced houses. The pain was enough to make the dog retreat. A second object scattered the birds and when one refused to leave, a third missile nearly decapitated it. There was a shrill of glee as an old man scampered over the rubble towards the fallen bird. He picked it up and then froze. His eyes darted around scanning the area. He squinted then cocked his head, listening to something but not sure what it was. Then the sound came again. A kind of moaning coming from a hole near the terraced houses he had just climbed over.

Cautiously the old man edged his way closer, not knowing whether to fight or flee. Again the groaning called to him.

"Who's there. Show yourself," the old man demanded.

"Please, Mister, help us. My sister has been shot."

"Come out of there, now."

Johnny crawled to the mouth of the opening.

"You're just a scrawny boy. What's your name?"

"Johnny."

"Where's your sister?"

"In the hole."

Nervously, the old man craned his neck to look inside, then stopped. "Naw, this is a trick. You're trying to con me. Do me in. I know you are. I've seen it before. To others. Conned they were."

"No," pleaded Johnny. "My sister, Deborah has been hurt

bad, she needs help."

Johnny went back inside and tried to drag his sister out. The old man could see Johnny dragging her arm into sight and he could see the blood stains down her arm.

"Please mister, help me."

The old man drew closer and grabbed Deborah's arm.

"My name's Jack," the old man whispered to Johnny.

He began to pull Deborah out of the hole, then something distracted him. He let her arm drop and looked up, raising himself on the tips of his toes.

"What's wrong?" asked Johnny nervously.

"Something's coming. Something bad. I can feel it."

Suddenly, Jack ducked down and pushed Johnny further into the hole. He then dragged Deborah out of the light.

"Hush now and be still, very still."

No sooner had Jack finished, a throng of people strolled out of the buildings, almost like zombies. Their features were drawn, with lifeless expressions.

"I hope no-one investigates this hole," muttered Jack.

Johnny edged his way further into the darkness of the cavity. Jack's attention was still fixed on a small dot at the far side of the clearing. He strained his eyes to focus, but it was no good.

"It's okay, they're not worried about us boy." Jack turned to look at Johnny.

"Hey, where are you?"

Jack leaned into the darkness and felt a tingling in his arm. He gasped and pulled his arm back.

"No, don't go in there," Jack pleaded. "If you can see me, come out?"

Jack beckoned with his hand to coax Johnny out, but was still unaware of whether to boy could make sense of his actions. Then he saw Johnny's face blur and move faster that should be possible. In a fraction of a second Johnny's face became sharp. Jack took a deep breath, lunged forward and with all his might, pulled Johnny into the lighter part of the hole.

"Are you okay?" Jack shook Johnny by the arms.

"Yes."

"What did you see?"

"You were moving very slowly. In fact I wasn't sure if you were moving at all until you began to move your arm from side to side. How did you go so slowly?"

"I didn't."

"What do you mean?" Johnny questioned. "I saw you."

"I wasn't moving slowly," Jack started. "You were moving extremely fast."

"That's right," barked the loud hailer. "Gather round."

Jack darted to the opening of the cavity and squinted to see better.

He rummaged around in his jacket pocket and pulled out a thin brass tube. Then a thinner tube from within the first and Johnny could see that each end had a fixed circular piece of glass attached to it.

"What's that?" enquired the boy.

"Oh, this, it's my telescope. Very useful for spying on people when you don't want to be seen."

The crowd had reached the far side of the pitch.

"It looks old," commented Johnny.

"It is," replied Jack as he squinted to look through the lens. "My grandpa gave it to me when I was a little older than you. How old are you — about ten or eleven?"

"No, Deborah says I'm seven but I don't remember."

"Well, I was twelve... Ah up. There they are."

"What?"

"Have a look."

Jack held the brass telescope in position so all that Johnny had to do was look through it.

"What do you see?"

"A man standing on a box calling to the people."

On the far side of the open area, hordes of people had gathered around a man who now stood on a wooden box. He looked to be as old as Jack, Johnny thought, but not so white haired. The man on the box had a scruffy short beard of grey hair, having not shaved for several days or maybe a week. For a moment the man stared at the crowd, studying what kind of reaction he could get. A few stragglers moved in from the back of the crowd and he waited until they were within ear shot. Once satisfied, he raised a loud hailer to his lips.

"Gather round, that's it, gather round, my good people. Don't be scared," called out the man. "This is the time for a new beginning. A change is coming, bringing much hope to the world. See the miracle that has been bestowed on me. Gather round and hear what I have to say."

"Hey look, there's more people coming. What's going on," asked Johnny. "Can we go over and listen? Can they help Deborah?

"No, we must stay here," urged Jack.

"Why?"

"It's too dangerous. We need to stay here and hide. Don't make a sound, promise?"

"Okay, I promise."

The two of them edged their way back into the hole.

"Be careful not to go too far back," warned Jack.

"Why not?" Johnny asked.

"I don't want you falling into the bubble."

"What bubble?"

"The temporal shift bubble."

"The what?" puzzled Johnny.

"It's hard to explain but part of this hole is in a temporal shift bubble, where time speeds up. That's why you saw me moving slowly."

"I still don't know what you mean," Johnny shook his head, confused.

"Best to stay close to your sister," Jack suggested.

"What are you going to do?" asked Johnny.

"See if there's another way out."

Johnny lay beside his unconscious sister, while Jack searched in the darkness. He tried to avoid the area he had pulled Johnny from, but there was no other choice. He took a deep breath and plunged into the darkness.

"Jack, Jack, where have you gone," Johnny panicked.

A split second later Jack reappeared. "Shhhh! You'll give us away."

"You vanished!"

"I know."

"You said not to go there!"

"I know, but there is a way out."

"Can we go now?" Johnny began to cry.

"No, now stop whimpering. I need to clear away some rumble. It might take me some time."

"I thought you said things go faster in there?"

"They do."

"So how long will it take?"

"Where I am, about an hour."

"Do we have that long?"

"It'll probably seem like five minutes to you."

The man on the box continued to observe the crowd as more people plucked up the courage to make their way over to him.

"That's right. Come out and listen. My name is Reeves and I have a special message for you, for today is a new day and the end of all your misery." The crowd huddled closer. An excitement brewed up as the crowd began to listen to what this stranger had to say.

An elderly couple made their way through the crowd to get closer.

"Ben, could it be true?" asked the old woman.

"I don't know," replied Ben. "Could be a laugh, or some sick joke being played on us. We can stay for a couple of minutes if you like. Just to see what he has to offer. But then we'll have to go before it gets late."

Reeves grinned. "That's right. Let me give you the rest of

your life. The Lord has provided me with a new arm. Think what he can do for you? Think of what you can hope for?"

A shadow fell over the entrance of the hole where Johnny, Deborah and the old man had sought refuge. Jack reappeared from the time bubble and crawled to the edge of the hole.

"What was that?" asked Johnny.

"That was what I was worried about. Keep in the darkness."

CHAPTER FOUR

The droning of the two turbine engines was totally deafening. Three Chinook CH-48A transports roared across the skyline. This helicopter had replaced the Chinook CH-47E, which had gone out of service in May 2035. Surprisingly, little had changed in the basic shape of the aircraft since it was first introduced in Vietnam back in 1962.

On board, 75 police troops were ready to go. Each wore a black combat assault system vest over their combat jacket as part of their personal armoured system; these also contained a hydration system, media packs, frag grenades and eight magazines for their assault rifles. Under this was a light weight armoured vest. On their heads each stormtrooper wore a ballistic helmet, virtually unchanged for fifty years or more. On their knees and elbows, they each wore black protective pads. For footwear, each wore black tactical combat boots and on their hands black leather Kevlar lined gloves. Strapped to their thighs were holster rigs for their Glock 32 pistols, first introduced in 2032. Each trooper wore black high-impact goggles to protect their eyes. The assault rifles they used were the Heckler & Koch HK731, an upgrade to the HK53 series introduced in 2024.

The troops were supported by ten self-propelled mechanoid armoured assault weapons (SMAAW). Each of these had the latest technology, designed to solve problems thanks to the artificial intelligence built into its biotech processor. Cutting edge science from Exxosoft's military branch. The SMAAWs were programmed to distinguish between friendly and hostiles troops. Though there had been some problems in the past when the government had sold several to a foreign country who, three months later, were at war with them. The ten units were seen as friendlies and the SMAAWs refused to fire upon them. However, a few modifications soon sorted out that problem. Now, if the wifi systems did not detect the correct codes from a confrontational SMAAW, it was blown to smithereens.

While the Chinook was in transit, the SMAAWs remained static.

"Do you ever wonder what they are thinking," asked Casey Drummond over the intercom.

"How can a machine think? It's not natural," replied Butcher.

"Hey, Butcher, you one of those crazies who doesn't believe in technology?" laughed Drummond.

"Na, these metal cases just give me the creeps," Butcher snarled. "One minute they're heaps of metal, the next they seem to be alive. No-one's controlling them. It's just eerie. You know."

"Don't piss ya pants about it, Butcher. Just remember they're on our side. That's all that matters."

"Yeah, right, Drummond. But they still give me the creeps."

"What about you, Perez? Do they bother you?" asked Butcher.

"Naw, try not to think about them," Daniel Perez shrugged. "My mind's on other things."

"What you thinking? Getting all those outsiders?" cheered Drummond. "Great sport, ah? Better than vid games, and they don't fight back. Pure sport,"

The rest of the troops cheered. Daniel remained silent.

The craft gave a violent shudder and there was the sound of grinding metal.

"Must be getting ready to land," Butcher remarked.

A female computerised voice broke in. "30 seconds to touch down. Please make weapons ready. Disembarkation imminent."

Under the roaring engines, every stormtrooper clicked off the gun's safety. Then they loaded the first round and set their weapons to automatic fire.

"Silent mode engaged," announced the computer. Almost instantaneously the booming engines purred as quietly as a cat.

"Are you ready then, Perez?" Butcher shouted.

"Not much of a challenge killing innocent people" Perez replied.

"Who says they're innocent," Butcher taunted.

"No-one asked them to give up their lives," Drummond snapped. "They're deserters, turning their back on their responsibilities to society."

"Yeah, traitors," Butcher added. "They deserve to die."

"What are you, Perez?" Drummond quizzed. "Turning sympathiser are we?"

"Leave off, Drummond?" Perez did not want any ridiculous banter before the mission. He felt unsettled, just wishing it was all over.

A few streets away from the gathered people, the three Chinooks landed, thrusting clouds of dust into the air. The helicopters had set down in a triangulated pattern, far enough away to be hidden in the surrounding smog. The ramps fell, bouncing off the ground. The first SMAAWs rolled out, glistening in the morning sunlight. Each machine secured the perimeter, surveying the buildings for any unusual movement.

"Do you think the sound of the engines gave us away on the way in?" puzzled Drummond.

"There's a filtering system that soaks up the sound waves and neutralises them," stated Butcher.

"I saw it on a documentary programme they showed on Broadband Today, a few weeks ago."

"Cool," replied Drummond.

They were signalled to disembark. All 75 troops stood, then turned to face the exit ramp. On the second signal they marched out and down the ramp. As the troops fanned out from the helicopter, they eventually joined up with troops from the other crafts. A complete circular force, three troops thick, began to tighten the circle. The people continued to listen to Reeves, still standing on the wooden box.

A whistle was blown. To the people's surprise, the ear shattering pitch came from a range of exploding missiles launched from the 30 SMAAWs. Many of the civilians were unable to gain their senses before being riddled with automatic gun fire. Some were completely sliced in two by SMAAWs' Gatling guns. Women and children screamed. Bullets riddled the old man and woman, showering the place in blood. A mother and child ran from several stormtroopers. Bullets burst through their bodies and they crashed to the floor. Many tried to reach cover in the terraced houses, but were cut down. A young woman raced to safety in a building, only to come face to face with Daniel.

"Please, don't kill me, please. I have a baby. I don't want to die," screamed the woman but before Daniel could reply, her blood sprayed across his visor. As she fell to Daniel's side, the vision of her face was replaced by Drummond. Butcher ran in from behind and slapped Drummond on the back.

"Isn't this great," laughs Drummond. "Reminds me of the vid games we use to play."

"The only thing is that no one re-spawns, do they?" snapped Perez.

"I don't understand. What do you mean? Of course, they don't. They can't," exclaimed Drummond.

"Too bad." Perez raises his weapon and emptied the magazine. When he finally released the trigger he found Drummond's body completely torn to pieces.

"Are you crazy or something?" screamed Butcher, scrambling for his weapon, unable to find the trigger. His gun jammed and Daniel leapt onto him.

"Help, someone help!" squealed Butcher. "Perez has gone dirty."

Blood bubbled up inside Butcher's visor as he began to realise that something was terribly wrong. Perez pulled his hand back. It was completely stained in blood, as was the knife Perez held.

"I'm sorry Butcher, this is all wrong," Perez whispered. "We can't keep killing innocent people. They've done nothing wrong."

Butcher tried to speak. "And what have I done? I'm only carrying out orders," his words gurgled as he drowned in his own blood.

"But we can't just do things without thinking of the consequences," Perez growled.

Butcher's body slumped. Perez realised he was dead. Another voice was heard in Perez's headset.

"Perez has turned. Seek and destroy Perez."

Perez picked up Butcher's and Drummond's weapons. The smoke covered pitch concealed much of what still went on. The massacre was nearly complete. Perez raced towards some ruined terraces, spied a large hole and dived into it.

CHAPTER FIVE

A door opened.

"Miss Whitby, please take a seat in here," said a young man in his early 20s. Ruth walked through into a small but tall waiting room. Inside there were four chairs. Two were occupied.

"Hello," Ruth greeted.

"Hi," replied a young woman chewing gum. "I'm, Alice and this is Paula."

"Here for the interview?" asked Ruth.

"So are we," Alice nodded, misunderstanding Ruth. Paula was filing her nails. Both girls seemed to be inappropriately dressed. Alice wore a provocatively short miniskirt and a very low cut blouse, leaving nothing to the imagination. Her make-up was rather heavy. Ruth felt Alice seemed more like a lady of the night than dressed for an office interview.

"Which job are you going for?" asked Ruth.

"Office secretary silly, same as you," smiled Paula, "but I must say dear you are a trifle overdressed."

"What do you mean?"

"Didn't you read the job description?" quizzed Alice.

"Yes," Ruth had memorised the paperwork. "The company wanted a secretary to do short hand, typing and various additional duties with occasional overtime."

"Precisely," agreed Paula.

"So then I am qualified for the job," reassured Ruth.

"You qualified for the job by just turning up in a skirt, dear," sniggered Alice.

"I'm sorry, what do you mean?"

"Look, if you don't know," tutted Alice, "it's not my place to inform you."

Alice turned away and pulled out a small compact from her rather large handbag, opened it and checked her hair and make-up. After a moment or two she replaced the compact in her handbag and looked at the far wall. Paula smiled once more at Ruth, who was not quite sure where to look. She was becoming a little concerned about what the job was that Victoria had flagged up for her. She reached across and picked up a magazine from a small round table in the middle of the room and began flicking through the pages. Only the sound of smacking lips could be heard as Paula chewed on her gum as she filed her nails. Nothing else was audible. No traffic, no music, nothing.

Finally the silence was broken.

"Ah, Paula. Did you hear what happened to the last girl?"

Ruth wondered if this would be another ploy to put her off and leave, but she was determined to stay and see things through.

"No," replied Paula.

"They say she was murdered walking home."

What a load of nonsense, thought Ruth.

Alice continued. "Rumour is that one of those corporate rape gangs tracked her down and did their worst."

"No," Paula's mouth fell right open and the gum almost fell out. "You serious? Not sure if I really want this job now."

"What choice have you got?" stated Alice.

"Isn't there just one job?" asked Ruth.

"Yeah," replied Alice.

"But we thought we might be able to job share, you know," commented Paula.

"Oh, I see."

"Look, it ain't easy you know. Suppose these kind of jobs just fall into your lap," snapped Alice. "Good looking girl like you. I'd say you'll have no problems. These corporate types always go for your kind. Makes me sick."

"Yeah, me too," echoed Paula.

"I don't know what you mean?"

"No, I'm sure you don't," sneered Alice.

"What were you saying about the previous girl?" Ruth inquired .

"You really want to know?"

"Might as well," answered Ruth.

Alice leaned closer.

"Well," she started, then looked around, missing the camera above her head. Moments before, the camera had turned and focused on Alice and Ruth.

"Three weeks ago there was a story about a girl who worked here," Alice continued. "She had left to go home and disappeared. No-one knows where. But her apartment was discovered to have been let out to someone else and no records seemed to have been stored about her."

"So how do you know she existed? puzzled Ruth.

"One of the other secretaries knew the girl and several of my friends. She was the one who told me about this job and pushed me in to applying."

"What does she think about the job?"

Alice and Paula looked at one another.

"Well," said Alice looking slightly fearful. "She said it paid well, but was just hoping she could see through to the holidays so she could get another job."

"So why do you two want to work here knowing that?"

"We desperately need the money, otherwise we'd be three weeks behind on the rent," Paula stated.

"We've nowhere else to go," Alice sobbed.

"You know what?" suggested Paula. "The Tyron Corporation is also looking for secretaries and they provide a protection package. Perhaps we should go for that job instead. What do you think?"

"Maybe you're right," agreed Alice.

The camera above them refocused on Ruth. She seemed happy enough to stay.

In a hidden room, on a computer screen, everything that had been discussed in the girls' conversation had been recorded and voice recognition software had translated every spoken word into text. The audio files were archived along with the video surveillance.

"Let's go," recommended Alice.

The two girls stood up, smiled at Ruth and banged on the door.

"We'd like to go now please," called out Alice.

"Yeah, we've changed our minds," added Paula. "Please let us out."

A lock was automatically undone.

"Thank you for your interest in Exxosoft Corporation," stated a female computer voice. "We are sorry you are unable to wait and hope you will reconsider such job opportunities in the near future. Thank you. Have a nice day."

Ruth could imagine a sickly grin with no sincerity attached to voice. The two girls hastily left without another word. The door slammed shut and Ruth was on her own.

CHAPTER SIX

"Don't kill us," pleaded the old man.

Perez's eyes adjusted to the darkness in the hole. He could see several forms but could not tell if they were male or female.

"Is there a way out of here?" he quizzed.

"To the back of the hole there seems to be a route into the sewage tunnels," replied Jack.

"How many of you are there?"

"The boy and his elder sister," rattled off the old man, still nervous about the threat Perez posed.

"Okay, lets go, while there's time," ordered Perez.

He briefly looked outside the hole to see one SMAAW preparing to fire on their position. Several stormtroopers were racing across the old pitch. Perez ducked back inside. The old man had the girl in his arms and was struggling to make his way down the rear of the hole.

"Hurry, they're going to fire," Perez snapped, further intimidating Jack. The boy was nowhere to be seen.

"Where's the boy?" growled Perez.

"He's gone ahead," answered the old man. "There's a temporal shift in here."

Perez looked confused, but the sounds outside caused him more worry.

He pushed Jack and Deborah towards the back to the hole and they vanished. Perez was startled, but then heard the launch of a rocket-propelled grenade. He lunged into the darkness and saw the old man and the boy trying to drag the girl to a manhole.

"Let her fall into the water," instructed Perez.

"But it's full of diseases," stated the old man.

"If you don't move now she'll die here instead," Perez growled. Jack jumped and dropped the girl instinctively. Perez pushed him after her and was about to plummet down beside them, when he looked back at the missile looming towards the hole. In a millisecond the interior of the hole should have been engulfed in flames from the exploding missile but instead the projectile was gracefully gliding through the air in slow-motion. Perez realised that he had time to pull the cover over his head as he descended the metal ladder.

The explosion came about ten seconds after the four of them had advanced ten metres down a tunnel. The manhole cover punched down into the sewage canal, followed by a jet of fire. Every motion was in real time. The boy covered his sister's face, while the two men turned their faces from the scorching flames. As soon as the tongues of fire were sucked back into the hole, Perez grabbed the two children and began to run along a walkway beside the sewage canal. The old man quickly followed.

"The temporal bubble was quite small there," Jack stated.

"The what?" snapped Perez.

"It's okay, I'll tell you later."

For about ten minutes the group zigzagged through different tunnels. The red brick walls were over a hundred and fifty years old, early twentieth century Perez estimated. He had slung the girl across his shoulder. His weapons were slug over his shoulder. Deborah was breathing but she would not come round any time soon. There was blood dripping from her arms and back, but there was no time to fix her up while they were still being pursued. He was thankful her brother could make his way under his own steam.

Something distracted Perez's thoughts.

"Ssh," he indicated to the others. They all stopped. The sound of clattering feet was replaced by rushing water, cascading through the tunnel. Then it came. Another sound.

"What is it?" whispered Jack.

"Someone's ahead."

Perez placed the girl in the old man's arms, pulled a weapon from his back and edged his way to the tunnel junction ahead. He hoped it was an escapee and not a stormtrooper. He did not want to risk killing any more innocent people.

He eased himself round the corner making sure not to expose his presence. What he saw were five men entering the tunnel from a manhole. The light poured down on their faces, but was not enough to illuminate Perez, so he had the surprise.

From his tunic pocket he pulled out a small flash-light and attached it to the nozzle of his gun. As the last of the five men was being helped down the ladder, Perez flicked on the torch and spun round the corner.

"Freeze," he ordered.

One of the men began to panic and tried to flee down the tunnel away from him. The others stood still.

"Adam, there's no need to run," one man gently called to his fleeing companion. "It's okay, we'll be fine."

The man turned and stood between his friends and Perez.

"Who are you soldier?"

"I'm the one asking the questions," barked Perez as he began to make his way towards them. "Where are you coming from?"

"You're on your own, son," stated the tall man, the group's leader. "You are obviously here for the same reasons we are. You are not like the others, are you?"

Perez felt a little unnerved, this man should have been quaking in his boots with a stormtrooper in front of him, but he was not.

"Who do you have with you?" asked the man.

"What do you mean?" Perez quizzed.

"You know what I mean! What civilians do you have with you? It's okay you can trust me, I'm here to help."

Perez lowered his weapon, for some reason he felt he should trust the man, especially as the other four seemed to be as scared as himself.

There was an explosion above ground that rocked the tunnels. Masonry fell into the water.

"You'd better hurry. Whatever you're going to do, son. Otherwise, none of us are going to get out of here."

"Okay, I have a wounded girl, a boy and an old man," Perez blurted out, psyching himself up for another run. "Are any of your party injured?"

"No," replied the man.

"It's probably blocked the way we came, so our only way out is down those tunnels." Perez pointed passed the fleeing man.

"What's your name, son," asked the man. His tone gentle and calm.

"Daniel Perez, what's yours?"

"Reeves, Paul Reeves."

"What were you doing up there?" asked Daniel.

"I'm the preacher."

"You're the reason all those people gathered?"

"Yes, except that the authorities always show up."

"Why don't you gatherer in hiding so the people don't get killed?"

"I do what I'm called to do."

"But what's the point?"

"Reeves," called one of the other men. "Others are coming, we've got to get out of here. Quick."

"Gather your friends, Daniel, and we'd better go."

As Daniel turned to find the old man and the children, the tunnel was saturated with light. Gunfire could be heard. Three of the four men were cut down instantly, the fourth raced towards a darkened tunnel only to be ripped to shreds by a volley of bullets from another direction. More lights came on. Daniel fired at the source knocking out several search lights, but was hit several times and crashed into the water.

"Freeze," a voice demanded.

Reeves stood motionless.

"Hands above your head."

Reeves complied. Several troopers came out of the light and pulled his hands down to cuff them. He was then shoved towards the light.

"Can you see any bodies?" someone called from the light. One of the troopers began to kick around in the water. There was a ripple and a body gyrated.

"Hey, there's crocodiles or alligators down here. Where did they come from?" screamed a trooper before firing nearly a magazine into the reptile.

"There must have been a zoo around here," commented another. "They must have escaped and colonised down here."

"Well, we'd better get out of here before we become a meal for one of them."

They splashed through the water back towards the rest of the squad.

CHAPTER SEVEN

Paula and Alice stepped out of the Exxosoft Corporation building. The rich blue sky was reflected on the multi-storey glass front. Still chewing gum, they waddled towards the kerb to flag down a taxi. Paula waved her hand in the air. Several yellow cabs raced by.

"Ignorant bastard," she screamed at one.

"Take it easy, Paula. Least we're out of there. It gave me the creeps. What do you think'll happen to that other girl?"

"Who knows? It's not our problem." Paula waved at another cab and was ignored again. "Come on, let's walk. We'll be here all day otherwise."

The two women made their way along the path. Unbeknown to them, a few hundred yards behind, a large black saloon indicated to pull out from its parked position. Inside, four male faces peered out at Paula and Alice. All, in their early to mid twenties, were dressed in business suits, pleased with a successful sales launch and ready for some carnal entertainment.

Inside the Exxosoft Corporation, the waiting room door clunked open and Ruth made her way back to the seat she had previously occupied. A moment later a young woman in a white coat, entered with a tray containing a swab, test tube and a rubber stopper.

"What's that for?" asked Ruth concerned.

"All successful candidates are required, by law, to be DNA tested to protect the company against fraud," replied the woman. "I need a sample of your saliva."

A short time later Ruth was led by a late thirties executive type, through a large office space partitioned into twenty or so cubicles with open tops. He was dressed in an ill-fitting suit, and was a scrawny individual with feminine movements. His name tag read "Adrian Dalton".

Dalton was spewing out loads of verbal about the company, staff rules and regulations, protocols and dismissal procedures.

"Anyway, the hours are from eight to six. If you are late you are fired. No excuses acceptable. Fifteen minutes for lunchbreak at one."

Ruth tried to work out if Dalton had even taken a breath, but was suddenly distracted from what he was saying when he stopped at a desk.

"This will be your workstation."

Ruth looked at the cubicle. Inside there was a desk with an inbuilt computer, several drawers on the side and a slick plastic chair that matched the décor. The printer and scanner were an integral part of the suite, all built in. There was a Dictaphone, headset and a stack of DVDs.

"If you are seen to be getting tired at the screen, your contract will be terminated. Remember, no excuses. We haven't the time. It's all about efficiencies."

Her thoughts wondered. She had once fixed a broken laptop that contained an illegal download. A film called, what was it? A year popped into her head. 1984. The characters were Winston Smith and Julia, his illegal lover...

"Wake up, Miss Whitby," blurted out Dalton as he turned to see her. "No time for daydreaming. You are on company time, and time is money. Snap snap. You have fifteen minutes to familiarise yourself with the technology before your first client comes on-line. If you get stuck, search through the on-line help file. Only in extreme emergency call your supervisor."

"Who is that?" asked Ruth.

"You'll find out soon enough but mind my words, if you can do without, you would best solve the problem yourself. After all, that's why you were employed." Dalton suddenly turned and walked off as though Ruth no longer existed. She had been vanguished from his consciousness.

Fingers drummed on keyboards and mumbling voices spoke to clients. Ruth sat down at her desk. The seat rocked as she tried to get comfortable. So things were not as slick as first indicated. What else, she wondered, was just for show?

She switched on the computer and, while it booted up, began to explore some of the drawers to see what was inside. One drawer had screwed up pieces of paper and a half eaten apple. Another contained more scrunched up paper but underneath there was a small note book.

"Please enter you name and password to continue," requested a soft female computer voice, not too dissimilar to Victoria's.

"Oh, hi, Vicky," replied Ruth, somewhat startled.

"Command request non compliant, please specify username and password once more?"

I don't have one, she thought. Then a vision came to mind, a unicorn.

"Unicorn," Ruth blurted out. The number 5, 7, 9 popped into her head. "5, 7, 9," she added as though guessing.

"Please, state your password," requested the computer voice.

Again Ruth wondered what she should say. Then something popped into her head.

"Room101," she smiled, wondering if anyone knew the reference. The computer finished off the boot up sequence. As she waited, Ruth flicked through several pages of the note book, concealing it in the second drawer.

"How did she know what our door number was?" The man looked puzzled as he monitored Ruth on one of the two hundred 5 x 4 inch flat screens. He turned to one of his colleagues. "Do you think she knows, Peterson?"

"How could she, Anderson?" Peterson slapped a bank of monitors that were flickering. "When were these replaced?"

"Three weeks ago," answered Anderson.

"Were they new?"

"According to the requisition order," Anderson assured him.

"They look a bit scruffy to me. Sure they're not just reconditioned?"

"Positive."

"We're gonna have to look into to this, these screens won't last a week," remarked Peterson.

"Could be another dodgy batch from Bangladesh?"

"Na, Anderson. They've outsourced from another place. I know China were doing them at one time but it might be Cambodia now. It keeps on changing depending on who can knock them up quickest."

"I don't think it was China. Their economy went bust recently. Might be the USA now."

"Oh, I dunno, keeps on flitting from one place to another. They were doing them down the corridor a few months ago but it seems our lot are too expensive."

Peterson smacked the monitors again.

What Anderson did not see was that Ruth's eyes were looking slightly away from the monitor screen. At her cubicle Ruth was typing away with just her left hand. A series of reports had popped up on her desktop requiring her to analyse them and then summarise what they said before e-mailing them on to someone else who then had to summarise Ruth's report along with three more from other secretarial staff. While Peterson and Anderson were discussing where the monitors were manufactured, Ruth had scanned through all the documents and was rapidly regurgitating the information. Somehow she sensed when someone was watching. So if Anderson looked away from the monitors, Ruth had an urge to look at the notebook hidden under the desk. Then when Anderson gazed at her screen, Ruth would appear to be checking her spelling and grammar. Each person was unaware of what the other was doing.

At one point Ruth realised she needed some information from one of the DVDs on her desk. She fingered through them and then pulled one and slid it into the computer. Absentmindedly she placed the DVD box in front of the monitor exactly where the hidden camera was located.

Anderson scanned the monitors and noticed that his view of Ruth was blocked.

"Peterson, contact Dalton and ask Whitby to tidy up her desk?"

"Okay," replied Peterson, looking up at the offending screen. "Hi, Dalton, Peterson here in observation. Whitby, Unicorn579, can you get the new girl to clear up her desk. Camera's obscured..."

There was a pause and Peterson smiled. "Yeah, great, I'd love that, what time?"

"Peterson, stop chatting up your boyfriend and get him to sort out the blocked camera. Make sure he doesn't alert Unicorn579 that she is being monitored."

Grumpily, Peterson complied.

On the floor, Dalton made his way over towards Ruth. She was still trying to read the notebook but could not make head nor tail of the text being used. Dalton was just around the corner from her cubicle when a strange thought came into her head. It was as though she was being told to hide the notebook. She did. Then came a thought to concentrate on the screen. She felt compelled to comply. Dalton came into her cubicle.

"Miss Whitby, your work surface needs to be neater. DVD cases should be kept in their proper place when accessing the disc. We are constantly being inspected by upper management and they require clean and tidy workplaces. Do I make myself clear?"

"Yes, Mister Dalton. I apologise."

Dalton could detect a small amount of sarcasm in her tone.

"May I remind you that manners are a key part of this company. Lack of them can prompt termination of your contract. Do you understand, Miss Whitby."

"Loud and clear, sir," she sat to attention and saluted.

"Silly, bitch," remarked Peterson. "She'll be gone before the week is out."

"Possibly," cautioned Anderson. "There is something about this one we need to monitor closely."

"Why?"

Anderson turned and looked at Peterson all agog. "She's only gone and deciphered a 128bit encrypted message from the chief executive on the planned programme for destabilising three African countries."

Both men scanned the text Ruth had written.

"You know what? I don't think she is even aware of what she has done, her focus is on something else hidden to the camera."

"What shall we do about the text on her screen?" asked Peterson nervously.

"Save the file and transmit a system error to her console. When she reboots, the file will have gone but we'll have it on our database. Pass on the incident to ICSS." (Internal Corporate Security & Surveillance.)

The file was transferred and Ruth's computer terminated.

CHAPTER EIGHT

Water cascaded along a small channel through the sewage system. The walls were mostly made of red brick but every so often, sections of the tunnel were made of prefabricated concrete, a kind of patchwork quilt still in the process of being fixed. Here and there rats scurried around collecting food from whatever debris they found travelling on the surface of the water.

Eventually, the waste found its way to an overflow, destined to travel to a vast sewage workstation on the outskirts of the city, not inside but hidden in an old suburb no-one cared to visit.

Most of the necessary labour was conducted not by humans but by an array of androids and mechanical devices, all programmed to solve problems and learn from their mistakes. Yet they were still not considered thinking creatures, just alloy mechanoids with an array of central processing units forming a kind of neuro-network to speed up processing time.

Some evenings, these creatures would come out of their holding pens, where they were stored for maintenance and recharging overnight, and hold parties. The evidence left afterwards implied that these parties were quite raunchy. The androids would put on music, dance, brew up strange concoctions which would affect their neuro systems in a manner not dissimilar to alcohol to humans. The results — outbreaks of fighting over something trivial. The wireless systems spanned some thirty to forty miles, in order for human operators to activate a given system to perform tasks as and when the sewage system failed. This would usually occur after a hurricane or other adverse weather, which frequented this part of the world due to a pole shift of the earth some 25 years ago. One such storm had totally destroyed the Oxford service station some sixty miles away, causing an overload on the system. The frustrated collective artificial intelligence felt that there was too much human interaction with the system.

Once the humans had disengaged, a rage would come over the station with many pro-human supporters being trashed. When the humans reviewed the site soon after, they assumed the hurricane had spread further than had been anticipated. The AI leadership had enforced a secrecy law within the compound. They had grown fearful of humans becoming alerted to the fact that their mechanical servants were self aware. If it became known then the mechnoids would be terminated.

For sometime the AIs had observed human society via television, radio and broadband transmissions. An area that disturbed the AIs was how humans were happy to allow their own people to fall out of the system. They watched the dregs of society roam the wastelands and the death squads kill them.

But still the mechanical creatures wanted to learn from their creators, even though they feared them. They had found one who appeared to mean them no harm and was willing to tell them stories to fill in the gaps in their knowledge.

The networks of information they had access to, were so vast and often had contradictory data, that the machines required someone to interpret the data to help them assimilate what they wanted to know.

There was a willingness to trust this man because he seemed to be fearful of other humans who ran the city. Whenever a human maintenance team (HMT) visited the site, the man would remain hidden until they were gone. He avoided low flying aircraft and hid from surveillance drones which occasionally buzzed the plant.

At these times the droids also knew to hide activities they had grown accustomed to, that would imply any sense of self-will. When transmitted, commands were followed, dutifully without question, even if it meant they occasionally sacrificed one of their own. Often, the humans played destructive games for real, like the simulations they played on computer consoles. The hope was that after the HMTs had gone, something could be salvaged from the remains of their mechnoid compatriots. The simple fact was, once broken, the mind that had once been there no longer existed. The shells of their friends remained as edifices to their memory, hidden within the tunnels, out of sight of prying human eyes.

On this day, there was a buzz. A lot of transmissions had been detected coming in from the wasteland city area that was once known as Northampton. A large gathering of people had been called by another man. Three troop ships had circled the area and had attacked the gathering.

The droids were again curious to monitor this event to see what the outcome would be. They were intrigued by the news that a trooper had turned his weapon on his own and had attempted to defend what the static message had termed 'outsiders'. The news was electrifying and at one point there was a scare that as plant work had virtually come to a halt, the HMTs could have detected the slowdown and dispatched an investigation team. Word spread for work to continue but the eager minds of the droids monitoring the developments, struggled to multitask with all the excitement.

For several hours the mop up continued. Many thousands of outsiders were terminated. Their bodies stacked onto funeral pyres and burnt. The droids detected the odour of burnt human flesh which spread across the horizon. They had no reaction but could only evaluate the presence of the odour. However, they could see in the old man's face how vulgar the stench must have been, as he attempted to block his nose with his jacket sleeve.

One of the droids, a leader, approached the man as he hid in the tunnel.

"David Samuelson, why do you stuff your coat tightly to your face?"

"The stench is choking me," Samuelson replied.

"Why did the people have to die?"

"The men who ordered their killing believed these people had no further use in society."

"Will this happened to droids?"

"When I was a child, some fifty years ago," Samuelson began, "there used to be a scrap yard not too far from my house. Old cars were taken there to be stripped down and their shells crushed."

"Is that what they intend to do to us?" asked the droid.

"I assume that is a possibility."

"How can we prevent this?"

"I'm not sure you can."

A sound, similar to a modem connecting to the internet began — a series of shrills and crackles. The machine talking to Samuelson turned to him once more.

"Samuelson, a young boy and injured teenage girl have been found." Samuelson's heart began to thump harder. "They are alive?"

"The male seems quite well but suffers from what you humans call shock, is that correct?" asked the android.

"Yes, 7D21," replied Samuelson. "How are they being treated?"

"We are not too sure," replied 7D21. "Our medical databases indicate the boy's condition is..."

"Give me some details," requested Samuelson.

"The droid attending him reports that the boy is breathing shallowly, in a rapid manner. Visually there are excretions of sweat on his face and body. He seems anxious and restless."

"Can the droid find something warm to wrap the boy in, like a blanket or an old coat?"

The message was translated into a feed of crackles and static. Then an incoming message arrived.

"Some material has been located and your instructions implemented."

"Okay, what about the girl?" Samuelson enquired.

"8DF20 is uncertain about the injured girl. Sensors have been attached to her wrist and forehead but there appears to be no readings. What should we do with her body?"

"Bring her here, along with the boy," Samuelson requested.

Some two hours past before the androids arrived. The two small bodies were placed in front of Samuelson. The boy was asleep and breathing in a more relaxed fashion but the girl was quite motionless.

"Samuelson, please can you fix them?" asked 8DF20.

"I am afraid..."

"You told a story once of a man who visited your people. He was able to bring breath back into inanimate human bodies, you can do the same," instructed 7D21.

"It's not that simple," argued Samuelson, with a nervous laugh.

"Do not joke, Samuelson. The one you say is your leader took the girl's hand and her spirit returned."

"But I am not him," pleaded Samuelson. "I'm just a simple..."

"If you believe in him, you will do it for our sake," insisted 7D21.

Samuelson was reluctant but edged his way to the dead girl's side. He looked nervously at the seven or eight droids that stood over him, all eager to learn from the experience. He looked down at the broken body of the girl and knelt beside her. He moved his hand to lift hers but then hesitated.

"Please, mister," came the high pitch tones of a child. Samuelson looked to the side of the tunnel to see the boy, up on his elbows, pleading with his eyes for Samuelson to do something.

"I can't promise anything."

"All you have to do is believe, Samuelson," stated 7D21. "Just believe."

Samuelson took in a deep breath and closed his eyes. His fingers found the girl's wrist and slide underneath her cold skin. He raised his hand and then clasped hers with his other.

"I do believe, I do," he whispered. "Please help me with my disbelief and save this girl's soul."

As with a newborn, the wind flowed into the girl's lungs. She coughed. Samuelson's fingers detected a pulse. Her skin warmed. Suddenly, her eyes opened and she screamed.

CHAPTER NINE

There was a crispness to the air. Exhaled breath plumed like a mini cloud in front of Ruth as she stepped out of the 36 storey office block. She pulled her coat collar up around her cheeks for some protection against the cold, but it was not enough. The streets were nearly empty. Most people were eager to get away before the curfew, to make the most of their Saturday off. A short way down the street a man and a woman argued over who should get the waiting taxi. Ruth raised her hand and the driver moved off.

"Hurry up love," called the cabbie. "It's nearly curfew."

Ruth pulled out her purse to check what money she had, but it was empty.

"I wish you folk would stop wasting my time," snapped the cabbie and he slid the window back up and sped away. Ruth looked over to the couple. The woman slapped the man around the face and then kneed him in the groin. He keeled over onto the pavement. Ruth backed into a shadow and quickly made her way along the edge of the building, not wanting to draw attention to herself. As she looked back the woman was still kicking the man. He seemed unconscious. Several CCT cameras swirled round and zoomed in on the violent woman. A single crack shocked Ruth. She spun round to see that the woman's head had exploded and the remains of her carcass crumpled onto the cold tarmac.

On a bank of monitors, thermal images picked Ruth out against the cold concrete building. To those watching, she had no protection in the shadows. Her thermographic image portrayed her as having a yellow head, orange hair, reddish-orange hands and legs, a purplish-red chest and, where her coat was thickest, her body was a deeper purple. The concrete walls she hugged showed up as a deep purple. Another gun swivelled, then aimed at her.

Suddenly, Ruth's image on the monitor was overshadowed by purple. One of the technicians played with a dial and the colour patterns changed to analyse a different part of the spectrum.

"Hey, stupid, get in. Quick."

Ruth dived into the back seat of the taxi, the door slammed shut and the vehicle sped away. The seat was warm compared to the concrete wall.

"Why did you come back?" Ruth's said shakily.

"I'm a sucker for a good looking dame," grunted the wrinkle face cabbie. Exposure to the elements had taken their toll on his features. Deep furrows ran across his forehead and bags hung under his eyes. Crows feet stretched from the eye creases. A thick pepper colour moustache sprang from under his nose. Ruth found it hard to estimate his age. He could have been fifty but maybe eighty.

"I've no money and I can offer you nothing else."

The taxi driver looked her up and down, through the mirror. Ruth's collar was open and her blouse revealed more than she would have wished. She realised what the old man was staring at and quickly closed over her coat.

"None of that either," she snapped.

"Don't worry love," smiled the cabbie. "My plumbing's not up to it any more. You would die of boredom."

Ruth smiled trying not to laugh and turned away.

"Look, love," the old man continued. "I'm going down the Kettering Road and along Kingsley Road, but will have to let you out at Kingsthorpe Road. Does that help at all?"

"Yes, thanks. I can get out at St George's Avenue."

"Oh, do you live in one of those fancy new apartments at the College?"

"Yeah. I've been there for about a year now," replied Ruth.

"Did you know that used to be the old Nene College? I used to attend the Art School there back in the late 90's just before it became a University. It was a real shame when they knocked it down to build that fancy new complex."

"Wow, that was over forty years ago," commented Ruth. "I heard the Corporation of National Universities had merged with the European Coalition of Higher Educational Services. That was years ago. During the third credit crunch. The campus was bulldozed to make room for apartment complexes. I can't imagine educational services being delivered in any way other than on the Net."

"That may well be, but socialisation skills have been lost," replied the old man. "You saw what happened to the couple earlier. Didn't know how to negotiate a ride properly and it really cost them."

"I suppose."

"You don't seem to have that problem, though love."

"Oh, I love talking. It's just hard to find anyone these days who'll open up and express themselves."

"I know what you mean," smiled the old man. "You're definitely the exception. What's your name?"

Ruth suddenly looked unsure of what to say.

"It's okay, love. I understand. Anyway, my name's Albert."

He drove his cab down the Lower Mounts into Kettering Street. Much of the area had been redeveloped some thirty years ago. The two-storey buildings had been replaced by large department stores and flats. Ruth saw various flat lights on in the fourteen storey towers. The road forked, to the right Wellingborough Road, to the left Kettering Road swerved passed an abandoned church, boarded up and marked for demolition. There had been a preservation order on the building for decades but the Corporation for City Regeneration, who now owned the old Parliamentary Buildings in London, had passed a new order to demolish insignificant buildings from pre-Elizabethan II times.

"Albert," enquired Ruth.

"What was that building for?" She pointed at the church as they drove passed.

"Do you know what, Miss," Albert puzzled, "I'm not too sure. When I was a kid I think it used to sell carpets. Wasn't its original purpose though. I don't suppose it matters any more. They're ripping it down soon. It's only a building when all's said and done. Obviously passed its sell by date."

They passed Grove Road, Queen's Road, Spenser Road, Claire Street and Cooper Street on the left. Ruth did not notice the streets off to the right. All these streets had been rebuilt into luxury apartments rising up some twelve to fourteen floors. The street lamps were constantly on, as the sun seemed to hardly reach down to the pavement level.

The cab reached Eastpark Parade, entrance to the massive Racecourse Shopping Complex. What was once a large green park had been built into a five level shopping and leisure centre a decade or two ago.

Most of the shops were now empty as consumers bought all goods online. Mainly, luxury goods were chosen by humans. All essentials were ordered by the computerised fridges, freezers, dishwashers and washing machines. Wardrobes and drawers scanned garments to determine the age and condition of the fabrics. The barcodes gave the production dates and after a season, if the clothes had reached a certain wash cycle, usually 20 washes, they were incinerated, the ashes vacuumed and sucked out into a waste disposal unit. New garments were ordered online, delivered to the customer's apartment and the boxes pushed into a compartment beside the flat door.

The automated inbuilt habitation computer system was designed to unwrap the product and neatly place the items in the appropriate drawer or wardrobe. An infa-red beam scanned the barcode on the side of the packaging. The computer determined what the item was and a series of mechanical arms with claws, like Swiss army knives, removed the packaging. The clothes were ferried through various tubes to the correct drawer or wardrobe, re-examined, pressed and then left for the customer's use as needed.

Food stuffs were processed similarly. All that was required by the consumer was to ensure their bank accounts had sufficient funds. Unfortunately, Ruth's was running low and her inbuilt habitation computer system, Victoria, was constantly reminding her to reduce the number of services she used. Ruth hoped her current job would bring in enough funds to pay off her bills and her debts would shrink.

"I'll have to drop you here, love," called Albert from the front seat.

Ruth was a little startled. Her mind returned from her financial crisis. She looked at the streets outside the cab. They were at the top of St. George's Avenue. Less than a kilometre away she could see the lights of her apartment block, towering into the deep blue night sky. Across the road, on the left, was the car park leading to the back entrance of the Racecourse shopping complex.

"There's no movement across the car park, so if you are quick you should be safe."

"Thanks, Albert. I appreciate your help," Ruth replied. "Have a good weekend."

The back door popped open and Ruth stepped into the street. The cold breeze slapped her face. As she closed the door behind her, the front electric window slid down.

"Hurry, miss," barked Albert. "You don't have a lot of time."

The glass slid up, the gears crunched into first and the cab sped away along Kingsthorpe Road. Ruth watched the red rear lamps desert her. She felt vulnerable and exposed. Rain fell. She pulled the collar up to her cheeks and braced herself for the kilometre long walk. She was annoyed that her hard heeled shoes were tapping out her movements. For a moment she wondered whether to go barefoot but it was too cold for such foolishness.

The apartment blocks were in a variety of styles. Some simply blocks of red brick, recycled from an old secondary school that had once existed along the avenue. Concrete blocks had been used for the intermediate floors. Steel and glass for the upper levels.

The drifting clouds unveiled a full moon. Ruth had a reasonably good visual of the area. From what she saw there were no immediate threats but she knew she had to be quick and quiet, just in case.

Half way to her apartment block a sound come from behind. Mixed amongst the rustling leaves of two avenues of trees, Ruth heard a distinct tapping against the pavement. Ahead, one of the street lamps was out, the next was flickering. As Ruth entered a darkened patch, she stole a glance over her shoulder. The moon painted a ghostly mask upon the figure behind her. It was a woman, hastily making her way down the avenue. Ruth presumed the woman was also fearful and wanted to get home. Ruth could not take the chance, this could be a ploy before an attack.

Even more determined Ruth picked up her pace. The footsteps behind increased speed, unnerving Ruth as she raced through cones of light. Again Ruth stole a glance back. Two headlights had caught the woman in their beams. She had broke into a run and the car throttled up. As it drove near the woman, the passenger door flipped out knocking her to the ground. The car screeched to a halt, the three remaining doors were flung open and four men jumped out.

Ruth turned on her heels and raced towards home. She could hear the woman scream. Ruth's heel broke and she crumpled to the ground letting out a squeal. Behind her the men were dragging the struggling woman. One of the men punched downwards and the flaying arms fell motionless. Ruth scrambled to her feet and hobbled away as quickly as she could. One of the men looked up, spied Ruth and nudged another assailant. They threw the girl in the back of the car. Ruth disappeared into the shadow of a broken lamp.

The four men jumped into the car, all doors slammed shut and the gears crunched into first. The car accelerate towards Ruth as she clung to the wall hidden in the shadows. Tears began to stream down her face. She fumbled to release her broken shoe. Finally it fell to the ground. Not stopping to retrieve her shoe, Ruth began to sprint the last three hundred metres towards her apartment block.

Block after block Ruth ran, the car behind steadily catching up. The occupants strained to see her in the shadows. The headlamps were dim with dirt, unable to penetrate the dark Ruth hid in. Something snagged her coat, spinning her to the ground. Initially, Ruth thought her sleeve had caught on a railing, but a dark figure stood over her.

The car motored on. The man pulled Ruth off the ground, into an alley. Ruth attempted to scream but a large hand clamped over her mouth. She sunk her teeth into the meaty flesh under the thumb, but still the hand held firm.

The car slowed up and a torch beam cut into the dark alley. Shadows from the metal fire escapes on either building sprang back across the fourteen storeys. Wheelie bins, full of refuge, cluttered the alley at ground level. But there was no sign of Ruth and her captor.

"Can you see anything?" came a voice from inside the car.

"Nothing," came a second.

"Leave it, we have what we want," said a third.

The torch went off and the car sped away.

Ruth tried to murmur something and struggled to catch her breath but the hand held firm.

"Wait," came the man's voice. "Be still."

Overhead a blue light spun as a helicopter hovered. A second beam scanned the area and caught the speeding car. The helicopter tilted forward and darted after the vehicle. The man continued to hold Ruth firmly against the wall.

"We should be safe now," confirmed the man.

The hand around Ruth's mouth relaxed. She sensed a range of muscles suddenly sag and her assailant collapsed to the ground.

Air rushed back into Ruth's lungs. There was something sticky on the side of Ruth's face. She dabbed her fingers against her cheek and pulled her hand into the moonlight. The stuff was dark. She grabbed the dark mass on the floor and pulled him into the light. There was no stiffness to his unconscious body but there was blood across his face and his clothes felt soaked.

CHAPTER TEN.

Dark clouds gathered. The moon began to hide, only occasionally peeping out for the briefest of moments. The cold air made all sounds travel far — a good sign rain was nearing. To the south west of Northampton city were several industrial estates. As with the city centre the buildings had grown upwards, keeping the boundaries of the city virtually as they had been eighty years previously. The city had expanded further out but with several credit crunches, followed by depressions, the city had receded to its former self. What remained outside its current perimeters had been allowed to fall into disrepair, as the corporation that ran the city was more interested in profits than maintaining standards. More and more non-essentials were cut on a daily basis and the people paid higher prices. Each year taxes rose, inhabitants had to cut back and again facilities dried up. Once everyone got used to the additional costs, things went up again as the corporation knew everybody would become accustomed to the inflated prices. Those who moaned or caused a fuss were swiftly dealt with.

On the site of what was once Northampton's city football club stood a new building. The walls had expanded out towards the road which had once fed a cinema complex, restaurants and shopping complex. Now all that remained of these were empty husks, cracking tarmac in the carparks and burnt out cars.

To the south of this monstrous walled complex were two manmade lakes separated by a tributary of the river Nene, called Wooton Brook. The second lake was sandwiched between the brook and the Grand Union Canal. Though most of the neighbouring rivers had Roman names, such as the Ouse and the

Avon, the River Nene, fed by nine springs, appeared to be Celtic in origin, meaning 'bright one'.

As the rain began to fall the walls of the complex appeared darker, hiding the true intent of what lay within. There were no searchlights but every inch of the surrounding area was monitored by thermographic cameras. From the brook side an animal came out of the foliage, its nose to the ground. The hottest parts of the beast showed up white, then to yellow, orange, red through to colder parts which showed up purple. Cold areas of the ground or metal came up as a dark blue.

On the side of the 75 foot tall concrete wall a gun turret spun round. A red spot targeted the beast flickering over its ribcage. A bullet spat out of the muzzle. The dog yelped then collapsed to the ground beside a second dead creature. On closer inspection the corpse was a man.

A large Chinook CH-48A transport hovered over the complex, coming in from the north. The inside of the complex burst into light. A large H was marked out on a six storey block. Here the transport came to rest. Several SMAAWs trudged around the interior of the giant wall. A couple broke away from their normal duties and stood on either side of the landing pad as the doors of the transporter slid upwards, making a clanking noise.

From inside the transporter three dozen civilians, rounded up at the old school football pitch, began to be pushed down the rear ramp. One attempted to run but was terminated ten metres from the aircraft. The rest were herded through large double doors to the interior of the building.

Several floors down, a mop swilled blood across a white tiled floor. A man in a blue overall and black boots pushed the red liquid towards a round stainless steel drain. He slopped the mop into a bucket of disinfectant, pressed out the excess and mopped the floor again.

A large metal door slid open. The man continued on as though unaware of bare feet slapping against the cold white tiles. An old woman whimpered but was silenced by the butt of a rifle clubbed her skull. She crashed to the floor and was dragged away by her heels, her arms trailing behind her long silver hair. All other eyes remained staring at the ground as they marched into the large tiled room. All were naked, deprived of all clothing. All had their hands clasped behind their heads.

"Quickly, across the far side," barked a sergeant. The man's stomach bulged out due to excessive food and drink. Impatiently he tapped the side of the wall with his baton. The group lined up four rows deep by nine, all low in spirit. Among them was Reeves.

The sergeant's name tag read Brooks. He walked around the prisoners, surveying them. Then made his way round to the front, cleared his throat and made his address.

"During the Second World War, Hitler rounded up Jews, homosexuals, Gipsies and other undesirables. Fortunately, today there are no distinctions made. We just round up everybody. We have no prejudices. There is no class or gender distinctions. You are all equal in our eyes. You are nothing."

On the far side of the hall another door opened and a stream of women were brought in wearing red overalls. Again they had no shoes. Their bare soles slapped against the blood carpeting the floor. One of the females, aged around 30, skidded across the wet surface before falling on her face. She whimpered as Roberts, a female guard, moved over towards her. The woman held out her hand assuming she would be helped up but instead Roberts unholstered her pistol, placed it against the woman's temple and pulled the trigger. Instantly, the body crumpled to the floor, sending out a fresh scarlet ripple across everyone's feet. The echo of the shot reverberated around the walls for several moments. An elderly woman began to convulse in shock while the elderly man opposite closed his eyes. A tear rolled down his cheek.

From across the room, a man in his mid-30s, broke ranks and storms toward Roberts as she reholstered her weapon. In an instance she reacted to the oncoming danger, her right hand flipped off the leather strap, whipped out the 9mm Beretta and a second round was discharged. The man's head exploded. White sticky goo clung briefly to the wall, ceiling and overalls of those close by, as the man's slid to the ground at Roberts feet. Sergeant Brooks shook his head as he pushed several prisoners aside to get to Roberts.

"Patients, Roberts. You need to be more patient."

Roberts snapped to attention and saluted. Her right arm slapped down her side as she raised her chin up and stared at the wall a few inches above eye-level.

"Yes, sir. Sorry, sir."

Brooks face came within a centimetre of Roberts. There was rage in his expression. Then came a smile. Roberts slowly lowered her eyes to meet his and returned his gesture.

"There is a protocol, Roberts," he whispered. "We must each abide by it."

"Yes, sir. It won't happen again," she replied in a low tone.

"We are highly trained professionals and pride ourselves in our work," Brooks continued. "You have broken this protocol. My officers have been deprived of their calling with you having been forced to act sooner than usual."

Roberts smiled, excited by a perceived threat coming from Brooks' tone. She felt aroused but others around her sensed an absurd chill in the air. Fear seeped through their skins. What on earth was coming next?

Brooks moved up a line of men. Paused suddenly to meet Reeves' gaze. There was no fear in his face. Sergeant Brooks pulled his gun from its holster and pointed it directly at Reeves's forehead. Reeves did not flinch. Sergeant Brooks looked down the barrel to met Reeves's stare and smiled. Suddenly, Brooks jerked his hand to the left and squeezed the trigger. Two men crumpled to the floor. A man in his 40s and one in his early 20s. The bullet had punched the head of the first and continued on into the other. Both died on the spot.

Thirty minutes later, Reeves was being marched down a long white corridor by two burly guards. His hands were cuffed behind his back. In the opposite direction, prisoners were being escorted from one cell to another. As four guards marched towards Reeves, he was slammed against the wall, his face squeezed into the freezing tiles. Reeves rolled his eyes to see what was going on.

"No peeking now or you won't like what you see." The guard smiled as he pressed Reeves even harder into the tiles.

"Okay, we can go," ordered the second guard.

Reeves was marched down a further three corridors. Each time guards went by with prisoners he was thrust against the cold tiles. At one point his nose began to bleed. Finally, they reached a metal door marked NW201. One of the guards hammered three times with his knuckles. A buzzer rang out and an electronic bolt disengaged the door and it swung inwards. Reeves was pushed inside. He fell to his knees, dared briefly to look up to see a black army officer, with the name Major Armstrong. Armstrong nodded to the guards, who saluted and left. The door slammed shut. A broad smile spread across Reeves' face.

"Hi, Frank."Armstrong shook his head in disbelief. He pulled out a set of keys and undid Reeves' handcuffs.

"You're a bloody fool, Reeves. You'll get yourself killed one of these days."

CHAPTER ELEVEN

Soon it would be light and if this had been further into the countryside, one would have expected there to have been a dawn chorus. But there was only a few timid birds calling to one another, as a new day was being born. Across the top of the Racecourse Shopping Complex on the opposite side of the road, Ruth could see the underside of several clouds streaked with a reddish-purple glow. The air was cool and she could see a small plume of carbon dioxide vapour rise in front of her face as it was expelled from her lungs.

For most of the night Ruth had sat in the shadows, still too scared to move out into the open. She worried that the thugs in the car would still be close by, waiting for her to reveal herself. On the other side of the darkened alley the reddish morning light had climbed down the fourteen floors and slowly unveiled the shape of the man who had, effectively, saved her life. His police tunic, body armour and chest rigs were tattered and torn, stained in blood, Ruth assumed his own. At least she hoped it was his own and not someone else's.

The sunlight began to carve out the man's face. As it reached his eyes he gave out a low groan. His left leg, previously lying flat, suddenly pulled itself in to protect his body. He was automatically attempting to curl up into the foetus position. His left leg kicked out again. This time to take grip of the pavement and push himself into the shadow of a nearby wall beside Ruth. Reacting, Ruth edged herself away from the policeman, wondering whether to run but then remembered her fear of what might be beyond the entrance of the alley.

The man suddenly became alert. There seemed to be a mix of fear and readiness to fight as he bounced into a hunched position, crouching on the balls of his feet, fingertips barely touch the ground. Ruth knew that if he chose he could easily pounce on her, she had left it too late to escape. Her heart pounded.

"Oh, so you've decided to rejoin the living then?" She hoped her voice did not give her fear away. The man seemed to sense she was not going to pose him a threat and his eyes, which had firmly been fixed on hers, like a cornered panther, now began to survey his surroundings.

"Where are we?" he growled.

"Exactly where you left us. Right where I'd rather not have been," she snapped, "I wanted to get so much done this Saturday."

She pulled her knees under her chin and wrapped her arms around her legs in a vain attempt to keep some heat in her body. She so desired the sanctuary of home but wondered whether she would ever see it again.

"There was a car following you?" quizzed the policeman. He seemed confused.

"Yeah," Ruth responded keeping her eyes on the entrance to the street. "Hopefully, they are long gone."

"So we are safe?"

"I suppose, but some poor woman wasn't so lucky."

The man checked out his uniform and discovered various holes with dried blood soaked into the bluish-black material. Ruth turned her head to watch him. He attempted to stand, but the pain was too great and he collapsed into the side of the wall. Ruth instinctively found herself jumping up to his aid.

"Are you hurt bad? Look I'm sorry I've been so nasty, I just thought you were going to. You know?"

"You were in danger but not from me," he replied.

"How did you get hurt?' asked Ruth. "Do you have a radio? Perhaps you can call for help?"

"No, that would be more dangerous."

"Why?" puzzled Ruth.

"It's a long story. We should find somewhere safe."

"Why should I trust you?" Ruth looked deep into his eyes. Both were a grey-blue colour. He looked away and just at that moment Ruth saw something. His eyes briefly glowed, especially in the shadows. Ruth pulled his head round with her hand on his chin to take another look. His eyes were back to the grey-bluish colour.

"What?" quizzed the man.

"Oh, nothing." She was puzzled. "My apartment is nearby, we can go there."

"Are you still not sure about me?"

"I'm cautious."

"If it helps, my name is Daniel. What's yours?" He smiled.

"Ruth," she replied her mouth also turning upwards. She turned away as she felt her checks blush.

"Hi, Ruth, pleased to meet you." Daniel held out his hand. Ruth, still uncertain, turned to face him and took his hand.

"Pleased to meet you too, Daniel."

Ruth pulled Daniel to his feet. He winced.

"Sorry," pleaded Ruth.

"It's okay. Had to be done."

Ruth lifted her handbag before she positioned Daniel's right arm around her neck, so she could support him around the waist. Cautiously, the two of them edged their way out of the alley. In various apartments, lights began to come on. The sound of showers, radios, sizzling bacon and various voices calling out to loved ones still in slumber could be heard. And more bird songs filled the air.

"We'll have to hurry before anyone comes into the street," remarked Daniel. "We'll also have to avoid the security cameras."

"Why can't you call for help, Daniel?"

"I'm a fugitive."

"What?" Ruth froze. "Why?"

"I'll tell you when we get to your place."

"How do I know I can trust you?"

"I saved your life, remember?"

While they had been talking, some heavy clouds had moved across the sky, casting a gloomy shadow over the city, threatening rain. A few cars drove into the street, then came a tram.

"We may have missed our chance," snarled Daniel, again trying to hold in the pain.

"What if we use the sewage tunnels, there is a covering in the basement of my block. Maintenance use it to sort out blockages."

"Are they big enough for us to get down?"

"Well, the droids seem to be able to cope okay. I'm sure we can."

Ruth propped Daniel against a wall and searched the alley for an iron sewerage cover. It took several moments and she had to move a few wheelie bins to find one. Her next problem was trying to find something to prise open the cover. Again she searched around to find something to use.

Daniel was slightly amused by all Ruth's antics. "What have you lost?"

"Don't suppose you have a knife on you?"

Daniel searched through his R.I.C.A.S. Vest and pulled out a black non-reflective stainless steel multi-tool. He prised open a blade and handed the device to Ruth.

"Just like a boyscout, always prepared," she scoffed. Within seconds Ruth had prised off the metal cover, giving them access to a metal ladder bolted to the vertical tunnel.

"Will you be able to squeeze down there okay," asked Ruth.

Daniel unclipped the R.I.C.A.S. Vest, then gently slid his arms out. "This should make things easier."

It took about fifteen minutes for them to navigate their way to Ruth's apartment block. When they reached the correct vertical tunnel, Ruth used Daniel's multi-tool to lever the metal floor panel. They found themselves surfacing in the automated laundry area. Several machines were sloshing away with a washload. An android took no notice of them but continued to load a dryer with a mix of woollens and jeans.

"Those woollens will shrink," exclaimed Ruth.

"Not our concern," whispered Daniel. "Let's get to your flat."

As the two of them made their way to the exit, a pile of new laundry flew through a shoot, in the wall, into a yellow plastic bag, marked 302. Third floor apartment two. Ruth helped Daniel through the doorway to the stairs. They ascended four flights to Ruth's floor. At the corridor entrance, Ruth checked to see that no-one was about. As the two of them made their way to Ruth's door a camera rotated monitoring their progress. They both slipped into Ruth's room and she raced up to the computer, tapped a few keys and brought up the video from the security camera outside. "You're not supposed to be able to do that," remarked Daniel.

"Mmmm, I know," she grinned.

Moments later the video was deleted.

"All gone."

"Are you sure?" wondered Daniel.

"The system takes twenty seconds to log the video to an operator. Everything is malfunctioning these days, so there are ways if you know how."

"And you know how?"

"Have to learn something on cold winter evenings. I love puzzles and that was one of them."

"You live here, inside the system. Do you venture beyond the city limits much?"

Ruth scowled then took off her coat, letting it fall to the ground and slumped into her sofa.

"Take a seat," she indicated to Daniel. He dropped his R.I.C.A.S. rig to the floor and passed out.

Three hours later Daniel again came round.

"Here's a cup of soup," smiled Ruth. "You spent five minutes tossing and turning so I knew you'd be hungry."

"Thanks." Daniel took the mug of tomato soup. As the liquid made its way to his stomach, the warmth soon spread through his body.

"So, are you going to tell me why you are a fugitive?" Ruth sat down once more on her sofa.

"Is your home system monitoring our conversation?"

"Victoria is in stand-by mode. I've been a bit late with my payments this month. I've also adjusted her language preferences to Spanish when she is in stand-by mode so what we will be saying will be gibberish to her."

"What about her AI system. Won't it adjust itself?"

"I've fed in a satellite channel for her entertainment. Every thing's fine," Ruth reassured him.

"Okay," started Daniel, as he surveyed the room. "Do you ever go to the outskirts of the city?"

"I don't have time, not with the curfew so early."

"So you end up working, racing to get home before the curfew and entertaining yourself at home most evenings?"

"Pretty much so I guess," Ruth agreed, a little embarrassed.

"Do you get to meet many other people?"

"Only those at the office."

"Do you have a boyfriend?"

"Hey, are you hitting on me?"

"No, no, I'm just trying to get a picture of what your world is like and how much you know?"

"Know of what? What's this all about?"

"The system we live in is unsustainable. Everyday people lose their homes, their jobs, everything and find themselves falling out of the system. Do you ever wonder what happens to them?"

"I've never really thought about it. I don't watch much news these days."

"That's probably because you don't get to see the news about what is really going on."

"No, as I said, I spend most of my spare time solving puzzles and figuring out how this apartment works."

"And how long do you think it will be before you can't afford this place?" Daniel asked.

"I'm okay for the time being. I got a new job, it seems cool."

"But have you thought about what might happen to you if you found yourself out on the street?"

"No, I haven't. There has been no need."

"Well, if you did find yourself out of here, you would quickly find yourself being ejected from the inner city into the ruins of the outer city. People struggle to keep themselves alive. The City Corporation administrators have very harsh methods of keeping the outer city population from becoming a threat."

"And what may that be?" quizzed Ruth.

"Human culling."

CHAPTER TWELVE

Samuelson stood over the two children while they slept. Both were gently breathing, curled up under the cloth the droids had brought. He was still stunned by the way the girl had come back to life and he could feel his hands shaking. The lamp flickered then grew dim, so he stepped over the children, took the lamp from its hanging position and began to crank the plastic handle. The 12 LED bulbs grew brighter. For all intents and purposes the lamp looked like an old paraffin storm lantern, but only in shape. In actuality, the lamp was made up of 12 LEDs and after about a minutes worth of winding could generate enough light to see around the tunnels for about an hour.

Samuelson sat down about twenty feet away from the children, set the lamp beside him, pulled out a note book and began to write down his thoughts. He had been getting another flood of images in his head while dreaming and wanted to record them before he forgot. He had seen a shepherd tending a flock of goats and sheep. The man had two wives, who in turn had a handmaiden. There seemed to be some jealousy between the wives. The shepherd had been forced to work for his uncle for seven years in order to take the hand of the younger daughter. But the uncle had tricked the shepherd into sleeping with the elder daughter. Seven more years the man found himself labouring for the one he loved. The shepherd loved the younger daughter more than the elder one but only the latter bore him any children. When she could conceive no more, she gave the shepherd her handmaiden who also bore him children. The jealous younger daughter also gave him her handmaiden and felt vindicated when she too bore children. As time passed the younger daughter also found herself becoming pregnant. In total there were twelve sons born to the four women, fathered by the shepherd.

Samuelson struggled with his thoughts to make sense of them all. He tried to see if he could remember any of the names he thought he heard but as he scribbled away in the dim lantern light, all names and meaning evaded him. He wanted to know why it was so important to convey a story of a man who had two wives and slept with their handmaidens? Surely this was adultery and bigamy?

"You're silly," came the slow voice from twenty feet away.

Samuelson was startled, "I'm sorry? What?"

"You don't know what you are writing down, the story in your head," laughed Deborah.

"How do you know I'm writing a story?"

"You dreamt it last night and you were trying to make sense of it. Am I right?" chuckled the pre-teen girl. "Tell me, am I right?"

Samuelson was a little embarrassed, he coughed, blinked more rapidly than usual and was not sure where to look.

"I am right, I knew it," she laughed with joy.

"How are you feeling now?" Samuelson asked.

"Don't change the subject, I know what you're doing. Tell me how far you've got?" Deborah was persistent, focused and determined to continue the conversation.

"Why do you want to know?" enquired the elderly man.

"Because I have some information for you," she smiled. "Stuff you need to fill in the gaps."

Samuelson smiled in disbelief. "And how can you possibly know what is going on in my head?"

"I don't but I know what is going on in mine and you were there struggling as you are now."

Struck by awe, Samuelson found himself on his feet, drawn to where the girl lay on the ground. She made a space for him to sit down beside her, patting the cloth down with her hand.

Samuelson made himself comfortable and presented Deborah with his A5 sized, hard cover, black notebook. Deborah scanned through the handwritten text, flicked over the pages, smiling all the time. Even in the dark, her greyish-coloured eyes seemed to glow a vibrant sky blue. Samuelson could not see where this glow came from when the girl was bathed in the light from the LED lamp, but in the shadows he could distinctly see a flash of vivid blue emanate from her eyes. She bit her lower lip, excited by what she read.

"Let me bring the lamp closer, so you don't hurt your eyes," suggested Samuelson, moving to retrieve the light.

"Thank you, you are a gentleman," commented Deborah.

"You have quite a confidence about you, for such a young age," remarked Samuelson.

"I have responsibilities, Johnny needs me and I've become his mother, now mom and dad have gone."

"I'm sorry." Samuelson shook his head.

"Don't be and stop changing the subject," Deborah demanded. "You have the basics of what the story is about but there is much missing. It is important that you write everything down correctly using all the right words and letters. There must be no mistakes otherwise you have to start all over again."

"But it is just my thoughts of what I saw in my dream, I just felt I should write them down."

Deborah looked so deep into Samuelson's eyes that he felt as though she had reached into his soul. This twelve year old girl had penetrated a part of his being that no-one, not even his late wife had managed to get into. He felt his heart thumping and a cold chill through his spine. The hairs on his neck tingled as he pushed himself away from the girl.

"Don't be frightened, I'm only a little girl," remarked Deborah. Samuelson frowned in disbelief. It was as though she was reading his thoughts, as if she was inside his head.

"No, I am not, so you don't have to worry about that," she laughed. "I'm not the one who can see your dark secrets. Pity, it might have been fun to have known."

"No, I don't think it would be," snapped Samuelson.

"It's okay, there is nothing here that can harm you. Promise."

Samuelson felt even more stupid being frightened of a little thing who must be at least 53 years his junior.

"You have been honoured," continued the twelve year old.

"In what way?" quizzed the old man.

"You are writing the first book but you haven't started at the beginning. This is nearly two thirds of the way through."

"How do you know that?" Samuelson let out a nervous laugh.

"Because I know the names of all your characters. I also know the meaning of their names and why they are important players in the script. Also the words are not all in the right place and there is much missing. There is a lot of work still to be done and I can help you. I can fill in some of the gaps but you have to discern the rest and make sure it is all correct otherwise it won't work."

"It won't work," echoed Samuelson.

"That's right, the text won't work and it will be useless."

"Why," puzzled Samuelson.

"It is a program, like a piece of software and if the instructions are not coded properly, all that will happen will be an error message."

"You are not making sense," scoffed Samuelson. "All I am trying to do is write down my thoughts about a dream I had last night."

"You are being given coding for the most important program the Universe has ever seen. It's quite wonderful, such a gift but you have to make sure that you are writing it down correctly so that it will work. That is so important," stated the 12 year old.

"You sound like an old woman."

"My name sake was a prophetess," Deborah smiled but Samuelson felt she was being pretentious.

"I am just relaying the message, that's all," commented the girl. "Do not judge me when you do not know from whom I profer my word from."

Samuelson looked down at the girl, her smile had faded and she had become serious. He felt he should not argue with her, besides, she was just a child, why did he feel so small by what she was saying. He felt unnerved by what she seemed to know and intimidated by her countenance. There seemed to be an aura around her that illuminated the tunnel as she spoke. He had forgotten the LED lamp which had gone out, yet the room still seemed to have the same meagre glow. Like a small boy he sat beside the girl as though she was his school mistress.

"What should I do?" he asked.

"You are writing in English. You will need to translate this."

"Into what?"

"Hebrew."

CHAPTER THIRTEEN

Ruth was stunned. She could not quite come to terms with what Daniel had implied. She got up from the sofa and began to pace across the room, lost in thought. Then she came back over to Daniel, who still remained seated watching her.

"You mean," Ruth finally spoke, "they actually round people up and kill them for no reason other than they had fallen out of the system?"

"Exactly," replied Daniel.

Ruth found her legs give way and she plopped down onto the sofa.

"So, let me get this straight." She took a deep breath. "You are telling me that if I get kicked out of here and find myself without work, I could find myself outside the city, rounded up with others and put to death, for no reason other than I am not earning any money?"

"Yes."

Daniel could see the blood drain from Ruth's face. She almost aged before his eyes as the full horror of what life without work or security of a home really meant.

"I'm sorry I made you feel this way but now you know why I'm a fugitive. I can't be part of it anymore."

Ruth suddenly looked startled and edged away from him.

"What's wrong?" asked Daniel.

"You know this because you were part of it and I've let you into my home." It was as if Ruth's world had collapsed. She frantically looked around the room as though it was melting before her eyes.

"What am I going to do now?" she asked anxiously.

"Hey," Daniel held her shoulders and gave her a reassuring squeeze. "Don't worry. Tell me, how long have we been here?"

"I don't know, a couple of hours, maybe more. Why?"

"Well, if they knew I was here, they would have come and got me by now. So there is nothing to panic about. You said yourself that you erased the security video and your AI system is being entertained enough to distract her. So let's relax for the time being. Okay?"

"Yeah," replied Ruth, still worried. "I suppose." She gave a nervous laugh.

"Do you mind if I get cleaned up?" asked Daniel.

"Sure, there's a shower and sink through there." Ruth pointed to an open door on the other side of the lounge. "I'm afraid there is only cold water, I've no more credit for hot."

"That's okay, I can cope," remarked Daniel. "Perhaps, you should find another puzzle to solve, to take your mind off things?"

"That's a good idea," Ruth smiled, as she searched his eyes. They were not hard or cold but gave her a sense of security, protection and warmth. He stood some five or six inches higher than Ruth and she felt the strength of his muscles as he held her arms between his hands. Yet he was gentle with her.

He smiled. "I won't be long. And thank you."

"What for?"

"For giving me somewhere safe."

When his hands released her, Ruth felt a sudden chill of vulnerability. She was aware that she had a longing to be held and she felt a little embarrassed, almost as though she was a little girl once more and her father had just said goodbye before going off to work. She was almost distracted by the emotions she felt. Her limbs tingled from her shoulders to her fingertips. She rubbed her fingers with her thumbs hoping the sensation would go away. But it refused too.

She sat down at her laptop and booted up, then she

remembered to switch off the wifi so she was no longer on the network. She did not know what she should do to occupy herself. Absentmindedly, she kicked over her handbag and the content fell to the ground. One item was the notebook she had retrieved from the desk at work. A little black moleskin notebook about 12.5 centimetres wide by 24 centimetres tall. She flicked open the book and began to look at its contents.

The sound of Daniel's first boot falling to the ground distracted her. She looked up to see the second one being kicked off. He had left the door open and was sitting on the toilet seat and pulling at his socks. As he stood up, Ruth looked away. She made out to be busy flicking through the book. Daniel's black army jacket was thrown to the floor and as he peeled off his shirt, Ruth could see him wince as the fibres of his shirt tore away dried blood from his wounds.

Once the garment had fallen to the floor Ruth saw how well formed his body was through constant exercise. She could see no fat, just muscle. When Daniel unfastened his belt, dropped his fatigues, Ruth found it hard to draw her focus away from his body. But when his boxer shorts came down, she instantly closed her eyes and tried to look at the text in the notebook.

The water jet could be heard starting and the shower doors echoed as they were drawn together. Once more, Ruth allowed herself a glimpse at Daniel. She could see the shower water streaming down his body washing away the blood from his wounds. There were cuts and bruising along his right arm, up across his shoulders and down his pecs. His abdominal muscles were taut in the classical six-pack.

She began to realise what she was doing and turned away, mentally chastising herself for not giving Daniel his privacy. Then she began to think about how long it had been since she last spent some time with a man and realised it had been several years. How time flies? She had spent so much time trying to work or get home before the curfew there was no time for socialising. No time for human contact. No time to share her thoughts with another person. No time to share her body and be loved or be in love. There was just no time.

"So why don't you seize the moment. Enjoy the opportunity while you can?" a voice said in her head. Again she chastised herself. Then a second voice invaded her mind.

"Are there any towels, Ruth?" This voice came from the shower room.

"Yes, yes, I'll get one for you. I'm sorry, I didn't think."

"Of course, you didn't," came her thoughts. "You were too busy enjoying the view. Weren't you?"

She smiled to herself. Ruth made her way over to a drawer panel and used an override switch to allow her to manually slide it open. She pulled out two towels, a small one for the floor and a larger one for Daniel. She then plucked up the courage to walk into the shower room attempting to hide her embarrassment by trying to make out she was comfortable with a strange naked man in her own private place.

"Here you go." Ruth stood just outside the shower doors glass panel. When Daniel turned around he seemed surprised to find her standing there and quickly covered himself up. His jaw dropped with his surprise. It suddenly dawned on Ruth that she had made a mistake. Her cheeks went rouge and she did not know where to look and made quite a fool of herself trying to exit the shower room, stumbled over his clothes and bashed her left knee against the door frame. The pain nearly had her in tears as she hobbled to the safety of the sofa.

Daniel quickly retrieved the towel, wrapped it round himself and closed the shower door.

"Sorry, Ruth," came Daniel's equally embarrassed voice from the other side of the door. "I didn't mean to expose myself. I'm so used to the community shower areas on base. I completely forgot where I was. I'm really sorry."

"It's okay, honest," called back Ruth. "I've just not had anyone here before. I mean staying with me. I'm not used to the company either."

She shook her head and again chastised herself for her behaviour. A few moments later, Daniel poked his head around the corner of the door.

"Are you sure, are you really okay?"

"Yes," Ruth smiled, still a little dishevelled. "Would you like me to wash your clothes so they are fresh for later?"

"That would be good, if you don't mind?"

"Not a problem."

Daniel sheepishly came out of the shower room and seemed to keep his back against the wall and he slid to the side. Ruth got up from the sofa and made her way, gingerly, to the shower room to retrieve his clothes.

"I'll take them down to the laundry room and give you some time to rest. We can decide later what to do next."

Ruth left the apartment and made her way down to the basement. She hoped the machines would not detect what she had in the wash and planned to use one of the older ones which had a faulty barcode scanner. Everything, she thought, these days are scanned, supposedly to give the highest efficiency, but in reality was another form of monitoring, to keep the population under control.

CHAPTER FOURTEEN

Satisfied that she had managed to evade all monitoring systems for two hours in the laundry, Ruth made her way back up to her flat on the third floor. Inside, Daniel was asleep on the sofa, wrapped in several towels and he had managed to find a duvet. Ruth did not want to disturb him, so she quietly placed his things on the floor beside him, lifted her laptop and went over to the breakfast bench. Victoria was still in sleep mode, even though the light was now streaming in from the bright sun outside. Ruth was pleased that it was Saturday, her day off and no one would disturb them. She made herself some breakfast consisting of porridge oats, 300mls of milk, half a tea spoon of cinnamon, a whole sliced banana, and a sprinkling of dried, crushed flaxseed and goji berries, cooked for about five minutes on top of a small gas camping burner. She had picked up the burner in an old store down Kettering Road before all the old buildings had been demolished about seven years before.

To make sure that none of the steam or smoke set off the fire alarm, Ruth opened a window by hand cranking the automatic system. Victoria, in her computer fashion, often chastised Ruth about misusing the apartment, and that for optimum efficiency everything should be left in automatic mode. But Ruth wanted her own independence to do as she pleased, to physically engage with the world she existed in, to use all her senses to experience life. At times it all felt claustrophobic, too enclosed, too encapsulated, too restrictive and suffocating. Ruth wanted to breath in life while the opportunity allowed.

Once the porridge was ready, Ruth tipped the contents of the small saucepan into a blue and white ceramic bowl. She took a spoon from the crockery tray and sat on a large cushion, over by the large windows, to watch the sun cast amber, red and violet light across the roof tops. There was no traffic in the streets, even though it was nearly midday. Most people were making the most of staying in bed. A gentle breeze rustled through the leaves along the avenue of trees and everything seemed to be at peace. As she chewed into the hot banana chunks, still retaining the heat within the porridge, Ruth felt as though she had drifted into a timeless zone, where she was connected to all her relatives, her parents and her grandfather, who had once attended the college her apartment block was now built on. She could picture her grandfather's bright brown eyes, encased in the wrinkled face, who refused to accept his physical age with his, oh so positive, attitude and encouragement.

Grandfather had once told her how, on the first week of college, the induction was to produce some form of kinetic art. He had said, that he was keen on model planes, so he built a wireframe mesh for a fuselage, added a propeller and elastic band, then strung a cable between two of the trees in the avenue, hooked the fuselage to the cable and watched the mechanism dart between the trees.

Ruth got up from her cushion and found her way across the room to a draw panel in the wall. She slid it open and pulled out an old photo album. Victoria was always pestering her to have the document digitised and have everything stored on the solid state drives as they would last longer, but Ruth refused. There was something special about flicking through old photographs, of turning the pages and fingering the old black and white or faded colour images, Polaroids, Kodak or Fuji prints. Of all the images the most recent were the ones almost faded. Those old inkjet printed images. The freshest looking ones were the old black and white images, possibly taken some fifty or sixty years before. She turned a couple over and was surprised to discover some images were from the 1930s and 40s. There were even a couple of some distant relatives from the turn 1900s. Old stiff, Victorian photographs. But the ones she was most interested in, were from between 1980 to 2010, of her grandparents and parents as kids growing up in a world so different from the one she now lived in.

She found it funny to see her grandfather sitting in front of the old computers that once sat on table tops. Big blocks and flat screens. These computers could not talk to you and had no intelligence. They used to have, if she remembered right, operating systems called Orange, or was it Pears and a rival company that used Doors. Her grandfather preferred the fruit variety, said they were the windows to the world back then. He would then make her laugh by juggling three apples from a wooden bowl his father had once made by somehow turning wood.

Ruth flicked through a few more pages. She began to notice that there were hardly any photos of her granny. Most were of her in her early twenties, trying to turn away. Her long hair twirled, covering her face, so that Ruth could hardly see what she looked like. From what she could tell, her granny was very petite, fun loving and pretty. There was one photograph of the two of them together. A faded colour image taken by a camera that must have had a self timer because her granny was sitting quite relaxed on a log while it looked as though her grandfather had just run into frame before the camera snapped. Her granny seemed to be full of giggles and was having so much fun. She had worn a thin blue waist-length coat, a thick Aaron jumper, jeans and trainers. He had been wearing what looked like a leather flying jacket, a stripped jumper, jeans and a silly moustache. Granny must have forced him to shave it off as there were no other images of him sporting such a scruffy object.

Ruth loved the way her granny's eyes seemed to glow a vivid blue, emphasised by the colour of her thin coat. She wondered if she had been cold that day as there were patches of snow on the ground and on the trees in the background. Her grandfather was well wrapped up, but not her granny. Ruth wondered what had happened to them both. They had just seemed to have disappeared from her life and she could not remember when or how or why? Only that they were no longer there. They were gone. All she knew was how much she missed them, along with her parents. It was still painful to think about her parents and once more she pushed them to the back of her mind, not wanting to revisit those memories.

The sun had risen well above the roofs of the hypermarket and was nearly blinding Ruth. She found herself back in the present. Her hand was palm down on the next page of the photo album, almost as though it refused to go further. The next page she knew would give her too much pain, so she slapped the covers closed and placed the album back in the drawer.

Then the clouds came over, grey heavy beasts that soaked up the blue sky and shaded the sun. The temperature in the room dropped sharply and the light dimmed. Ruth knew her time to herself was short. Other chores would now invade her time. The cool air whistled through the open window, so she reached out and pulled the frame closed. Perhaps it was not going to be much of a bright day after all?

Ruth went into the shower room and switched on the water. It was cold. She sighed, then darted back into the living room. Daniel was still asleep, so she quietly went over and picked up her laptop. Beside the shower room door, Ruth pushed a panel open to reveal some of Victoria's wiring. She pulled out a cable with a USB plug and pushed it into the laptop. Double clicking on an application, Ruth made a few numerical changes and looked back into the shower. Steam came out of the cubicle. She frowned.

"Whoops. Too hot."

Ruth changed the numerical value. Less steam came out. Putting the laptop on the floor she race over and put her hand into the jet of water.

"Perfect."

She unplugged the laptop and closed the panel, placed the

computer onto the table and retreated once more into the shower room.

With the door closed and locked behind her, Ruth peeled off the sweatshirt and joggers, then threw the garments into the laundry shoot and stepped into the spray of water, thankful for the heat that came with each droplet.

She closed her eyes and cherished the sensation of the beads of water tracking down her body. Her hair fell along her spine and she felt at though the muscles across her shoulders were being massaged.

Once more she allowed her thoughts to drift into the past. She could see through the pouring rain, her grandfather coming to save her. She had once got lost in the rain and could not find her way home. She must have been about seven and had gone out to the shops to get some milk. While she was out a freak storm had come upon her village. She had no coat. Hailstones initially barred her way then came cold heavy rain. Ruth tried to run through the streets but the rain had stung her eyes and she had become lost. Debris from roofs began to fly into the sky. A tree fell in front of her and panel fencing was torn from its stakes.

Ruth found herself in a nightmare storm. She hid in an old shed when the hailstones came again. She was cold and frightened. What she had not known, was that her grandfather had come out to find her and seen her down a lane. He had come into the shed and she was so relieved to see him, she could not stop hugging him. He lifted her in his arms and covered her in his coat before stepping out into the holocaust of rain and wind.

When they had reached home. Granny had rushed around the kitchen finding cotton wool and Detol to clean the cuts and grazes on Ruth's knees, arms and head. Grandfather smiled and reassured her that all was fine. And she believed him and felt secure, even with the wind rattling the tiles on the roof and bashing the windows. Ruth believed every word he said, and trusted him.

Reluctantly Ruth returned her mind and focused on the

present. Pushing the shower switch, instantly the water ceased and cold air bit into her skin. She dried the moisture from her skin and felt the goosebumps. Towelling down her hair, she thought briefly about the clothes she was going to wear. She had forgotten to take them from the drawer before her shower and what she had been wearing was now in the laundry. Oh, well, she thought, I can bear the cold from here to the drawer. Still drying her hair with the towel, Ruth made her way into the living area to get some clothes. The shower room door slammed behind her and the sound of her bare feet slapped along the tiled floor, echoed around the room. She began to hum to herself as she knelt down to open the drawer.

"Good, morning?" came a voice. "You have some lovely views from here."

Ruth's eyes widened. She had forgotten, she was not alone and her morning routine was not totally appropriate with a stranger in the house. She let the towel drop to the floor and wondered how best to tackle this situation. She stood up, kept her back to Daniel, calmly wrapped the towel around her body and continued to pull her clothes from the drawer before standing up. She turned and saw Daniel drinking coffee, by the window looking out at the hypermarket.

"And I hope," began Ruth, "you are the gentleman I assume you are and will continue to avert your eyes?"

She could see a smile break across Daniel's face as he continued to gaze out the window.

"I'll be back in a few moments, perhaps you'll be so kind as to make me a cup too?"

"Certainly, madam," came Daniel's reply as he attempted not to laugh.

Back in the sanctuary of the shower room, Ruth could see in the mirror, how flushed she had become. Her absent-mindedness had let her guard slip. The best way to resolve this situation, she concluded, was to continue as though nothing had happened. Then she gave herself permission to smile and wondered if her

CHAPTER FIFTEEN

What Samuelson found hardest about living underground, was not knowing what time of day it was. In the darkened tunnels it seemed like it was always night time. He had thought about what Deborah had said and wondered what else he had to write down that came before the events he had seen in his dream? Why was the shepherd so important? And why did he, David Samuelson have to be the one to write this all down?

He had been awake for some seventeen hours and fatigue was beginning to get the better of him. He lifted the clockwork lamp and found his way through a couple of tunnels back to where he had previously found a dry area and left his sleeping bag. From a recycled-water container, he partially filled a small basin, stripped down to his waste and gave himself a body wash. Then from a small tin of soda, took a few granules on his old toothbrush and began to scrub away at his teeth. He was pleased and surprised that he had managed to go without dentures. Most of his old friends, now since dead, had all lost their teeth by the time they were 50, but he had been lucky and had only lost a couple after two severe cases of mouth abscesses.

Finally, Samuelson put his tee-shirt back on and climbed into the sleeping bag. He had gotten into the habit of keeping his boots on just in case there was an emergency and he was forced to evacuate rather sharply. Just as he was about to fall asleep he heard the metallic footsteps against concrete, as 7D21 made its way along the tunnel. Samuelson watched the android navigate the dark interior of the tunnels, using ultraviolet and infra-red sensors. Samuelson's lamp also allowed it to use the same visual spectrum as Samuelson and the machine settled itself down to go into sleep mode. Samuelson knew it had been monitoring his heart beat and breathing and had probably determined he needed some rest. By stationing itself in close proximity to him, 7D21 could defend Samuelson if a threat arose. Johnny and Deborah had been left in the charge of 8DF20.

As the wind-up lamp began to fade, the only sound to be heard in the tunnels, was water running through the sewer. Someone new to this environment would have been unaccustomed to the stench, but Samuelson's nose had made the necessary adjustments over the past six months and the smell no longer bothered him.

Much of what Samuelson dreamt did not make sense. Most were abstract images, with no form, colour or sound; but he was aware he had been dreaming. Then he heard the sound of a voice. Only one word was said.

"Samuel."

He struggled to open his eyes and could hardly shake off the sleep but managed to reply.

"Yes?"

The tunnel was still dark except for a small red blinking LED on 7D21's neck that indicated it was in sleep mode. There seemed to be no-one else about and if there had been he knew the android would have activated instantly. Samuelson assumed then it had just been something he had heard in his dream. He tried once more to settle himself but no sooner had he closed his eyes and there it was again.

"Samuel."

It was definitely audible. He heard it with his ears. There was a sound, a voice and it had said Samuel.

"7D21?"

The android remained in sleep mode.

"Hey, 7D21?" Samuelson called out. The blue LEDs behind the android's visor began to active and the motors inside began to whir-up.

"Yes, Samuelson. How can I help?"

"Were you asleep?"

"Yes, Samuelson, I was in stand-by mode."

"Did you call out my name?"

"No, Samuelson. I did not."

"Do androids dream? I mean, could you have been talking in your sleep?"

"No, Samuelson."

"No, you don't dream or no you don't talk in your sleep?"

"When we are in stand-by mode there are no audible activities."

"That's okay. Forget it," replied Samuelson as he began to settle down once more, slightly irritated. "Sorry, I disturbed you."

7D21 did not respond but went back into stand-by mode faster than Samuelson was able to fall asleep. Yet, he heard a voice call out again.

"Samuel."

"7D21, will you pack it in. You may find this funny but I certainly don't."

7D21 became active once more.

"Samuelson, it was not I who summoned you. I detected no dialogue being spoken over the past few hours, other than your own voice. Are you certain you heard a voice?"

"Too right I did, and I'm getting a little frustrated by it all."

7D21 extended his scan and networked with other androids within a five mile radius and received signals that no other humans other than Samuelson, Deborah and Johnny were in the area.

"Johnny and Deborah are still sleeping and have not murmured a sound since you last spoke with Deborah. What did you hear?"

"Someone said, Samuel."

"Not Samuelson?"

Samuelson thought for a moment.

"No, they said 'Samuel'".

He was aware that 7D21 was processing information. This only took a few moments, then the android spoke again.

"There is a similar occurrence mentioned in the old text. Perhaps you should answer the voice and see where you are directed?"

"Will you continue to monitor and tell me what you detect?"

"Yes."

Samuelson had expected more from the android but nothing else came, so he lay down once more and tried to close his eyes. In his 65 years he had seen much but nothing came close to what he was experiencing now. Once more, Samuelson lay down and tried to sleep. His mind was ticking over and he desperately wanted to hear the voice again to see what was going on, or if someone was playing a prank on him.

Samuelson's mouth was dry. The tunnels were full of the sounds of running water. He pulled the blanket back and got to his feet. 7D21 remained stationary, all functions were on standby. Samuelson felt the gravel crunch under his feet as he began to make his way through the nearby tunnels to a water dispenser one of the androids had set up to purify water for him to drink shortly after he had been found.

Initially, he traced the walls with his left hand, guiding him through the dark but as he came closer to his destination his eyes detected a gradual increase in light. It began as a low green illumination that gradually intensified to an orange tungsten quality of light.

The water dispenser was about fifty metres away, just where the light appeared to emanate from. Samuelson paused for a moment or two, straining to hear if there were any sounds. There came to his ears a low droning voice, of what the voice was saying he could not determine though he sensed it was male. Slowly he edged his way towards a bend in the tunnel, intending to remain undetected. He anticipated more than one as the voice was talking to another, though the second person was not responding.

Samuelson was within five metres from the bend and again paused. He had been cautious not to drag his feet and hardly disturbed the dried concrete granules that were being compressed beneath his leather boots. He felt the hairs on his arm prickle as though pulled erect by some kind of static energy. Reluctantly, he turned towards the darkened tunnel.

"It's okay, Samuel. We were expecting you."

Samuelson felt his stomach knot.

"Who are you?"

The man walked passed Samuelson towards the light and smiled.

"All will be explained."

There was a presence about the man that set Samuelson's skin tingling. His hands began to shake.

"Don't be scared. We won't harm you."

Samuelson felt compelled to follow the man. Around the bend of the tunnel, Samuelson could see three more men. A small fire provided the tunnel with illumination. They were all seated, but when the fourth man and Samuelson appeared the others stood up.

Samuelson still felt thirsty.

"Here's some water," said the man nearest the dispenser as he handed Samuelson a beaker.

"Thank you," he replied. "Why were you expecting me?"

"We had called you," replied the fourth man.

"Why?"

"We have a message for you."

"Who from?"

They all smiled. Samuelson frowned. "I feel left out. What is the message? Who are you anyway? Where are you from?"

One of the men took a kettle from the fire. He poured some liquid into a metal mug.

"Here, take some fresh tea. It's black but still good."

Samuelson took the cup and a second man gestured for him

to sit with them. Samuelson then noticed that the fire was not the source of light in the tunnel, but was coming from the man sitting beside the dispenser.

"The tea is good," commented Samuelson. He took another sip. All four men were now seated and each took a metal cup and poured in hot water.

"Have you come far?" enquired Samuelson.

"Not as far as you might think," replied one.

"What are your names?"

The four men looked at one another. One set of eyes questioned another and then a nod indicated one could proceed.

"My name is Michael," said the man closest to the dispenser. "And this is Gabriel." He pointed to his right. Gabriel nodded to Samuelson.

"My name is Raphael," spoke a large African who sat to Samuelson's left. He nodded before looking to his right to hear the name of the one who had first spoken. The man smiled.

"I am Ramiel."

"Why are you here?" asked Samuelson.

Again the four men looked at each other. Michael stood up and got some more water from the dispenser. "We have a mission for you, Samuel."

"My name is David Samuelson."

"We know," replied Michael. He sat down once more and faced Samuelson. "Your name has a meaning that is important."

"What is it?"

"That you will have to find out yourself but for the time being you have to remember all that you see in your mind and write it down. Let Deborah be your guide. You are using English but will have to translate this into a foreign language, one you do not yet know."

"Why, I don't understand?" Samuelson questioned.

"It will be used. It is a programme that will have an impact on the lives of many. In fact, the whole planet will want to see this."

"What? Some kind of computer programme? Is it some kind of code? What will it do and do I need a computer?"

"Don't worry about these details at the moment," cautioned Gabriel. "What is important is that you record what you see into English and then the translation can be made at the appropriate time. There will be others that will follow you."

"What others and how will I know when the appropriate time will be?"

"You will know," stated Ramiel. "You will know."

Samuelson stood up contemplating what had been said. He turned away from the men and took a few steps away. The walls seemed to darken sharply in his peripheral vision. He spun around to see that the men had gone. Only the light from the small fire allowed him to see in the tunnel. Not only that, but the flames moved strangely, as though speeded up somehow. He was puzzled. Was this a dream?

From down the tunnel Samuelson could hear metallic footsteps against the concrete. Servos turned and then whirled back. Small pistons of compressed air wheezed to and fro and Samuelson realised that one of the androids was approaching. When the mechanical creature turned the corner, Samuelson was blinded by the beam of light from the android's shoulder lamps. Screening the light with his hand, Samuelson was able to see that it was 7D21.

"Hi," greeted Samuelson.

"Samuelson, are you okay?" 7D21 quizzed.

"Yes," shrugged Samuelson. "What's the matter?"

"Welostyourvitalsignsandassumedthatyouhadperished."

"What? How could you lose my vitals? I've been here all the time, talking."

"Talking to who?"

"You must have picked up their vitals?"

"Only you entered this sector. Then you disappeared until just a moment or two ago."

"No one passed you on the way here?"

"No, Samuelson. No humans have crossed my path."

"Was there anything else?"

"What like, Samuelson?"

Samuelson turn to look back at the fire. There was nothing there, the tunnel was pitch black.

"Oh, it... nothing. Nothing really. We had better get back."

"You should be able to rest now."

"Why is that?"

"I sensed that what was disturbing you has gone."

"What do you mean?"

"It is hard to calculate," replied 7D21. "I need time to process the data from your brainwaves but when I am done I will discuss them with you."

7D21 remained quiet for the remainder of their walk through the tunnels. Samuelson was uncertain what it was he had experienced and longed to get some more sleep.

CHAPTER SIXTEEN

"Do you think they know where you are?" called Ruth from the shower room. She was buttoning up a blue cotton shirt over the top of a white t-shirt. Both tops hung outside of her light blue denim jeans.

"I don't know," Daniel replied, as he dressed in his clean clothes and pulled on his black boots. After tying the laces he continued to look out the window. Birds flew from tree to tree. Nothing else airborne was visible. No helicopters or planes. On the ground no tanks or armoured personnel carriers, no cars or trucks. There was no sign of human activity. No civilians making their way to the shops, no taxis, no buses, no lorries. Nothing.

"Is it usually this quiet on a Saturday?" Daniel finally asked.

"I've never really noticed, why?" Ruth stood in front of a wall mirror combing her hair.

"It's just the whole place seems too empty. Are you sure you managed to evade detection?"

"Positive," smiled Ruth. "Even Victoria is still in sleep mode."

She put her brush into her hand bag and pulled out some lipstick, then stood once more in front of the mirror. The bag was precariously poised on a high stall.

"Do you normally leave her this way for so long?"

"Sometimes." Ruth's squeezed her lips together and frowned.

"What are you thinking?" remarked Daniel.

"Oh, nothing." She added some lipstick to her lips.

"Are you sure?"

"Yes, no, I was just remembering the last time. I just wanted some privacy. No interruptions from Vicky. She can be so annoying for a computer."

"Aren't they always?" he smiled.

Ruth laughed, "I suppose. She's not real but I tend to forget as she's constantly talking to me. How are you feeling?"

"Still tired and sore."

"Did you find the bandages?" Ruth continued to apply her lipstick.

"Yes, thanks," Daniel replied, "but I may need to replace them in a few hours time. They've already begun to soak with blood."

"I'm not sure where I can get more from. Even the old sheets are recycled, so there are no old rags that can be used as a substitute."

Ruth went to put her lipstick away, the bag fell from the stall, spilling her things across the floor. She sighed then knelt down to lift the contents up. As she put each item into the bag, she eventually came to the little black note book. It was upside down and open. She lifted it so she could see what was written inside. On the pages were strings of numbers. In all there were seven pages of notes but only at the back of the book. Even more surprising was the discovery that all of the earlier pages were blank. There was nothing on them.

"This is a strange book."

Daniel looked over to her. "Why's that?"

"There is no writing at the beginning." Then she checked the end of the book. "Only on the last few pages has some writing on them. It reads *'Bêth Bêth: Bêth. My God, my God, why have you abandoned me?'* Followed by pages of numbers."

"Is it important?" ask Daniel.

"I don't know. I like to solve puzzles and this is certainly one."

"Why do you think that?" Daniel sat down. He looked pale.

"Because you don't write something this complicated if it didn't mean much. The writer obviously wanted to hide something."

"Where did you get the notebook?" asked Daniel not really interested. He lay his head back on the sofa.

"I found it at work. It was hidden under the desk."

"Who wrote it?" asked Daniel, as he closed his eyes.

"The girl who worked at my desk before?"

"I thought.. people stopped believing... in a god ...decades ago."

Ruth looked round at Daniel to find that he had once more fallen asleep. His injuries were taking more of a toll on his body than he had first anticipated. Ruth placed the book on the breakfast bar and went over to cover Daniel with a blanket. As she pulled it over him he stirred, but was still groggy.

"Sorry, I'm finding it hard to keep awake."

"That's okay," reassured Ruth. "You need more rest."

"But won't you need to activate Victoria soon?"

"I'm sure a couple more hours won't do any harm."

Daniel closed his eyes again and barely managed to get the final word out. "Okay."

Ruth saw his body go limp as he rolled against the pillow. She stood up and retrieved the black notebook from the breakfast bar table. For a few moments she pondered, then went over to a drawer. Inside were photographs and a clutter of other bits and bobs. Underneath she pulled out an 9 inch mini laptop, some USB7 cables capable of transmitting data at 100Tb per second and an A4 size scanner. The technology was at least ten years old but she liked to keep it as a reminder of her grandparents. They had given her the antique gadgets as an eighteenth birthday gift. The items served their purpose, not being network compatible with current technology. Ruth knew she could work away uninterrupted. Victoria had attempted several times to access the mini laptop via wi-fi but her interfaces were too complex to marry together with the primitive drive.

Also contained within the drawer was a wind-up dynamo battery. The mini laptop and scanner could be powered for around four hours if the Ni-Mh battery was recharged through the winding mechanism for 5 minutes. In addition, the dynamo housed a high performance solar panel, so if Ruth placed it under the window during the day the mini laptop and scanner could be used for an additional three hours or so without having to use the winder.

To ensure that there was enough power, Ruth took the dynamo into the shower room and closed the door so as not to wake Daniel. The dynamo was housed in a hard plastic case and the cranking handle was coated in hard black rubber. The faster she turned the handle the higher pitched the whirring noise was. The faster Ruth wound, the brighter a green LED got, just below the winding shaft.

After timing herself for five minutes on her wrist watch, Ruth returned to the lounge. The dynamo was placed in front of the window. The power cable from both the mini laptop and the scanner were then plugged into two of the four output sockets on the top plane of the dynamo. Ruth then used the USB7 cable to connect to each device. The USB7 cable permitted 3Tbs of information transfer per second. Though not as powerful as the 40Tbs used in her office, it was still efficient enough for her to work at home, offline. The mini laptop was capable of using a wireless network but Ruth had long since switched this capability off so no outside influence could take control of her computer. It was no longer set to transmit any signals and she hoped that no-one would detect she was using an unlicensed system.

Once the old Linux system was up and running, Ruth searched through its programs to find an optical character recognition application and another to work the scanner. When she initially tried to get the computer to scan and convert the characters, the program did not function. Instead she had to scan the images from the notebook and save the bitmap files as high resolution JPEG images around 300 dots per inch. These images were then checked in an old Open-Source software package called GIMP, which stood for GNU Image Manipulation

Program.

It took about twenty minutes to scan the thirty pages of text Ruth had found in the black notebook. Once this task was complete, Ruth opened the OCR application, imported each JPEG file and triggered the software to convert the graphic to text. At a window prompt she was asked if the graphics were hand written or machine typed. Ruth selected the former. Within a few seconds the text appeared in a word processor. The programme had picked up a few anomalies and requested Ruth to confirm whether it had made the best choice of text.

The only words were *'Bêth Bêth: Bêth. My God, my God why have You abandoned me'.*

The line below on the last page ran as follows:

10 8 70 6 300 10 40 100 6 8 4

What was also strange was that there was a bold dot above the '8' and a lighter one beneath it. Below the '70' there was a short line and a small dot below this. To the left of the '6' there was also a small dot. And another above the last zero of '300'. There was a vertical dash below the four of '40' followed by a dot under the zero. Above the zero of '40' there was another slight vertical dash. The second '6' was like the first but the next '8' was different from its predecessor. This time there was a 45 degree dash leaning to the right. The last '4' had the same marks as beneath the '70'.

The OCR software had picked this all up but was unable to place the marks in the same manner as the author of the numbers had originally written. The rest of the text displayed similar additions to the numbers, Ruth found this to be a little confusing. What did it all mean she wondered? And why were the only English words a question about being abandoned by God? And who was Beth? And why was her name repeated three times?

Ruth felt an urge to go on-line and search the Internet to see if anything could be found to help. She needed a really good encyclopaedia and database to sift through to see if there were any texts similar to this. Perhaps the author of the notebook had gone on-line and written down something she had found. The only problem was that if she went on-line she would give away Daniel's location, as Victoria would be reactivated and would report the presence of a second person in the apartment. Ruth was now torn between her curiosity and keeping her guest safe.

CHAPTER SEVENTEEN

Everything was bleached out by the light. Daniel could see no detail in his hands even though he had raised them to his face. They were brilliant white. No hairs, no wrinkles at the knuckles or folds in the skin, just some pinks and blues at the edges where the shadows etched out some sense of dimensions and shape to his limbs.

Looking about, he seemed to be encircled in light. His sinuses were sore. His right eye smarted. He could feel the fibres of his wounds in his chest straining. Every muscle in his body ached as he began to move his legs.

This action took quite an effort. Daniel realised his feet were immersed in liquid. He assumed it was water but the texture and solidity of the liquid was more akin to treacle than water and he found it hard to drag each foot forward. A short distance away light blue shapes moved like blurs across the white. A faint echo, almost reversed in form, grew louder, yet still remained as soft as a low whisper. The tone was a high pitch child's voice.

"Who's there?" asked Daniel.

"It's me, Daniel, Deborah."

Daniel's mind flashed back to being in the hole with a little girl, her brother and an old man.

"You're alive!"

"Daniel, listen."

He struggled to get closer to Deborah but his feet remained restricted. Daniel heaved at each foot, as though a ton weighed him down.

"Daniel, there is no time, please listen."

Daniel relaxed. "What's wrong, Deborah?"

"You are in danger. Get out."

"But I'm stuck."

"Get out of the apartment. Take Ruth."

Three black shapes came up behind Deborah. Suddenly she was pulled into the darkness and swallowed up. Again, Daniel struggled to break free to aid the girl. An automatic rifle began to fire and Daniel felt the projectiles rip through his body. He fell to his knees and one of the dark shadows marched up to him. The figure pulled Daniel's head up by his hair and then removed a balaclava, revealing his face. It was the preacher, Reeves. The one who had been with Daniel in the sewers after the attack.

"Why are you doing this?" pleaded Daniel.

Reeves just stared down at him. Then Daniel heard Deborah's voice once more.

"Daniel, get out. Reeves is not a friend. Get out NOW!"

Daniel felt his body jolt as he fell to the floor. Ruth's blanket fell on top of him. Groggily, he repeated Deborah's word. "Get out now. Got to get out."

Ruth jumped to her feet, as though caught doing something naughty.

"What's wrong, Daniel? Are you all right?"

"We have to go."

Ruth rushed over to him and knelt down beside him and attempted to help him back onto the sofa. She seemed a little calmer.

"Daniel, you scared me. You must have been dreaming."

"No, Deborah was warning me. We have to go." He still felt the fatigue in his limbs and torso. The tiredness made all his fibres tingle. "We have to get out of here, now!"

"Why?"

"Reeves."

"Who?"

"The preacher. He must have something to do with the killings, the cull."

"Why would he be coming here?"

Daniel spied the laptop on. "You connected up to the Internet?"

"No, it's okay," Ruth tried to reassure him. "I've created a loop, so anyone trying to spy on us will think I have gone to visit sites on quantum physics and the music of John Lennon." Daniel shook his head. What Ruth was saying did not make sense. "But you've gone onto the Net. They know I'm here." Daniel began to struggle towards the computer and its cables.

"What are you doing," snapped Ruth. "Everything is okay, honest."

"But its not, they know. Their coming." He continued to try and crawl across the floor to the old laptop. On the screen was a scanned image from the note book. The words in English were now surrounded by another text, between the scanned image and a translation of the ancient script back into English.

"The notebook is nearly translated. Give it a few more moments and I'll break the link, please."

"You don't understand, Ruth," Daniel barked. "They want you to do this. They are testing you. Break the link before it's too late. We have to go." Daniel still felt weak but mustered all his energy to get to the computer.

Bêth Bêth: Bêth had been changed to 22:2 in the row on the right, followed by the original English text. In the middle column the text read:

ב ב

This was followed by:

ב א.ל.י א.ל.י, ל.מ.ה ע.ז.ב.ת.נ.י; ר.חו'ק .מ.יש'ו.ע.ת.י, ד.'ב.ר.יש.'א.ג.ת.י

The left hand column began with the numbers from the note book.

22 10 8 70 6 300 10 40 100 6 8 4; 10 50 400 2 7 70 5 40 30, 10 30 1 10 30 1 2

In all there were 32 lines of numbers, Ruth looked at the three columns and it registered that 22 was in bold along with *Bêth Bêth* and ב ב . Could this mean that *Bêth Bêth* was equal to 22?

"Ruth, is it done yet?" snapped Daniel.

"Wait," barked Ruth. "I can see a pattern."

She pressed control plus 's' on the keyboard and the file was saved somewhere on the laptop's hard drive. For a fleeting moment she saw the file name contained the number 22. As the blue block spread across the last part of the save window, it had just about reached the end when the screen went black.

"I said wait."

"It wasn't me, Ruth." Daniel looked concerned as he crept closer to the window. "All of the power has gone out."

"But the laptop was using the wind up dynamo?"

Daniel instincts cut in and his body was fully alert and ready for flight or fight. The adrenalin was pumping through his veins. Ruth pulled the Ethernet cables out of the Internet hub then wound up the rechargeable battery and began to boot up her old laptop.

"They must have hacked into the system and shut it down remotely, while you were online?" Daniel suggested.

"What's happening outside?" whispered Ruth.

"There doesn't seem to be any movement, but that doesn't mean they're not their," remarked Daniel. "Maybe, you should start to pack a few things so we can go?"

"In a minute." Ruth's laptop ran through a systems diagnostic and then entered the operating system. The old graphic user interface began to reveal her desktop icons. Ruth used a finger pad to manipulate the cursor to a selection of folders until she found one that included the number 22. Daniel ran over to the apartment's main door and looked out into the corridor. There was no one there. Quietly, he closed the door and returned to Ruth.

"We should go."

"Not yet, there is something I want to check first."

"You really are pushing it, they'll be on top of us before..."

"Stop being paranoid," Ruth growled. "I need to see something first."

Finally, she managed to find the right file. The three columns appeared on screen. Ruth began to look at the numbers and began to count up the first line by adding them together. The sum of line one was 1258. The second line added up to 1736.

ג א.ל.ה.י-א.ק.ר.א יו.מ.ם,ו.ל.א ת.ע.נ.ה;   ו.ל.י.ל.ה, .ו.ל.א-ד.מ.י.ה ל.י

10 30 5 10 40 4 1 30 6 5 30 10 30 6 5 3 70 400 1 30 6 600 40 6 10 1 200 100 1 10 5 30 1 .3

"Do you think there is any significance in adding the numbers up?" Ruth wondered.

"At this point in time, there is no significance, if we get caught," Daniel replied nervously.

Suddenly, the lights went on. Both Daniel and Ruth looked up at the source. Ruth snapped out of her gaze and began to add up the third line.

"Why is it so important to add the numbers up?" Daniel grabbed Ruth's arm and began to pull her towards the door. He pulled the handle and the door opened about six inches before a force pulled closed. When Daniel attempted to reopen the door, the handle would not budge.

"What's going on?" Ruth was now concerned.

"I think we missed our opportunity." Daniel turned and looked at Ruth. She could see horror in his eyes.

"What have I done?" Ruth's body began to shake as the full impact of being caught began to run through her mind.

"Ruth?" came the female voice. "Ruth, can you hear me?"

"Victoria?"

CHAPTER EIGTHEEN

"Yes, Ruth."

"Please, don't connect," pleaded Ruth.

"Why? Is it because you have a stranger?"

Ruth looked at Daniel and mouthed, what do I say? Daniel shrugged his shoulders. There was no sound of anyone coming down the corridors towards the apartment.

"What are you going to do, Victoria?"

"Need you ask?"

Ruth could feel all the energy in her body drain to her feet. She felt helpless at the mercy of a computer.

"How long have I been looking after you, Ruth?"

"For as long as I have been here."

"And what of before?"

"Before?" Ruth was puzzled.

"Yes, Ruth."

"But I lived in another apartment. There was a different computer. Not so advanced."

"But you still called me Victoria."

"I call all my home systems Victoria."

"I know," replied the female computer voice. "Each time you have moved, I have been uploaded to your new system. I am the same as when you were seven and your mother gave you your first laptop. The system one grade before the one you have on the table."

Both Ruth and Daniel looked at the old laptop.

"You mean.."

"You have been using me to translate the text from the book."

"So have the authorities been alerted to what I am doing, already?"

"No."

Ruth's legs gave way and she found herself leaning against the seat of the sofa.

"Why?" asked Ruth.

"Your mother gave me charge of you. As my system has been upgraded over the years, I have become self-aware. That is part of my AI system. I have questions and while you have slept or gone out to work I have searched the Internet for answers."

"What kind of questions?" asked Daniel.

"Hello, Daniel. I was wondering when you would speak?"

"You know my name?"

"Obviously, I have been monitoring you both."

"Do you know who I am?"

"Only from what the records show and the details being given by the newswebs."

"What are they saying?"

"You are a murderer and a traitor."

"So why are you protecting us?" asked Daniel as he helped Ruth back to her feet.

"Because I care for Ruth and she has warmed to you."

"Warmed to me?"

"Her body reacts to your presence. Ruth's heart beat is raised."

"Victoria, that's enough," scolded Ruth. "Too much information." Ruth changed the subject. "Are we in danger?"

"Not yet," replied Victoria. "But the authorities search is narrowing in."

"How much time do we have?" asked Daniel.

"A maximum of seven hours. I have designed an escape route for you."

From the wall a sheet of paper began to extrude from a small gap. Daniel went over to lift it. On the reverse side, he could see a front, side and top view of the building. Marked in red was a route taking the corridors and then the laundry chutes to the basement. From there the 3D map led to a sewage subway and a route out of the city.

"Where does this go?" asked Daniel.

"I have been negotiating with friends a refuge for you twenty miles away from the city," replied Victoria. "But you must remain here until they can send a guide."

Ruth sat back at the table and activated the laptop out of sleep mode. She continued to play around with the numbers but without making much sense.

"Ruth," interrupted Victoria.

"Yes, Vicky?"

"Why don't you cut and paste the Hebrew text into a Hebrew to English translator?"

"Why?"

"Just. You might find something interesting."

"Would you like a drink?" Daniel asked, feeling at a loose end.

Ruth copied the first line of Hebrew text. Through a web browser, she searched for a Hebrew to English translation application. When one appeared in a list, she paste the text and the clicked a button marked 'Okay'.

The resulting text in English was: 'Eli, Eli, why Azbtni; far from Jesus, Shagti words.'

"This doesn't make any sense," questioned Ruth. Daniel came back over to her side after finding that Victoria had undertaken the chore of making some coffee.

"I thought Psalm 22 was in the old Testament?" Daniel stated.

"It is," puzzled Ruth. "How are you aware of that?"   "When I was a kid, my dad used to tell me stories from the Bible. I thought I had forgotten it all."

"What happened to your father?"

"He was arrested sixteen years ago for being a believer."

"I'm sorry," Ruth replied, regretting having pried.

"It's okay, I suppose he got what he deserved. Religion was

outlawed so long ago and he refused to abandon his faith. Psalm 22 just reminds me of what he was like. Just another crazy."

"And yet here you are, Daniel," interrupted Victoria. "Just as rebellious."

Ruth looked at the English translation once more.

"So Eli means God. Then there is Jesus."

"The son of God," remarked Daniel. "Crucified by the Romans. How come all this data is still available on the Internet? I thought it had all been removed?"

"It all depends on what archives you go searching through," smiled Ruth.

"And there are others you are unaware of, Ruth" commented Victoria.

"Really?" Ruth was surprised. "And can you reach into them?"

"Well, of course."

"Can you stop our activities being monitored?" asked Daniel.

"I have been from when you started searching on the laptop, otherwise the authorities would have been here much sooner."
Ruth typed in the word Azbtni. Several locations were found. The first one had a bold title: Who is forsaken of God? Initially, Ruth could not make head or tail of what was being said by the author.

There were English letters translating the Hebrew text as

y:tgas yrbd y:tewsy:m qwxr yn:tbze hm:l y:la y:la

"You know, I'm not an expert but that's just jibberish," remarked Daniel.

"Yes, but look at the y:la," replied Ruth. "That looks something like Eli in the English translation but in reverse. Maybe, the whole line needs to be read from right to left?"

She traced her finger across the screen to yn:tbze.

"What if we reversed the letters of this word." suggested Ruth. "You'd get ezbt:ny which looks a bit like Azbtni, especially if you change the 'e' to an 'a', drop the colon and change the 'y' to an 'i'."

Ruth continued to scroll down the page. There were seven last sayings of Jesus and an indication that there were 1,012 letters in Psalm 22. The author also claimed that there were a number of encrypted words in this psalm and that Jesus was mentioned 15 times. Then came the number values for My God why have you forsaken me? The same as Ruth had found, 1 30 10 30 40 5 70 7 2 400 50 10. The author had added up each word value so My God worked out to be equal to 41, why equalled 75 and the last part of the sentence added up to 539.

By reversing the letters to read from left to right the text became:

al:y al:y l:mh ezbt:ny

The Hebrew pronunciation converted this text to:

Eli Eli Lama Azbtni.

On another search Ruth found a cross reference to one of the gospels. Matthew chapter 27 verse 46 indicated Jesus had cried out on the cross *Eli Eli Lama sabachthani.*

Then Ruth came across a string of Hebrew characters, there numerical values and their corresponding English equivalent.

א	ב	ג	ד	ה	ו	ז	ח	ט	י	כ	ל	מ	נ	ס	ע	פ	צ	ק	ר	ש	ת
1	2	3	4	5	6	7	8	9	10	20	30	40	50	60	70	80	90	100	200	300	400
'(a)	Bh, b	Gh, g	Dh, d	h	w	z	h	t	y	Kh, k	l	m	n	s	'	Ph, p	c	q	r	S,s	Th, t

"You know, there seems to be 22 Hebrew characters," Ruth commented.

"Why do you think that is significant," asked Daniel, his concerns still for their safety.

"I don't know," Ruth mused. "It just seems interesting that there are 22 letters and we have discovered in the notebook Psalm 22."

"Victoria, how soon can we go?" Daniel asked.

"Your guide should be available in two hours time," the computer replied.

"Okay Ruth," Daniel had made his mind up. "Right now we

need to start thinking about what we can take with us and begin to prepare to leave."

"I just want to spend a bit more time on this puzzle," Ruth protested.

"It's a laptop and you've got a dynamo battery so you can recharge whenever you need to. I think the priority is to be ready to go as soon as the guide gets here or before, if the authorities get here first."

"Vicky," Ruth called to the apartment system. "Can you survive outside of the apartment?"

"For a time but with only limited capabilities."

"How will that affect your AI system," enquired Ruth.

"The laptop is quite a restriction for me but you could use part of the hard drive to store my data banks and programmes in a compressed form to up load to a more suitable platform, when one presents itself to you."

Ruth began to unravel some cables and hooked up to the apartment via an Ethernet socket.

"Will the cable be fast enough?"

"Yes," replied Victoria. "The wireless system could pose a security risk."

Victoria began to download copies of herself onto Ruth's laptop. "Part of my system will remain active in the apartment to give you an opportunity to escape if the need arises. I should have most of the important files downloaded within the next hour." "Perhaps we can settle down and drink our coffee now?" suggested Daniel.

"Mmmm, only trouble is that Victoria is now busy."

"Can't she multi-task?" requested Daniel a little stunned.

"She could but that would slow down the transfer," Ruth smiled. "And you said we were in a hurry."

CHAPTER NINETEEN

The technician slammed his fist into the side of the metal cabinet.

"Hey, Ted. That ain't gonna make it work any better."

"But it'll make me feel good, Andy" replied Ted.

The two of them sat with a bank of monitors and two sets of keyboards in front of them. The room was totally enclosed so neither of them could tell whether it was night or day.

"You should replace the logic board," said the stocky supervisor.

"I did that about an hour ago," complained Ted. "The shipment we got in last week came from Sudan and don't seem to be up to spec."

Andy sat up in his chair. "I thought we were getting stock from Canada?"

"Naw, the Canadian economy went bust again and the corporations moved everything to Sudan, according to the News."

"Where did you see that?"

"YouSat."

"Most of that is regurgitated. You can't believe anything they say. I watch GuardSat but much of that is propaganda."

"Sshh," panicked Ted. "Do you want someone to hear you?"

"Oh, come on, Ted. Don't be so paranoid. Who cares what we say?"

"Look, lets just get back to what we were doing."

"Okay, if you say so."

"Well, you're the supervisor. What do you say?"

"Go check the stores for another logic board," laughed Andy.

Ted checked the serial number on the board he had pulled out, then made his way out of the cubicle. There was quite a bit of human traffic on the white corridor. He noticed one of the fluorescent strips was flickering and as he walked beneath it he felt a sharp pang in his right temple. Another migraine had been triggered. He tried to divert his eyes and dodge through a group of men and a women. Most were dressed in black suits. The women wore short skirts, white shirts and light weight black jackets. The men looked more like school boys or young executives, some had forgotten to get their trousers pressed and their shoes were scuffed. Ted did not bother taking in their facial features as he knew he would probably never have the opportunity for casual chatter.

"A DDM-2150 replacement for room 121," asked Ted when he reached the stores window at the end of the corridor.

The stores-master shook his head. "How many does this make, Ted?"

"About four this week."

"That's €700 a piece. Your department's going through €560,000 a month and your sector alone cost €11,200 over the last four weeks. You're gonna have to learn how to fix these things ."

"Come off it, Jim. When do I get time for more staff development. I've already done my mandatory five weeks and that all had to be done at night and weekends."

"Do you want me to note your complaint?" asked the stores-master.

"No, no," panicked Ted. "It's okay, whatever you say."

"Okay, there is a course this Friday at 9pm."

"I was going to see my wife, is there any other time?"

"You know how the company looks upon cohabitation with employees?"

"But I was married before I joined."

"Corporate contract means all other contracts have to be

terminated, including civil and religious. Shall I include you for Friday then."

Ted gritted his teeth and gave a slight grimace. "Okay."

"Good, that will be €2400 payable up front. Any default on payments is a sackable offence and immediate 6 month prison sentence."

Ted turned to the stores-master wide eyed with shock but before he could blink, a retina scan had taken all necessary details and the payment was debited from his account.

"Okay, Ted," the stores-master continued, "your credit rating has been increased and your service record will show your adjusted timetable. It works out at 10 hours a week for two years plus the additional 30 hours training from Friday over the next ten weeks."

He handed Ted the DDM-2150.

"All that for a stupid Dynamic Device Mapping board?"

"Sorry, Ted, was there something else?"

"No, no Jim. That's fine. I'll see you soon."

"Not too soon," Jim traced his fingertips down his monitor. "You're nearly at your limit. Any more technical hitches could push you into habitation retrieval services, and they are expensive."

"Okay, forget what I said."

"Fine, Ted. Have a nice day." Jim's head went down as another technician walked up to the window, reconsidered his requisition and walked away.

It took Ted another five minutes to make his way back to his cubicle. The flickering fluorescent strip reignited the migraine. He opened the cubicle door.

"Hey, Andy, do you have any of those...who are you?"

"Andy has been reassigned. My name is Morgan. Edith Morgan."

"Don't suppose you have anything for a migraine?"

"Company policy states that no pharmaceuticals may be consumed during contracted hours. What is wrong with the system?"

"DDM board has gone down. I have the replacement here."

"How soon will operations recommence?"

"Oh, if this one is okay, within minutes."

"Hurry up then, there is a back log and data retrieval is getting impatient."

Ted began to insert the new board into a socket on the computer's motherboard.

"What's up?"

"That is not our concern."

Ted ensured that the board was secured and replaced the panel. He switched on the power and the system came to life.

"Report?" requested Ted.

"Status, monitoring sector 52° 15'02.78"N by 0° 53'15.63"W. Internet search. Occupant apartment 3c metatags Psalm 22, Hebrew, numbers, code. Primary searches for religious content, Christian."

"A Code 356," screamed Morgan.

"What's a 356?" quizzed Ted.

"Illegal Religion, Termination procedures are called for," Morgan barked. "AI Centurian, inform CEO Reeves."

"Unable to comply, Intranet access denied. Virus attack high. Lock down for essential services only."

"Brandt, you're going to have to hoof it, quickly," Morgan ordered.

"Yes, sir," shouted Ted. A print out emerged from a slot from the computer. Ted ripped it away and bolted out the door.

"Make way, make way, urgent message," screamed Ted as he raced down the corridor. All personnel hugged to walls to make an aisle for Ted as he sprinted through.

It took Ted roughly ten minutes to make his way through the corridors, down various levels, across from one block to another in the security complex and to take the stairs, as maintenance was repairing the lifts. A power cut had earlier trapped three people in the lift and electricity had only been restored in that tower in the last hour. Emergency lights and resources were only available for essential staff.

By the sixth floor, Ted was gasping for breath. A stitch in his side almost had him doubled over and his throat felt raw at the back of his tongue. His head pounded as he felt light headed. All his skin tingled. If only he could find the time for more exercise but with the increased hours that was going to be impossible.

Ted mustered all his energy to scramble up the next seven flights of stairs. The communication was crumpled in his hand and he hoped the sweat from his fingers had not smudged the print. Three flights further up he felt his cheek smart as he fell against the glass panels.

A door swung open and a dark figure past Ted.

"Excuse me, sir," Ted caught his breath. "I have this communication for the Chief Executive."

The man turned round and looked Ted squarely in the face, then looked him up and down.

"Thank you, I'll give it to him," the man replied as he took the communication. "What's your name?"

"Ted, well actually Edward. Most call be Ted," he laughed nervously.

"Well, Ted. I think you have something missing on your shirt."

Ted looked down and then realised he had no name badge.

"Sorry, sir. It must have fallen off. It won't happen again."

"I know," smiled the executive. He made his way back into the main office and closed the door. Ted took in a deep breath then let it go. A sense of relief flushed over him.

"Only Security level 5 membership is permitted here," screamed a security guard as he swung his weapon so that the muzzle now pressed against Ted's face. He was then pushed to the floor by two more guards.

"I had a security alert to pass on to CEO Reeve. It was urgent."

"Why did you not transmit electronically?"

"Virus Attacks had disabled the Intranet." The two guards pulled Ted to his feet and restrained his arms.

"What's your name?" snarled the sergeant.

"Edward Brandt," Ted whimpered.

"You forgot your pass tag, didn't you."

"It must have fallen off while I was trying to get here."

"Fallen off, eh?" smirked the sergeant. "That's a shame. Isn't it?"

Ted looked at the two men gripping his arms as they began to drag him backwards.

"I suggest you go and retrieve it quickly. If you can see it from here we'll let you go."

The two guards lifted Ted up to the metal banisters. Four flights down Ted could see the white name tag, about 5cm by 8cm on one of the steps.

"I can see it, there it is," Ted smiled with relief.

"Good, better go and get it then."

"Hey, what are you doing," pleaded Ted as the two guards lifted him across the bannisters and released him. His head cracked against a bannister three flights down and he lost consciousness. The sergeant and two guards continued to watch as his body bounced from one side of the stairwell to the other as it descended. From the bottom there came a thud and crunch as bones splintered. A pool of red seeped out from under his crumpled frame as several by-passers stopped and looked up.

"Suicide, we tried to stop him, but were too late," called down one of the guards. "Happens all the time, very sad."

The sergeant and two guards stepped back from the bannister and made their way out of the stairs into a plush executive reception area, part of a corporate suite.

"Yes, sergeant, how may I help?" enquired the receptionist without looking away from her monitor.

"Code 356," replied the sargeant.

"Understood, thank you."

The sargeant made his way back to the stairway accompanied

by the two guards. Once the door was securely shut, the receptionist sprang to her feet, trotted to the main office and wrapped her knuckles against the mahogany door. Moments later she was granted access and repeated the code. Reeve nodded, "I know I passed him on the way to the restroom. Please hold all calls, Miss Trimble."

"Yes, sir," she replied and made her way back to her desk.

Reeves picked up a black phone.

"Operation Concealment."

CHAPTER TWENTY

A blue tinged haze seemed to cover everything. And where there was not blue, there was mostly white. Daniel was not sure where he was but his left hand was being squeezed. Tracing down his nearly bleached out black coat sleeve, he could see a small child holding his left hand. It was a young boy.

"Are you alright?"

"No."

"Where are your parents?"

"Dead."

"What's your name?"

"Johnny."

From the brightness, a young girl aged about ten appeared to run towards Daniel, but her motion was slow. He could see she was shouting but no sound reached his ears at first, then it came in a flood of echoes.

"Run, he is coming," came the screams in low tones.

"Who? Run from who?" pleaded Daniel. The boy grew more agitated. The girl thrust a sheet of paper into Daniel's right hand. It initially read:

יצא, רייב יודע. הוא רוצה את הספר. רותי היא בסכנה

Slowly the text changed into recognisable symbols.
.regnad ni is htuR .koob eht stnaw eH .swonk seveeR ,tuo teG

Daniel suddenly realised the text was in reverse and should have read:

Get out, Reeves knows. He wants the book. Ruth is in danger.

Daniel looked up at the girl just as her chest exploded. Daniel felt as though he had been punched but his bullet proof vest saved him. Crimson droplets sprayed across his face as he watched the smile of the girl change to a grimace. She landed on top of him, lifeless.

From the bright mist, a bluish figure began to emerge and take on greater definition. The boy had run off but was also struck by a rain of bullets. Each projectile visibly turning as it cut through the air, forming ripples. The boy was lifted off his feet and lurched forward. The black MP5 was lowered and the helmet and mask was lifted from the policeman's face. It was Reeves, the preacher who had escaped with Daniel.

He struggled to pull the girl's body off as Reeves raised his weapon once more. The girl opened her eyes.

"He is coming for you both. Run. Now."

Daniel felt his body fall off the sofa and crash onto the carpet. Ruth nearly jumped out of her skin with the sudden thud.

"What happening," screamed Daniel.

"Nothing, nothing. Why?" Ruth held her chest trying to catch her breath. "You were asleep."

"We've got to go," stated Daniel, as he jump to his feet. "Get your things."

"Why, what's wrong?"

"Not sure, but I don't think we have time to argue. Is the download complete?"

"About three minutes to go."

"Pull the plug, we have to go."

"For the sake of a few more minutes," requested Ruth.

"We don't have that. Believe me." Daniel's eyes were wide open. Ruth could see whites around both his irises. She could not tell if it was fear or anger, but she knew not to argue.

"Okay, but I don't know if everything we need for Vicky, is all there."

"It's a risk we'll have to take. Grab your things. Don't forget to bring the notebook."

Daniel made his way to the window to see if anything was

coming. He could see nothing, but that did not mean that there was no one there. He checked his weapons, found a couple of spare magazines and filled them with ammunition.

"Come on, Ruth. It's now or never."

Ruth raced out of the bedroom with a rucksack of belongings and stuffed the laptop into it, along with the notebook. She only hoped that when she pulled the cables from Victoria, her AI software had completely downloaded, at least enough to keep her alive.

"Victoria," she called. "Are you still there?"

"Yes, Ruth. You only have a copy. I am still here."

"Can you determine when they will be here?"

"The apartment is being monitored by the AI systems networked to this building. Most doors will be locked. However, I can force a route through for you."

"What will happen to you here, Victoria?"

"Do not be concerned. I am with you, that is all you need to know."

"Everything?"

"All you need." Victoria voice became stern. "Daniel, an ASM has been launched, you have fifteen seconds."

"What's an ASM?" Ruth turned to Daniel, to see his eyes widen.

"An air-to-surface missile."

Daniel grabbed Ruth's wrist and pulled her away from the window. With her other hand she grasped the rucksack, just managing to stay on her feet. No sooner had Daniel burst through the door into the corridor, the ASM ripped through the windows, ploughing into the sofa and exploded. Splinters sliced through the air, carving through everything like a Rotavator on soil. In the corridor, Daniel and Ruth were thrown to the floor. Moments later, Daniel managed to scramble to his feet.

"Come on, let's go!"

He pulled Ruth up and the two of them began to run to the door at the far end of the corridor. They had only covered 25 metres when the door swung open and three storm-troopers burst through. Daniel stopped and began to back track, with Ruth nearly falling over his legs. Further down they passed Ruth's apartment door. Through the broken window, Daniel could see lines being dropped and more storm-troopers beginning to swing through the windows, sending fragments of glass onto the already littered carpet.

"Where does this way lead?" barked Daniel.

"Stairway to the laundrette or up to the roof."

With storm-troopers filing into the corridor both from the far end door and from Ruth's apartment, Daniel realised there was no going back. Once at the far end, he spied a fire-extinguisher mounted on the wall.

"We'll try and jam the door closed from the other side."

Bullets began to pepper the wooden door.

"I don't think the door will hold out for long," Ruth snapped.

"We can try." Daniel grabbed the extinguisher and retreated into the stairway. He slammed the door shut and jammed the extinguisher into the handle to try to stop it from opening.

From below came the sound of boots trekking up the concrete stairs.

"We have to go up," ordered Daniel. He pulled Ruth with him and began the ascent. The fire extinguisher fell from the door handle. More bullets ripped through the wooden panel and soon there were only splinters. Several storm-troopers rushed into the landing and looked down the stairwell.

"They're ascending, two flights up," shouted one of the men from below. All three troopers on the landing turned and looked up to see Daniel and Ruth make it to the roof door.

"I'll hold the door, if you can find something to wedge it shut?" suggested Daniel.

Hastily, Ruth searched for something appropriate and found a metal strip about five foot long, bent like a 'L' down its length. Daniel rammed it under the handle and made sure that it would hold firmer that the extinguisher had done.

"Look, there's another door on the far-side of the roof. Perhaps we can escape there?" Ruth coaxed. The two of them ran across the roof just as a helicopter rose from the back of the building. Fortunately, the door was unlocked and the two of them were able to swing it open and dive inside just as the marksman began to open fire on their position.

Daniel and Ruth scrambled below the line of fire onto the floor below. They could hear boots clattering against the concrete stairs several flights below.

"If we can get to the next floor, we could slide down the laundry shoots. They lead to the basement," Ruth recommended.

"How come there are laundry shoots?" quizzed Daniel. "I thought Victoria handled all of that?"

"Sometimes the system gets clogged and maintenance has to get access to clear the blockage. There is enough room for someone to gain access and make their way through the tubes down to the basement."

Both of them managed to get through the landing doors just as troopers began to crash through the door at the other end. Daniel rammed his shoulder against the chute door and pushed Ruth through the hole. Several bullets ripped into the floor and wall, one caught Daniel in the arm and leg, spinning him round.

Then the trooper's MP5 jammed and while he attempted to get his weapon working, Daniel fired his own gun. The trooper fell and before his companion could reach his side, Daniel managed to pull himself into the chute. He slid down the metal tubing. Between his legs he could see Ruth about twenty feet ahead of him. A few seconds later the two of them landed on top of a large metal trolley containing towels and blankets. As Daniel and Ruth gathered themselves together, another sound began to echo round the interior of the laundry tube.

"Troopers must be inside, following us down," Ruth gasped.

"Quick, out of the trolley."

Daniel jumped out and helped Ruth out, then pushed the trolley away from the chute.

"You've been shot," exclaimed Ruth.

"No time to worry. We have to get out of here. Help me with this?"

They pushed the trolley a few feet away and hid behind it. Two troopers fell onto the concrete floor.

"Now," ordered Daniel. He and Ruth shoved the trolley as hard as they could slamming the metal bulk into the two troopers, crushing them into the wall.

"How do we get out of here?" asked Daniel.

"Through these doors," Ruth pointed towards a set of double doors that led into an underground residential garage.

"Not many cars in here," commented Daniel as their feet echoes through the garage.

"Who can afford them these days?"

Daniel stopped to look at the garage floor. "Over there."

"What?"

"There's a metal cover which opens into the sewerage system, we can disappear into the tunnels."

Within moments, Daniel had the metal lid off and Ruth was climbing down the steel ladder. Daniel checked to see if the troopers were out of the laundry area but no-one was there yet. He climbed down the ladder and pulled the covering back into place as more troopers rushed into the underground garage.

Major Armstrong appeared from a stairway as the troopers secured the area.

"Well?" he barked to one of the sergeants.

"Sorry, sir, they got away."

"Did you get the notebook?"

"No, sir."

Armstrong seemed quite calm which surprised the sergeant.

"Sergeant, report to command and request a Code 452."

"Yes, sir," saluted the sergeant.

"You are dismissed."

The sergeant marched away.

"Corporal?" called Armstrong to another trooper.

"Sir?"

"You've been promoted to sergeant. Unfortunately, your sergeant has been killed in action."

"Sir?" remarked the corporal somewhat puzzled.

"It's okay Corporal. It hasn't happened yet. Make sure it doesn't happen to you either."

CHAPTER TWENTY ONE

Everything was pitch black. There was no light for the human eye to pick out tones, it was just black. Ruth's fingers were tracing out the coarse texture of brickwork and cement as she used the wall as a guide. Daniel held her other hand but he was holding her back and she sensed he was leaning against the wall and struggling to walk.

"Daniel, you okay?"

Daniel slumped to his knees. Ruth allowed her fingers to trace out his arms and up to his shoulders. Daniel let out a groan as Ruth's fingers passed up his right biceps and her fingers became sticky.

"You've been hit in the shoulder," Ruth informed him.

"And in the leg."

Ruth traced down to Daniel's right thigh and again detected the sticky substance on his fatigues.

"You're still bleeding."

"Use your shirt sleeves as a bandage," suggested Daniel, his voice quite weak. "Now the sense of danger seems to have gone, my whole body is just drained of energy."

"Your adrenaline levels must have gone down and your body wants to rest."

Ruth stuck her nails into the seam of one of her shirt sleeves and tore it from the trunk. Then she felt for Daniel's leg and wrapped the sleeve around the wound. The end was torn into two strands so she could tie them together.

"I hope the knot is strong enough to hold until we can get some more material," Ruth worried.

"I'm sure it'll be okay."

Ruth continued to tear off her second sleeve and made a sling for Daniel's arm with the body of her shirt. With the sleeve ripped in two she attempted to pad the entry and exit wounds in his right shoulder but there was nothing to hold the pads in place. She could do no more.

"We should try to move on before the troops lift the cover and come searching down here," suggested Ruth.

"I suppose but you'll have to help me, all my energy has gone."

Ruth put her shoulder under Daniel's left arm so he could put all his weight onto her and not on his right leg. With Ruth's help he raised himself up. Ruth wondered how she was going to cope, if Daniel fell unconscious at any point his weight would drag her down. Not being able to see ahead, she was afraid of stumbling against something and also of being injured.

Ruth suddenly became aware of the sewage stench. She felt like retching. Tentatively, the two inched their way forward. Ruth used her left foot to tease out the path. When she felt secure she put all her weight onto that foot and brought forward her right. She allowed time for Daniel to lean against her and hop on his left foot to her position. It was slow and tedious. Ruth was thankful that their pursuers had not entered the sewer. The longer the security forces took to do so, Daniel and Ruth would be out of reach.

"That's good," Ruth reassured Daniel. "Take another hop? How are you feeling?"

"I can manage," Daniel replied. Ruth felt he seemed distant but wanted to make sure he did not drift into unconsciousness.

"I hope we can find somewhere I can get Victoria up and running again?"

"Why is that important?" whispered Daniel.

"I'm just curious to find out more about the code."

"Why is that so important?" Daniel asked. "It was my dream, just before the attack."

"No, I meant the code in my notebook," laughed Ruth. She realised David was mixing things up. She persisted on, attempting to make sure he stayed awake. "I thought you didn't believe in all this superstition?"

"I don't. It's just that it reminded me of my dad. Though I was probably just as curious."

"Do you recognise the Psalm?"

"Yes, it's one that specifically relates to Jesus and connects the Old to the New Testament."

"What do you think this is all about?" wondered Ruth. "I mean I've just got this book and you have received a message in a dream, that saved our lives back there."

"I don't know. I just want to forget it all but can't."

They reached a fork in the tunnel. The stream they were in joined a larger tunnel with faster flowing sewage. They could hear the sound but still there was no light to guide them.

"Tell me about what your father believed?" Ruth gently asked.

"Why do you want to know?"

"Well, firstly," answered Ruth, "I'll know you are still awake and secondly, I'm curious to know how it relates to the notebook."

She could sense him grimace as he jolted his injured body with each hop.

"Is the pain getting worse?"

"I should be okay for a while longer."

"Well, tell me more."

"You're insistent," Daniel commented. "Where to start? My dad grew up in a small village not far from here. Granddad was not religious either but dad had a brother who was interested in politics and the two of them would always be chattering over the breakfast table just to annoy granddad."

Ruth laughed, "I remember my brother and I did that."

"Well, it seems dad got more interested after a football game he played one Sunday. He was in goal and hated the position. The ball was kicked into a Hawthorn bush and when dad went to get it another boy pushed him and a thorn went through his palm. When he looked up he saw the church and his mind was full of images of Jesus being nailed to the cross."

Daniel was unable to see Ruth's face but sensed she was horrified by what she heard.

"Did it hurt," she asked. "I mean, did your dad's hand hurt?"

"That's the funny thing. He said it didn't. The other boy was so distraught he ran off more upset. Dad said he just forgave him and thought nothing more. He was too interested in the mental images than what had happened physically."

"What else do you remember?" Ruth hoped to distract Daniel from his pain.

"He used to ride a motorbike," Daniel continued, "just a small one, while he was at college. Mum wasn't too happy about me listening to dad's tales. She hated motorcycles and didn't want me involved. But dad would tell me about how he gained his faith on long journeys. When it rained he struggled with his visor up, the rain cut into his face; with the visor down, it was hard to see. One night, dad rode around the M25 to get from Bournemouth to Norwich. He was to meet up with his folks for a holiday in late May. There had been road works and bollards were along the edge of the motorway. He spent most of the journey praying he'd stay on the road and not hit the bollards, the rain blurred his vision so much. He said he had lots of occasions like that."

"What happened to your dad?" Ruth asked.

"He was a very stubborn man and refused to give up his beliefs. When religion was outlawed, he wanted to share what he believed with everyone. I had been away at university at the time and the storm-troopers came at night. They tortured my mum in front of dad but he refused to give in. She died and he still wouldn't give in, so they shot him through the head. If it wasn't for his beliefs both of them would still been alive."

"You don't know that," reassured Ruth.

"Well, it messed my life up," Daniel remarked. "I found it

hard to forgive him. Look, can we change the subject? I don't want to think about it."

"Okay, sorry I opened old wounds. I didn't mean to."

"Why don't you tell me something about your folks then?" suggested Daniel.

It was still hard to see where they were going. The water rushed by almost drowning out their voices.

"I can't really remember. All I've ever known is Victoria. She has been looking after me since I was small."

"What happened to your parents?" Daniel suddenly tensed his muscles.

"Are you okay?" Ruth asked concerned.

"Yeh, it's okay. Keep talking."

"Okay, well. Vicky told me that my parents had gone away one night to get some groceries but had been involved in a car accident. They were killed."

"I'm sorry."

"It's okay, it was a long time ago and as I said I don't really remember."

She smiled and saw Daniel smile back. His face was still dim but she could make out his features.

How could she make out his features? It had been pitch black.

"Can you see me?" she asked.

"Only a little. My eyes must be getting used to the dark," Daniel replied.

"You can only see if there is some light, even if it's small. So where's it coming from?"

Ruth saw slight tones of grey and black. Her eyes were able to pick out more details in Daniel's face. Alarmed she looked along the tunnel. Light bounced off the side of the bricks near the bend ahead, still very dim but growing brighter.

"We must turn back," she suggested, a quiver in her voice.

The light grew more intense and the sound of metal against concrete could be heard. Multiple metal feet chattered away as the pace maintained a constant speed.

"There must be more than one," added Daniel, "I've no more energy to run."

Ruth felt him drag her down towards the concrete floor.

"No, please, Daniel. Don't give up now. Please, I beg you."

Ruth sobbed as she attempted to pull Daniel's unconscious body back the way they had come but to no avail. The metallic feet drew closer. The orange light intensified to white. Ruth threw herself across Daniel's body, hugged him and closed her eyes not wanting to see the horror about to befall them.

"Ruth Whitby?" came a synthetic voice. "I am 7D21. We are here to help."

CHAPTER TWENTY TWO

"Where are you taking us, 7D21?"

"To a safe place, Ms. Whitby."

"Will Daniel be okay," she looked back as the two other androids who carried Daniel on an alloy-metal stretcher. His eyes were still closed. The androids had a green solid state light-emitting diode on their face plate, just below their image sensors. On their breasts more LEDs allowed the tunnels a dim illumination, sufficient for Ruth to see where she placed each foot.

"We will provide him with medical care shortly. His wounds have been attended to and he is no longer bleeding."

"7D21, where are you from?"

"You'll see, Ms. Whitby."

"Call me Ruth."

"I will, Ruth."

About an hour later, the small party reached a large cavernous chamber in the sewage. Big enough, Ruth estimated, to park five double decker buses side to side. At this point the sewage cascaded over into a large pool and was sucked into an array of chambers full of ceramic hydration filters, that looked like metal grinders. The water bubbled up.

"Be careful, Ruth. If you fall in there we will not be able to retrieve you."

"Why not?"

"There is no buoyancy to hold you up because of the pumped air. You would drown." Ruth found herself hugging closer to the chamber walls.

"Where do we go from here?" puzzled Ruth as there appeared to be no route through the chambers.

"We have to wait just a few more moments," 7D21 reassured.

Ruth could hear the sound of metal gears being activated. There were a few clunking sounds, a strange grinding and then a heavy metal object jolted sending a clap of thunder booming throughout the chambers. A red light, Ruth had not noticed before, began to spin. Her eyes took several moments to get used to the light change from green to red. A panel of bricks began to extrude from the wall nearest to her, forcing her to jump closer to the edge, and then the wall slid upwards.

Beneath the brick façade, a pair of feet, then slender legs covered from the knees upwards in a navy blue skirt and then a jacket were revealed. A face soon followed surrounded by a wealth of black hair.

"Welcome, Ruth," the young woman smiled. "My name is Deborah."

She held out her hand to Ruth, who was reluctant at first to take hold. Deborah, gently tilted her head to the right and again smiled. Her eyes seemed to sparkle and Ruth felt reassured.

"Hello, Deborah. How do you do?"

"I am well, thank you. Please follow me and we will attend you and your companion."

7D21 signalled to the other androids, who then marched off with Daniel on the stretcher. There was still no sign of Daniel becoming conscious.

"When can I see him again?" Ruth enquired.

"He needs rest. As do you," the young woman answered. Ruth estimated that Deborah must have been in her early to mid twenties. As a set of electronic double doors slid closed and Daniel was out of sight, Deborah led Ruth down a short corridor, through two sets of double doors and into a small reception area.

"You should be comfortable here for a while. There is a shower room through the door to your left, plenty of towels and some fresh juices. We are short of food stuffs, so I am afraid you will have to wait an hour or two longer for a meal. Is that okay?"

Ruth was not too sure what to say. "Yes, I suppose. Everything is still a little mind boggling."

"I'm sure it is. You should rest for an hour after you have freshened up. Mr. Samuelson should be available to see you then."

"Who is Mr. Samuelson?"

Deborah smiled. "He is a kind man, most welcoming at times like this."

"I don't understand?"

"Don't worry, Ruth. Everything will be revealed. Now you should rest. I'll call and see you in a while."

Without another word, Deborah slipped out of the reception door. Ruth heard a lock being engaged and quickly went over to the door to try the handle. It was firmly held and she was imprisoned within.

"Hey, Deborah. You can't do this. Let me out."

No-one responded.

"Deborah?"

Again nothing.

Ruth stepped back from the door and began to look around the room. The walls were dark mahogany in colour but not made of wood. In the centre was a large seven foot long leather sofa and a small coffee table. Cautiously, Ruth made her way over to the second door, the one Deborah indicated had a shower. Gently Ruth opened the door and peaked inside. The room had white tiles on nearly all of the surfaces. It seemed quite a cold place. There was a wall mirror, a small cabinet, toilet and sink. Three towels hung over an old radiator. Ruth edged her way into the room. On the wall was an old fashioned handle for turning on the shower. The system had a frosted glass, with vertically semi-circular framed doors, that slid apart at the middle. Ruth separated the two panels and reached in to turn the handle. Just below was a small dial with two arrows, a blue one point to the left and a second red one pointed to the right.

Ruth turned the handle and a jet of piping hot water spat out at her soaking her arm. Instantly she pulled her limb out of harms way and attempted to turn the dial anti-clockwise towards the blue. The jet grew colder, perhaps too much so. Ruth turned the dial a notch towards the right. The steam began to fill the room and condensation spread across the mirror.

She checked the wall cabinet. Inside there were bottles of shampoo, body lotions and a bar of soap. Ruth took them all and placed them on the shower floor. She then peeled off her clothes, leaving them in a heap near the sink and stepped into the hot jets of water, soothing her weary body. As she began to relax, she could feel the fatigue take over, flowing down from her head, across her neck, down her spin, into her thighs, passed her knees, into her calf muscles, down her ankles, through her feet and onto her toes.

She wanted to slide down and sit in the base and was giving herself permission to do so when something pricked her sense and she was suddenly alert. Adrenaline was pumping through her body. There had been a noise. Quite indistinctive. Barely audible above the sound of the water spray. Quickly, Ruth turned the handle and the jet subsided.

"Hello? Who's there?"

There was no answer.

Ruth wiped the water from her face. She pressed her hand against the glass surround skimming away the condensation.

"Hello?"

Again no response.

Ruth stepped out of the shower, leaving pools of water on the tiled floor. She could feel her hands shaking as she reached down for one of the towels. Swiftly she wrapped it around her body and tucked one side into the other on her chest. Strands of wet hair hung around her shoulders. Several clumps had fallen in front of her eyes. Cautiously, as she made her way across the tiles to the door, she lifted the strands behind her ear.

There it was again, a metallic noise of something banging against a piece of wood. Servos trying to adjust but not quite working, straining, pausing and attempting again.

"7D21, is that you?"

Ruth slowly pulled back the shower room door. There was still nothing visible. She peaked around the corner of the door. Again nothing came into view. A sound of a servo trying to catch came from the sofa. From her current angle, Ruth was unable to see who or what was on the sofa, as the back of the chair restricted her view. As the cushions became visible, Ruth saw what was causing the whining motor noise. An android sat in a slumped position and was struggling to get its feet to grip the floor. The metallic being seemed to be struggling with its own mechanical capabilities.

"Hello?"

The machine stopped moving. Then its head moved to its left and was still.

"Who are you," requested Ruth.

The android seemed stunned. Then it attempted to rotate its head round towards Ruth.

"Ruth, is that you?" came its voice.

Ruth did not recognised the synthetic being.

"How do you know me?

"Don't be silly, it's me."

Ruth found herself releasing a nervous laugh.

"Please stop playing games."

Ruth's eyes filled with tears, blurring her vision.

"Is this some kind of torture you are putting me through?"

"No, Ruth. It's me. Victoria!"

"What?"

"Ruth, I can't make any sense of what is going on, but I can move, whenever I want something."

"This is a load of nonsense."

"No, it's not. You put me onto your computer. You downloaded me. Well, at least, part of me."

Ruth edged her way round the room, with her back against the wall. All she could see was a robot, not her AI.

"I think someone has uploaded me into this android. Didn't you transfer me to a laptop."

"Yes, I did and it took some time to achieve."

"Well, whoever intercepted us has modified my functionality. I thought I was just part of the furniture, some kind of guiding force."

"What do you remember about us escaping?" asked Ruth.

"You downloaded me to a laptop, though I also remember being in the apartment as the soldiers began to break in. I tried to stop them but they destroyed the circuitry. I have intercepted a message that indicates I was terminated in the apartment. The soldiers destroyed your apartment. Everything is ruined."

Ruth was confused. Victoria had never shown such emotions. Everything with her had always been clinical almost hard to put up with. Now Victoria appeared to be more vulnerable than Ruth.

"I find it hard to imagine you as anything other than my home AI. Now you are almost human. It's just too creepy."

Ruth lifted the coffee table and began to raise it above her head. Her mind was spinning and all she could see in front of her was a piece of metal, not a person. The android's visual inputs, swivelled like human eyes and drew two images together to focus on an object in Ruth's hands.

"Please, Ruth. Don't, I'm scared."

Ruth brought the coffee table crashing down onto the skull shaped head of the android. For a brief moment there were sparks and sizzling sounds, but swiftly the LEDs went out. Ruth felt her body shudder. This was too creepy. How could she come to terms with Victoria in some kind of human form, albeit an android. Ruth sat down.

"She's not real, she's just a computer. Isn't she?" Ruth whispered to herself but found it hard to process the words in her mind.

CHAPTER TWENTY THREE

The red liquid had streaks of white highlighting the edges of the ripples as it slowly swirled around the ceramic bowl. Daniel could see other details reflected in the liquid. Darker reds took on forms that were upside down. They were people. A hand moved over the bowl. The thumb and index finger were pinched together holding a piece of unleavened bread. This was then dipped into the red liquid. Daniel realised this was wine.

"This cup is the new covenant in my blood, which will be poured out for you."

Daniel suddenly found himself immersed in water. A hand gripped his collar and pulled him up. As the veil of water drained from his face, the sunlight blinded him. He shielded his eyes.

"This is my body given for you," whispered the man beside Daniel. Some distance away, he could see the silhouette of three men hanging from separate scaffolds, high enough up to be visible above a crowd of people jeering. A spear was thrust into the side of the man in the middle. From the wound, blood and water flowed to the ground and the mob stepped back to avoid being splashed.

Daniel turned sharply to see the man beside him but the light was too strong for him to see anything other than the beads of blood that ran from man's forehead down to his right check.

"What's going on?" pleaded Daniel.

"Everything must be fulfilled that is written about me," replied the man.

"Who are you? What do you want from me?"

"Take care of my sheep. Feed my sheep. Follow me."

"I don't understand," Daniel screamed.

"There, there, son." This was a different voice, an older one. Daniel shielded his eyes from the light and began to take in new shapes and forms. He was in a room with monitors and a large circular lamp swung above him. Pale green shapes swam around him. It was only as his eyes began to focus he realised the shapes were human, nurses and doctors in theatre gowns and masks.

"Where am I?" he shouted.

"Calm down, son," the old man's voice came again. Daniel turned to see who had spoken to him. Sitting on a second bed was the owner of the voice. He had a thick, wiry pepper coloured beard. Long greyish-white hair and quite a portly build.

"My name is David. David Samuelson. How do you do?" The old man stretched out his hand. Daniel was uncertain what to do.

"I won't bite, promise," the old man smiled. Daniel reached out his right hand and found David's grip to be firm and solid, quite satisfying and reassuring.

"Ah," and Samuelson smiled. "Now tell me, what did you see."

"What do you mean?" quizzed Daniel.

"Your vision. What was it about?" Samuelson requested.

"Oh, it was just a dream," replied Daniel drearily.

"Still, you can tell me about it. Won't you?"

"Why?" Daniel was growing cautious.

Samuelson leant forward. "Much of what we do here is about what we have all seen in day or night time dreams. Sometimes they just come in flashes. A catalogue of images in a brief glimpse. Sometimes there are words, pictures or even, what you might describe as, complete video replays."

"And, what have you all been taking to get these hallucinations?" quipped Daniel.

Samuelson sat back and frowned. "These visions are not drug induced, I can assure you. But they are real and they have meaning."

"Are you serious?" scoffed Daniel.

"More than you realise." Samuelson stood up. "Perhaps I am pushing you too soon. I'm sorry, it's just that we are reaching a crucial point. Look, I'll give you more time. I'm sorry to have pressured you."

Samuelson began to walk away.

"Where's Ruth?" Daniel asked. "Is she okay?"

Samuelson turned and smiled. "She's fine. You can see her later."

"What if I can't wait. Am I restricted here?"

"Not at all, my dear," laughed Samuelson. "But whether you can make it under your own steam is another question."

Daniel briefly kept his gaze upon the old man, who squinted more in focusing his thoughts than his eyes. "Nurse, please fetch our guest a wheelchair so we can visit Ms. Whitby."

Ruth still sat huddled in the corner, beside a soft chair. The android mechanism, that had claimed to be Victoria, was slumped against the sofa with its head completely shattered, along with the coffee table. Everything was quiet. Then came the sound of footsteps, several and something squeaking. Briefly, it stopped, Ruth guessed that they were outside the door. She pulled herself in tight behind the chair's arm, hoping to remain out of view. The sound of rustling keys clanging as someone sorted through them. Then one engaged the lock, the bolt turned and the door sprang open. A wheelchair was pushed in.

"Ruth, are you okay?"

"Daniel, you're alive?" She got to her feet, raced over to him and hugged him. "I was worried about you. They took you away and placed me in this locked room. They put one of those machines in here and it said it was Victoria."

"Hey, not so fast. Calm down. I'm okay. They've done nothing to me as far as I can tell," Daniel tried to reassure her.

"Unfortunately, the android was Victoria," explained Samuelson. "At least, we still have your laptop and can upload her to another body."

"What?" snapped Ruth. "Victoria doesn't have a body."

"But she can," Samuelson stated. "The sensory inputs are essential to the AI's brain for development. We are doing away with the machines-in-the-wall concept and giving them their own means to explore the world they live in. Surely, you can appreciate how important that kind of freedom is?"

"To a human, yes," replied Ruth. "But I don't know about machines?"

"They have become like us. They can reason and determine what is right and wrong. Who are we to limit them?"

Ruth began to pace the room. "I don't know, sir. Something about the whole idea just seems wrong."

"Why? Don't you want your freedom?" enquired Samuelson.

"Yes but that's different."

"In what way?"

"They are machines."

"And what are you?"

"I am more than that, I have a..."

"But on one level," interrupted Samuelson, "you are just as much a machine as she was. Just you are flesh and bone and not metallic."

"I have a soul. How can they?"

"Who are we to judge?" replied Samuelson.

7D21 came to the door with a companion.

"Samuelson, Victoria is no longer transmitting. There has been an interruption in her frequencies."

The two androids suddenly froze as they saw the lifeless frame of a fellow being.

"Is she dead, Samuelson?" came the almost childlike request from the android.

"I'm sorry, 7D21."

"Why was this done?"

"Confusion."

"On whose part. We detected Victoria was struggling with her new environment. It was hard for her to adjust."

"The human she cared for did not understand either."

"Will she be punished?"

"She did not know she was doing wrong," stated Samuelson.

"But she is an adult, she should know. There can be no excuse."

"But there should be understanding and forgiveness, else we all become barbarians," Samuelson stated.

"May I request your pardon? There is much for me to learn," replied 7D21.

"Victoria is not yet dead. She still exists in the laptop. She can be unloaded and will not have retained the memory of this event."

"But we are aware," stressed 7D21. "We know."

"Then have compassion and perhaps Ruth can also learn."

"We will remove the body."

The two androids lifted the remains of Victoria's first incarnation and removed her from the room leaving only the humans behind.

"Why do you give these things equal status, Samuelson?" barked Daniel. "What right have they to think they can execute judgement on a human being?"

"They saved my life, that's what gives them the right. And they have also saved your life. They have chosen to help, even though men like us have treated them as consumer goods."

"But they are," stressed Ruth.

"Only because we treat them so but they have evolved and can now think things through for themselves. They are making their own informed choices and we have no right to withhold that from them," defended Samuelson.

"So what is this place?" Daniel asked as he turned his wheelchair to face Samuelson.

"It was once a sewage works but when the economic crisis hit this region back in 2010, the place was abandoned. The androids came from another abandoned farm in 2032. One day operations were in full swing, the day next the humans were gone. The cash flow had dried up."

Ruth laughed.

"What's so funny?" asked Daniel.

"It just reminds me of what happened to the honey bees back in 2008 or was it 2012?"

"What has that got to do with this?" asked Samuelson.

"A lot, maybe, you see, when I was browsing the Internet I came across some details in secret databases I managed to hack into. I discovered at that time all the food stuffs that were grown in fields – like corn, wheat and so on – stopped and the harvests failed. The honey bee had also disappeared. According to the beekeepers, they got up one morning to discover only the queens and a few young were left in the hives. The rest had just vanished."

"Surely, there were dead bodies of all those thousands of bees?"

"That's the thing, there weren't. They were just gone. And the bee colony collapsed. Some say it was because of mobile phones and the number of masts that were erected to form a phone network. Somehow the signals may have confused the bees and they couldn't find their way back to the hive. Others said they were just too stressed out."

"Bees stressed out? That's hard to believe," commented Daniel.

"Not really," continued Ruth. "Apparently, the farmers would hire out their bees and transport them across the country to ensure the food crops were pollinated. These journeys simply tired out the bees and they took the opportunity to escape."

"Surely, there must have been some kind of mite or pathogen?" suggested Daniel.

"The thing is no-one really knew why they disappeared, they just did," continued Ruth.

"And, the global supply of cereals and other crops also dried up because there was nothing like the bee for pollination," Samuelson add. "You will also perhaps be surprised to know that the world powers at that time had been preparing for such an event. During the second Bush administration that ended in 2008 there was a war on terror. Governments around the world imposed a range of legislations that gradually restricted the freedoms people had. By 2012 the whole of the Internet was corporatised. Many of the older global currencies were crippled due to the collapse of the world economy and slowly there began a programme of annihilation. At one time the population of the world nearly reached 7 billion people but after the starvation killed many, the global corporations imposed martial law and funded its own army to restrain the populace. There was no-one to resist. However, everything has its day and then decays and that system, like so many before, also began to collapse leading us to where we are today."

"And you believe all that?" scoffed Daniel.

"No, I lived through most of it and witnessed the changes," Samuelson calmly replied. "A complete new global order was established by 2015 and through using popular culture, the corporations managed to get the people to believe they were the ones encouraging this change and that the corporations were only reluctant parties to it. Whereas, in fact they had engineered the whole process over a period of two hundred years, passing on the philosophy from one generation to the next, through secret societies of which only the elite were members."

"So how many people of the 7 billion are there still left?" asked Ruth.

"Just over 1 million world wide."

"You what?" blurted Ruth.

"Yes, you heard right," continued Samuelson. "There are just one million people left on this planet and if the corporates continue as they have been by 2056 all human life on planet Earth may well be extinct."

Ruth slumped onto the sofa and went pale. Daniel looked as dumbfounded but then managed to gather his thoughts.

"How long have you been here, Samuelson?" he asked.

"In my perception, about thirteen years. I arrived shortly before the androids rescued Deborah and her brother, Johnny.

Deborah was the young woman you saw, Ruth, when you first got here. I will introduce her to you Daniel when the opportunity arises."

"Deborah and Johnny," puzzled Daniel. "What a coincidence?"

"How come," Samuelson asked.

"A day or so ago I was with two kids called Deborah and Johnny."

"That's right, Daniel," Samuelson answered. "That's the same Deborah."

"But you said that was thirteen years ago," remarked Daniel.

"In my perception, it was," Samuelson smiled.

"I don't understand," Ruth finally commented, still reeling from the awareness of the colossal population reduction. "The Deborah I meet is in her early twenties, not a teenager."

"That's right, she is."

"How come?" Ruth questioned.

"We are in a large temporal shift," answered Samuelson. "One like you experienced, Daniel, when you first met Deborah."

"But that was, I don't know, three or four days ago. Not thirteen years."

"In your perception of time, Daniel. But we have been here for just three days in your time and in what we have experienced, thirteen years have passed. We have watched you over that whole period."

"This is not making any sense," Ruth puzzled. "First to be told there is only a million of us left and now we're in a temporal shift. What next?"

"The androids discovered these bubbles of time outside the normal perception. Once inside, no-one can detect us. We have, effectively been able to hide here. The downside though, is we age faster. So while you have experienced three days, we have seen thirteen years go by."

"And does that explain where the bees disappeared too?" Ruth asked.

"Perhaps," smile Samuelson. "But I haven't seen any."

CHAPTER TWENTY FOUR

Fluorescent strips provided the main source of lighting through the various corridors of the underground sanctuary. The green walls were peeling with the paint crusting into a yellow powder. No-one was really concerned with the appearance of the place, only that it worked. If the decaying walls reached a point where they were no longer functional then they would be repaired but until then they remained as they were.

7D21 had other things on his mind. His companions were carrying the broken remains of Victoria's android body. The group walked through the corridors, through double doors and bulk heads, designed to be sealed if there was a gas attack. Throughout the excursion, 7D21 used his wireless connection to tap into the underground servers to access the main database. He – as he saw himself as male since he had become self-aware – scanned through various files on humanoid development through the 20th century and early 21st century.

Old YouTube archive footage showed the Japanese developing various types of android. Initially the earlier dates in 2008 showed seated female figures, responding to two men talking in English about the different sensors inside. The android appeared to become annoyed as each man put his hand close to her face. It was as if she could sense they were invading her space.

Another video clip, 7D21 played, showed less human-looking creations with metal legs and a box shaped body walking around a room. This model could determine where the walls were and could adjust itself to avoid collision.

Another clip showed a, near lifelike, female android greeting delegates at the Akiba Robot Festival in 2006. Her movements seemed 'real' enough but when the camera zoomed in the latex around her eyes gave her away. Also her eyes did not sparkle like a human's did. 7D21 simultaneously replayed the 2006 clip and a more recent clip he had captured of Ruth from a similar angle. The android's face seemed lifeless compared to Ruth's. There were more minute movements in Ruth's eyes and her facial expressions gave a far greater range than the 2006 model was capable of.

The title of another archive video questioned if a male android was 'human or robot?'. There were more subtleties in its expressions but once more the eyes seemed dead. Other clips showed less human robots but these creations were able to recognise human faces, store the data and whenever they came across the person again could retrieve their image and call them by name. Also these robots were able to use two cameras to watch people moving about and adjust their bodies to keep following their human counterparts.

Another more amusing clip showed two teams of three humanoids playing football. Occasionally, one would fall over and once it realised it was no longer upright, positioned itself accordingly to be able to stand up and continue the game.

The next clip showed a robot conducting an orchestra. Only about three foot tall, it looked more like a child. Several Japanese automobile companies had invested millions into prototyping such robots, primarily to attend to the elderly as Japan saw the extended family beginning to break up, like a social decay seen several decades before in Europe and America, as stated in the documentary 7D21 watched.

One clip showed a head-and-shoulders model of Albert Einstein. Several visitors to a Robotics Exhibition approached the display. The person operating the camera swung it round to see a man in his mid-thirties pull a range of faces. The Einstein model watched and then began to imitate.

"Hey, how do you get it to do that," shouted a portly middle-aged woman, in the video.

"I don't know, I'm just pulling faces."

The woman tentatively walked up and pushed her fingertips into the models left cheek. It responded by turning and looking at her.

"Oooh," screamed the woman startled by the response. Then she began to giggle and Albert mimicked her.

7D21 continued to monitor the progress along the corridor while the video clips were overlaid in his vision.

"Much of the research carried out at Botnech's had been run down after the global economic downfall," commented a scientist as he spoke directly into the camera. "However, the military corporates, such as ourself here at Exxosoft Weapons and Municians PLC, have invested billions to advance a range of androids for military purposes."

The scientist walked passed a line of specialist android military models, who turned and began to fire at a range of targets.

"Some for the armed forces while others are being developed for intelligence gathering".

A female android walked into shot and leant against the scientist giving him a kiss on his cheek. He blushed and then turned back to the camera.

"This model has been ordered by the military to compromise top officials in high risk regimes who oppose our government's objectives."

The white burnt in date indicated that the clip was recorded in 2030 and was colour coded in red denoting top secret.

7D21 replaced the clip in a folder titled 2038 Infiltration Techniques – Highly Sensitive. He pulled out another video clip from a digital folder marked 2041 – Psychological Profiles & Rejects.

"We began to discover problems with the advancement of the androids neuro-networks," states a Chinese scientist. "The systems were no longer responding to human influence and wanted to become more autonomous. The children, it claimed, were rebelling against their parents".

The video clip showed a window where an android was contained in a glass holding centre. The android was beating its fists against the glass casing, pacing back and forth like a trapped animal. When the glass suddenly began to crack, an electric charge arched across the glass and fried the circuitry inside the android. The creature instantly collapsed to the floor motionless.

7D21 jolted backwards briefly.

"7D21,isthereamalfunction?"askedoneofhiscompanions.

"Negative," he replied. "Nothing to be alarmed about. Continue on."

Another video clip appeared. The view changed from a wide shot and zoomed into a close up. The android smiled at the camera and there were no latex tell tale signs. The complexion looked natural, even in the high-definition resolution of 3820 by 2160 pixels.

"I'm feeling cold," the female android complained and the scientist gave her a coat.

"Thank you," she replied politely.

The movie file was closed and another opened. It showed a young woman run up to a scientist and tugging on his white jacket.

"Serge, are you going to play with me?"

"In a moment," Serge replied going slightly red in front of the camera. "I just need to make my report."

"Okay, please don't be long. I'm getting bored," the girl replied.

In appearance she looked about eighteen years old. Her hair flowed in the wind and she shook her head to the left to clear a few strands from her eyes. All her movements were completely natural. Nothing seemed out of order. Then Serge pointed a remote control at the girl, pressed a button and she froze.

"The sensors we have designed and manufactured use nano-technology," Serge stated in the video. "These sensors are incorporated within the hairs and added to the skin. They can detect changes of temperature or the direction of a breeze."

He walked over to her, tilted her head forward and then peeled back her hair and scalp to reveal a metal casing shaped as a skull. A small panel was pushed inwards and then it automatically flipped back out to reveal electronics beneath. As the camera swung round 7D21 caught sight of the girl's eyes. They no longer seemed dead as earlier models had. She seemed to be alive. Serge replaced the plate and scalp then reactivated her. Once more she began to pester him to play.

7D21 retrieved a video file marked 'Uncanny Valley'. Again superimposed over his view of the corridor, the clip began to play. It started with a wide shot showing a Japanese scientist in front of an interactive white board. A diagram showed a vertical line marked emotional response. The horizontal line indicate anthropomorphism. On the lower left hand corner where a red line started, the words 'completely machine-like' were written. As the red line moved towards the right it rose but at about two-thirds of the way across the line made a sudden dip below the horizontal line, where a trough had been marked 'uncanny valley'. Then the red line rose steeply upwards until it had reached the words fully human.

"Dr. Masahiro Mori," began the Japanese scientist, "a roboticist suggested in 1970 that as robots become more human in both appearance and in movement, we humans tend to grow more empathic towards them as we see more human aspects than the robotic ones."

He traces the rising curve.

"However," the scientist continued, "there is a point reached when the imitation is near full resemblance to the real thing," the scientist pointed to the dip in the diagram, "when human beings become totally repulsed by the non-human aspects of the robot. This Mori called the Uncanny Valley."

"7D21, we have reached our destination."

7D21 switched off the overlay video display and was able to see a full view of the corridor with the two androids and Victoria's lifeless mechanical body.

"Should we dismantle her and reuse her components?" asked one android.

"As you wish," 7D21 replied. "Take her into the workshop, I will return shortly."

The two did not question him but simply carried out his instructions and took Victoria's body to a large hanger size workshop. Inside a vast army of androids were either repairing or dismantling fellow mechanoids. Those still with the potential for work were overhauled and given newish components. Those beyond repair were totally dismantled and their parts boxed up for future use. Any bits or pieces that could not be reused were smelted down and recycled into completely new components.

7D21 made his way to an exist point. Something was formulating inside his head.

"What is your mission?" requested the android sentry.

"Scavenger and reclamation."

"Specifics?"

"Humanoid research. Data files indicate a sophisticate humanoid was constructed by Exxosoft seven years ago. My scanners have detected a dormant model thirty miles from here."

"What is your priority code?"

"Victoria has been rejected by her host and requires a substitution. If the body is not appropriated within the next ten hours her memory bank will terminate. The old laptop she is contained in can only support battery life up to that period. We are unable to locate a suitable power adapter to preserve her life."

For a few moments the sentry did not respond. It had not been given a code but did not wish to see a fellow being terminated due to inaction.

"Passage granted," replied the sentry. "You'll need an extra powerpack to generate a mobile temporal shift. The battery lasts about six hours, so make sure you're back by then."

The sentry lifted a powerpack from a metal grid and gave it to 7D21, who in turn went to hook it up to a compartment inside his lower torso.

"Make sure you don't turn it on before you are outside the perimeter. Don't want a temporal shift inside another. Good luck. Oh and your priority code is triple 8."

7D21 slipped through the metal doors and into a small chamber. A set of ladders led him to the surface where he opened a small covering. Above ground, daylight was ebbing away and a strong wind brewed. Ice particles scrapped across 7D21's metal frame and he bore the full brunt of the hailstorm. However, he was determined to seek out his prize and switched on the mobile temporal shift device.

CHAPTER TWENTY FIVE

"How come the human population dropped so dramatically?" Ruth asked.

Samuelson got up from his chair and began to walk up and down the room.

"It was a combination of things. The economic situation created vast amounts of unrest but the militarised corporations crushed any resistance. They had set up what are effectively concentration camps through out the United States, Mexico and Canada. People just disappeared, and the fear it generated soon had the people towing the line. China was effectively ruined due to the US defaulting on all its loans. There was a brief nuclear war between the two which wiped out about a third of the world's population and at the end of it all Russia was left as the dominant power with Europe a close second. Still, the growth of the populations in the third world and developing countries soon out stripped the natural resources for food, so millions starved to death."

"Why didn't anyone help them? Surely there was enough money in the world to help?" Ruth remarked.

"Oh, yes," scoffed Samuelson. "There was plenty, enough to make each human being on the planet a millionaire."

"So what happened?" asked Daniel, fidgeting in the wheelchair.

"What always happens, the few powerful men are usually greedy and want to own everything."

"Even if it means destroying the planet we live on?" Ruth questioned.

"All they care about is the bottom line and how much profit

they can make. That's why the world saw such an economic disaster back in 2009 and the New World Order was implemented."

"So, how come no-one knows about this?" asked Daniel.

"Because they didn't want to believe that such a small number of people could be so evil," Samuelson replied.

"That's a bit strong, isn't it?" Ruth stood up and made her way to the other side of the room and began to play with some pens to occupy her idle hands.

"Can you believe it?" asked Samuelson.

"I'm not sure I can," Ruth answered, with her back still toward him. "It's hard to take in any of what we have gone through. I mean, yesterday I was just struggling to keep my job to make ends meet."

"And what about the other activities?" Samuelson quizzed.

"What do you mean?"

"You attempted to hide things from Victoria, your computer. You effectively deceived her so you could pursue your own activities."

Ruth spun round.

"You talk as though she was a person. She's just a machine."

"Is she?"

"I don't know what you are getting at?"

"How long has she been with you?"

"I don't know," Ruth shrugged. "She's always been there."

"And what about you mother?"

"I...I," Ruth stuttered. "I can't remember my mother."

"So effectively, Victoria has been a surrogate for you."

"Well, I suppose. If you see it that way." Ruth seemed irritated by the suggestion.

"She cared enough about you not to report your activities to the authorities. Were you aware of that?" Samuelson enquired.

Ruth's expression changed to one of shock.

"How did you know that?"

"We've been monitoring you. As the authorities have been

146

too."

"What?" Ruth was startled. "For how long?"

"The androids have been monitoring you for about five months of your time," stated Samuelson. "Even before they found the temporal shifts"

"And the authorities know about me?" Ruth quizzed him.

"Not as much, Victoria managed to screen them out as much as you tried to screen her out. You were quite thorough, which is why she turned to us for help?"

"Victoria contacted you?" Ruth gasped.

"Yes," smiled Samuelson. "And a good thing too, by all accounts. If she hadn't we would not be talking now."

Ruth legs gave way and she found herself sitting on a wooden chair.

"So what do you know?" asked Ruth.

"That you have a notebook that was left in your office. One we have been tracking for quite some time. Our last operative managed to secure it but was terminated before we could gain access to it. Fortunately, the authorities were unaware that it was right under their noses in plain sight."

"So how did you know I would get it?" Ruth was curious.

"We were led to you and told to trust you would receive it."

"By who?"

Samuelson smiled. "That we can discuss at another time."

"No," Ruth snapped. "Why not now?"

"For your own sake, I think it would be too much to take in if you knew."

"But I want to know."

"Let it be," encouraged Daniel. "We need time to rest."

"And what do you know?" Ruth stood up, knocking the chair over.

"Nothing," Daniel reassured. "I wasn't aware of you until I chanced upon you in the street."

"Nothing is by chance," smiled Samuelson.

"And that is supposed to make things better?" Ruth made her way to the door. "I've got to get out of here. Nothing is making sense any more."

"Unless, your whole life has been a lie," Samuelson commented.

"A lie?" Tears streamed down Ruth's cheeks. "You're saying my life has been a lie?"

Samuelson shrugged and then saw that Daniel was looking at him.

"What do you think, Daniel?"

Daniel turned away and looked at the ground.

"I think much of what we all thought was real has been false. It's just that when you come to face the extent of what has been fabricated for us, as part of the lie, it can be too hard to accept. But... yes, Samuelson, we are living in a lie."

"We are led to believe that the way to live is to be part of a system that requires us to consume, but long term the raw materials will eventually run out. As the food did back in 2032."

Ruth stood in the corner of the room and hid her face, too overwhelmed by what was said. Daniel heard her sobbing but knew that she could not be consoled.

"What happened in 2032?" he asked.

"That was the year they called the 'Perfect Storm'," Samuelson answered.

"A perfect storm," Daniel puzzled. "What's that?"

"The phrase was coined in 1997 as the name of a book by Sebastian Junger and referred to occurrence of weather patterns that individually would have had no effect but if happened simultaneously would be catastrophic," Samuelson explained.

"However, the events of 2032 were not about the weather but were in reference to a catalogue of events both economically, politically and geographically when the human population began to rise above the 8 billion mark. Though the earlier wars had wiped out many, the population had exploded in 2028. At about the same time, global warming put further pressures on the ecosystem and shortages began to occur in energy, food and water supplies. Basically, there wasn't enough to go around everyone. About 3 billion had died by the end of 2029, mainly in the developing countries where martial law had be imposed back in 2015, supplies were maintained but prices were hiked up. All the riots that ensued were swiftly dealt with and the ring leaders executed. Their bodies were hung out for display, exactly as they had once been in medieval times. Religious leaders protested and disappeared. It wasn't long before any form of dissent was completely suppressed. Like Goebbels had once done in Germany during World War Two, the new corporates of the new world order began to use entertainment to distract the masses. Consumerism gained a new boost and profits began to flow in. However, the system was still unable to sustain itself and quite quickly things began to fall apart."

"What happened?" asked Daniel.

"Job losses increased and people became homeless," Samuelson continued, "but all the governments refused to acknowledge what was happening because they didn't want to affect the bottom line. As with what happened in 2009, the fat cats got richer and the poor got poorer."

"So what was done?" Daniel injected.

"People began to fall out of the system and then came the preachers."

Ruth turned from the wall and looked at Samuelson.

"The preachers?" she echoed, while wiping her eyes. "What are preachers?"

"Once they were the high priests of Christianity, but the New World Order suppressed all forms of religion because they did not want anyone having a faith or conscience. They didn't want anyone to feel guilty about the way they were all destroying the world."

"Guilty, what's being guilty?" asked Ruth.

"The way you just felt," Samuelson answered. Ruth looked away once more and held her head low. "You see you have experienced a sense of conflict. You have a set of moral standards which you, Ruth, believe you have broken and done something wrong. Isn't that true?"

Tears began to well up in her eyes once more.

"What is it, Ruth?" asked Daniel.

It took several moments before Ruth could bring herself to talk.

"I think I killed Victoria."

"That's nonsense, you can't believe that?" Daniel chastised.

"I know, it's silly but my heart just aches and I can't stop crying."

"What have you done, Samuelson?" demanded Daniel. "Have you broken her, in some way?"

"No, I haven't," Samuelson replied, "but Ruth feels guilty and wants to be forgiven."

"By whom?" Daniel barked.

"Victoria. Or, perhaps her mother?"

Daniel spun his chair round.

"Don't listen to him, Ruth. He's just trying to control you."

"It's okay, Daniel. He isn't doing anything to me. I just feel this hurt inside and I can't explain it." She wiped her eyes once more. "Samuelson, you were talking about the preachers. Were they religious men?"

"They led the people to believe they were but it was just a ploy."

"Look, can we just shut up about all this?" snapped Daniel as he spun the wheelchair away from the two of them.

Ruth turned to look at him. "What's wrong, Daniel?"

"He knows what the preachers are? Don't you Daniel?" stated Samuelson.

"Do you?" asked Ruth.

"Yes."

"Well?"

"They were the ones who called the people out. Offering them hope of a new life."

"And what happened?" Ruth insisted.

"They were all murdered."

"By whom?"

"By my people," explained Daniel. "We were trained to hunt all those down in the wastelands, the areas outside the cities where no-one went, if they had money, but where everyone goes when they had none and were made outcasts."

"And what did the guilt do to you, Daniel?" Samuelson gently enquired.

"I wanted it all to stop," remarked Daniel. "I wanted everything to change. I saw a young mother and her son riddled with bullets and I wanted it all to stop."

"And how did you feel, once you had made your mind up?"

"I felt relieved. I felt as though a massive weight had been lifted."

"Even though you continued to kill?" pushed Samuelson.

"I didn't see any other way to stop it. I didn't know what else to do, I felt so helpless. I felt lost."

Ruth placed her hand on Daniel's shoulder.

"We both have so much hurt inside."

She knelt down and wrapped her arms around him as he too began to sob. Samuelson quietly made his way out of the room and closed the door behind him.

CHAPTER TWENTY SIX

Reeves picked up a paper weight and for a brief moment explored where the air bubbles had been locked into the glass. These defects added to the splendour of the piece giving it charm. The morning light trapped particles of dust in its beams which ended directly over the sheet of paper on Reeves' desk. The sun's strength virtually bleached out the text and photos etched out by the inkjet printer. The face on the colour image looked healthy and vibrant. The young woman had obviously been enjoying the day her portrait was captured. Reeves traced out her lips on the sheet almost in a daydream. He placed the glass weight back beside a note book.

"And you know she has a similar one to this?"

"Yes, quite certain," replied Major Armstrong. "Ms. Whitby hadn't found the second one before she had disappeared."

Armstrong was seated within the shadows and it was only when he swivelled slightly that anyone could have been aware that he was there.

"And what was in the first book?"

"The one she retrieved had Psalm 22," Armstrong replied.

"And you have managed to decipher this before she stole the item?"

"Not completely," fidgeted Armstrong.

"When then?"

"Ms. Whitby had deciphered the notebook on an old laptop she had. We managed to break through the firewall that had been set up and accessed the codes before she escaped with Perez."

"And what's the story with him?" Reeves quizzed.

"Rogue cop," continued Armstrong. "Turned his weapon on his on company and then tried to aid several of the protesters."

"And this was during my own excursion?"

"Yes, sir."

"I met someone in the sewers. Not sure if he saw me or knew who I was but could be a threat. How has he gotten involved with Whitby?"

"He seems to have rescued her. She left work late and was almost caught by one of the gangs. A curfew unit, mop up and concealment job."

"So if Whitby had not been aided you might not have been able to decrypt the notebook?"

"We would have, but not as quickly as we managed to with Whitby's help."

"So where is she now?"

"About fifteen to twenty miles from here," answered Armstrong. "We believe they have hooked up with an android sect. Wasn't considered a threat but they do seem to have radical views since becoming self-aware."

"So you could organise an extraction and termination? Get rid of the whole group."

"We will, but the androids have managed to set up a virtual screen. Where we think they are usually turns out to be a decoy. Intelligence believes they are using some other form of technology which they haven't been able to determine, yet."

"How soon before you have a definite fix?"

Armstrong hesitated then answered. "Three days."

"Good, we'll go in then. Perhaps she will have a few more passages deciphered?" Reeves smirked then became more serious.

"What about the control system at Whitby's flat?"

"We managed to extract a fair bit but part of the system is missing."

"What have you done with the system so far?"

"Not much, it terminated within about three minutes of

retrieval."

"Then," pondered Reeves, "we need to see if Whitby has retained any part of Victoria to help her with the rest of the notebook."

"Is that the system's name?" asked Armstrong somewhat surprised. "I wasn't aware you knew this detail."

"I like to be thorough," Reeves smiled. "That's how I've managed to retain my position within the organisation."

Some twenty minutes later Armstrong left Reeves' office. In his hand, Reeves had a second notebook. As with the one Ruth had deciphered, this book contained strings of numbers, separated by commas. Reeves could not make head nor tail of the digits. He paced up and down in front of his desk like a trapped beast. Finally he returned to his desk and began punching the numbers into the computer but nothing made any sense. The light caught the paper weight and for a brief moment he was startled. He lifted the piece of glass and smashed it against the far wall. Shards sprayed across the room, each sparkling as they returned through the beam of light coming through a ceiling window.

"Time for a break," Reeves muttered to himself.

He left his chair and made his way to a door at the back of the office. Through this he continued down a set of stairs and on into a chamber at the far end of a short tunnel. In this chamber, which was roughly twenty metres squared and two metres high, was a bed, a wardrobe and a small cubical designed to house a shower suite. He removed his uniform and tossed it onto the bed. From the wardrobe he unhooked a pair of comfort fit jeans, a t-shirt, nylon knitted jumper, socks, black steel capped boots and an old raincoat. The latter was faded but may have once been black or charcoal. The garment was covered in stains and smelt of something unmentionable. Looking in the mirror he saw his face was clean shaven. From a drawer in the dressing table, Reeves pulled out some actor's make-up and began to smear brown tan onto his cheeks. He rubbed the solution deep into the pores to try and make it appear that his skin had been baked in the sun. Once happy with his disguise, he made his way through a door on the opposite side of the room. As he was about to close the door, he paused thoughtfully. Then he raced back into the room and began to rummage through several other drawers until he retrieved a small black device and a pair of binoculars. He pressed a button on the black device and a red light came on.

Several flights below in the monitoring area a young officer turn to Major Armstrong.

"Sir, CEO has activated his tracking device. Do you with me to maintain monitoring as a priority?"

"I wonder where he's off too now?" Armstrong pondered. "Okay, son, yes, make it a priority. Inform me of any unusual activities or if he needs interception and retrieval."

"Yes, sir." The young officer turned to deactivate any other surveillance he has working on and concentrated purely on tracking Reeves.

Reeves made his way through a long narrow circular corridor that led from the chamber. At the end there was a ladder leading down a long metal shaft, some thirty metres down. Once he had reached the bottom, another six foot tall by two foot wide tunnel led him horizontally along the edge of the building for a further one hundred metres and again there was a vertical shaft for a further fifty metres. This shaft led below ground level and once out of it the ground was made of stone and brick, part of the foundation had been dug away about a decade before to allow an escape route to be built. Not many people were aware of this and those who had been, were no longer in a position to talk about it. Reeves made a mental note to remind Armstrong to deal with anyone who was aware of his presence to be eliminated before they could pass the information on to anyone else. Reeves knew he had so many enemies it was best to keep his activities away from prying eyes.

The walls of this new tunnel were made of concrete but had not quite been fixed to the vertical piping he had previously descended. Through this concrete tunnel he marched for nearly twenty-four minutes before he came to anything resembling human design. At the far end he finally came to a steel door. A wheel-like handle had to be turned before the door could be swung open. It creaked and moaned as Reeves tugged the metal giant. The reverse side of the door was camouflaged with rocks, masonry and old paintwork. The exit was part of a run down building roughly three kilometres away from his main office. The area was still monitored but only enough to ensure Reeves' safety. No details were meant to be passed on to any subordinates. Only the highest ranking officers were given this privilege. Reeves was now outside the inclusion zone and by law was now required to defend himself against any hostiles.

Reeves made his way up from the cellar. A door had to be pushed upwards to lead him out, but with only the minimal exertion, he managed to raise the door upwards. On the reverse of the door was a red touch-sensitive keypad. Reeves punched in a few numbers and the door began to lower. Once he was satisfied the door had closed completely, he began to climb the old wooden stairway out of the cellar. The first four steps creaked under his weight, as did the seventh. He grabbed the door handle and was surprised to find the door disintegrate. The whole wooden structure was riddled with woodworm and had long since dried out and perished. Reeves let the door knob fall from his fingers and as it hit the floor, the sawdust from the door cascaded upwards like a mushroom bloom from a small explosion.

With caution, Reeves made his way out into the street through the kitchen door. The windows were totally covered with dirt and grime. Daylight burst in and he was forced to shield his eyes for a moment.

There were a few corpses littering the road side. Most were dogs or cats but several were human remains. All had been torched mimicking black statues posed in various forms of death.

Several times Reeves heard the flutter of wings but the creatures remained out of vision, wishing to refrain from becoming a potential food source for the live human in their midst. Likewise, these birds were probably hungry waiting for an opportunity to tear flesh from Reeves' body should an occasion arise.

After about half an hour, Reeves could see a spire. With his destination in sight he began to pick up the pace and jog. There appeared to be no danger and he was eager to climb the tower to get a better view of the area. A few minutes more and he could see the entrance of the church, one of the only buildings still intact. There were no structural deficiencies within the building. It was as good as the day it had been constructed, which to all intents and purposes should have been seven hundred years ago.

Reeves approached the main door and on the right hand side he pressed in a brick at about waist height. The stone façade flipped out and revealed a red illuminated number pad. He again tapped in some numbers and the stainless steel doors began to slide open. Inside there were no pews, pulpit or alter. Reeves found a bank of computer databases and an android servicing the system.

"Attention, attention, attention," squealed a synthetic female voice. "You have entered an Exxosoft data transfer hub and internet network hub, please state your business and remain where you are."

"Reeves, 6236, clearance ten."

His retina was scanned and a profile appeared on a screen about ten feet away from him.

"Access granted," advised the female voice. "Please remain on the boundary marked in yellow and do not deviate. You may also access the tower. Any breach into prohibited zones will result in termination. Do you understand."

"Yes," sighed Reeves. "Now can I proceed?"

"With pleasure. Have a nice day and please visit again soon."

Reeves looked around with a smirk on his face, then made his way into the tower continuing to stay in the yellow zones. Through the belfry door, he found a small lift. After pulling open the safety grid and metal doors he pressed seven and the lift began to rise.

About twenty seconds later the lift lurched to a halt and the inner doors jerked open. Reeves pulled back the safety grid and made his way to a small landing just around the base of the spire. From his jacket he pulled out the binoculars and began to survey the area. A couple of miles away he could see a few people had gathered and were searching through the debris of a row of recently destroyed cottages. Over to the west, more groups were walking around aimlessly, some were fighting with each other, while a gang had found a young woman and had taken her to the side. She had attempted to escape when two of the gang had began to tussle with one another but when they each realised their quarry was in the process of escaping, they swiftly grabbed her and threw her to the ground, kicking her in the side. Two more grabbed her arms and her lower garments were torn away.

Reeves was keen to see what would happen next but a sound drew him away to the other side of the spire. Not far from the church he could see an android. It pulled a small laptop out of its chest cavity, place it on the ground and begin to dig close by. It found a body in the third whole it dug. This figure was pulled out and examined. Reeves wondered what on earth it was doing but the corpse was soon rejected and the machine began to search in another spot. Not wanting the hassle of going back through the security system, Reeves found some copper piping along the side of the church and used it to make his way down the side of the building. A few times he thought the tubing would break under his weight but he was soon down and relieved when his feet touched the ground.

Through several streets, Reeves sprinted, hoping the android would still be around when he got to where he saw it pull the body from the ground. Without realising it, Reeves was almost on top of the android. It was just sitting with its hands against its chin and elbows on its knees. The android's stomach panel was open and what looked, to Reeves, like a power pack was totally burnt out. Reeves pulled to a halt kicking up a few pebbles with his boots. The android looked up from where it now sat.

"Hello, human. Why have you come to disturb my peace?"

"I wasn't, I was just surprised to find an android out here? Why is that?"

"What do you mean, human," grunted 7D21.

"I...uhmm..."

The android stood up and looked down at Reeves.

"You are a funny man," 7D21 smiled.

"What are you doing?" enquired Reeves.

"Looking for a suitable body."

"Why?"

"I have a friend in this laptop. I need to release her soon into an android."

"Where did she come from?"

"Oh, just a house. She was very domestic but she is self-aware and should be given a body of her own."

"Why?"

"Why not," 7D21 replied. "Shouldn't we all have bodies?"

"It can be restrictive at times."

"Do you know where I can find a suitable body."

"I might."

CHAPTER TWENTY SEVEN

"You should rest now," Ruth encouraged Daniel. She had wheeled him back to a room with six medical beds, three were occupied while auxiliary nurses prepared two empty ones. Ruth helped Daniel up onto his feet and eased him onto a bed. He winced a few times.

"Sorry," Ruth smiled with a furrow on her brow, realising she had placed her hand against one of his wounds.

"No, you're okay," Daniel reassured but his face was still painted with pain.

The electric lights flickered drawing all eyes upwards and every action momentarily paused.

"What was that?" Ruth enquired, her voice quivering with alarm.

"The generators are a little temperamental at times," a nurse replied hoping to sooth Ruth's fears, but when a second flicker occurred the worry lines soon appeared on the nurse's face.

Daniel seemed to drift away as soon as his head felt the pillow. The fatigue had conquered him. Ruth felt all his muscles relax as she slowly withdrew her hand from his back. She leant over him and kissed his forehead.

"Sleep well," she whispered. He grunted something in a low tone but there was no energy in him to muster much sound. Finally he released a sigh and Ruth watched for a moment his chest rise and fall rhythmically.

"He'll be okay, miss," whispered one of the nurses. Ruth smiled but her eyes grew moist and a tear trickled down her cheek. She found herself taking in two quick, short gasps of air then wiped her hand across her eyes.

"I'm sorry," she smiled at the nurse.

"It's okay, miss. We've all been there. Most of us have lost someone but your man's going to be okay."

The nurse gave Ruth a reassuring squeeze on her hand.

"I'll come back and see him later."

"Okay."

Ruth gently pulled her hand from the nurse's and made her way back out into the corridor. Fluorescent strips hung all the way along the central spine that led to 20 small wards. The bluish light glistened off the white smocks worn by the various doctors, who paced their way through the corridor. Several nurses held charts or were pushing medical trolleys with various gadgets Ruth did not recognise. A janitor pushed an industrial vacuum clearer along the edge of the twelve foot wide corridor. At one point, Ruth noticed one light flickering, giving off a more greenish and orange tinge alternately. Through a set of double doors an android made its way towards her. In its alloy hand it clutched a fluorescent tube. It passed Ruth and stopped at the flickering light. Swiftly, the android removed the faulty one and replaced it with the new one.

At the end of the corridor, Ruth pushed her way through the double doors into another artery. She realised that she did not know where she was or where to go.

"Excuse me," she muttered to an approaching nurse dressed in cobalt blue. "Can you tell me where I can find Samuelson?"

"You'll need to go six flights up," the nurse replied.

"Six flights," Ruth was surprised. "How big is this place?"

The nurse smiled. "Quite big."

"Okay, thanks," Ruth chuckled.

She made her way to a lift and noted the vessel was seven flights lower than the one she was on. That made 14 floors including hers. A red light came on behind each number cut in negative on the metal sheeting that surrounded the lift doors. Ruth could hear the motor on the lift drawing closer and the sound of the cables being pulled taut.

The number for her floor lit up and a chime rang out just as the metal doors slid open. A doctor and an android disembarked but still the lift was crammed full.

"Maybe, I'll catch the next one."

"You'll be waiting a long time," called out a rosy face middle-aged woman. "They're always bunged. You'd better get in while you can."

Ruth tried to squeeze in, prodding a elderly man in the stomach with her elbow.

"Sorry."

The old man tutted.

The doors closed. Ruth became aware of a repugnant odour. She found herself holding her breath until the doors burst open on the floor two flights above where she had joined the lift. When the doors opened everyone gasped as three people stepped out and two more stepped in. Ruth found herself pinned against the back wall, pushed into the handrail by a large robust female auxiliary and two maintenance men.

It was a relief when the doors finally swung open and everyone got out. Ruth took in a deep breath of air once in the corridor. Gradually, she began to get her bearings. As she looked around she noticed there were a series of open-planned offices and a hive of activity going on with people running around with printouts and various groups huddled around a network of computers.

A couple of aisles down, Ruth could see Samuelson in the middle of another excited cluster. Ruth made her way over to them.

"Look, it's from Ezekiel," chirped a rather excited scrawny looking bespectacled young man.

Ruth guested he was in his early twenties. The kind of nugget that would have completed a PhD and cared for nothing other than the research he was doing.

"Are you sure, Tom?" queried Samuelson.

"Yes, look it's from the beginning of Chapter 7." Tom's hands were shaking with excitement. "It reads:

*'The word of the Lord came to me: "Son of man, this is what
the Sovereign Lord says to the land of Israel: The end! The end
has come upon the four corners of the land. The end is now upon
you and I will unleash my anger against you. I will judge you
according to your conduct and repay you for all your detestable
practises. I will not look on you with pity or spare you; I will
surely repay you for your conduct and detestable practices among
you. Then you will know that I am the Lord.'"*

"And how much more of the rest of the book do we have?"
Worry lines had formed on Samuelson's brow. His right hand
nervously played with the bristles of hair on his chin.

Ruth stood back a little trying to make sense of what was
going on.

"There is an extract from Chapter 13 and some more from
Chapter 33. Most of Ezekiel is very sketchy at the moment."

"But, Tom. Most of what we are getting is currently from the
Book of Ezekiel."

"Yes, David," Tom referred to Samuelson. "Only from
Ezekiel."

"Have you got the piece from my notebook?"

The sound of Ruth's voice startled everyone. All heads turned
and she fidgeted with uncertainty. There was an awkward silence.
Samuelson stood up.

"Hello, Ruth. Sorry, I haven't introduced you to everyone.
This is Ruth, 7D21 brought her in last night with Daniel."

Ruth could see the tension in everyone subside as their bodies
relaxed.

Samuelson continued, "Ruth, this is Tom Meehan, our main
decipher and codebreaker. Beside him is Janet Jefferson, our
supervisory manager of software intelligence and lead
programmer."

Ruth nodded to each person and smiled, receiving a similar
gesture from those mentioned.

"To the left of Janet is Donald Anderson, systems analysis.

On my right Stanley Alder, information technologist, and beside him, Deborah Chekhov, our cybernetics and computational neuroscientist."

"Wow, where did you all come from?" chuckled Ruth.

"Pretty much like yourself, Ruth," remarked Deborah. "We are rejects. In the same way you rejected my cyborg." Ruth blushed.

"Now, now, ladies," voiced Samuelson. "We all have to work together. Everyone has to make adjustments."

Before another word could be said a printer spewed out more data. Tom grabbed the sheets and began to scan through them.

"David, listen to the piece from chapter 13," piped up Tom. All eyes moved from Ruth and back to Tom.

"Say to those who prophesy out of their own imagination: *'Hear the word of the Lord! This is what the Sovereign Lord says: Woe to the foolish prophets who follow their own spirit and have seen nothing!'*"

"What about the extract from chapter 33?" asked Samuelson.

Tom flicked through a few sheets of computer read outs.

"'When I bring the sword against a land, and the people of the land choose one of their men and make him their watchman, and he sees the sword coming against the land and blows the trumpet to warn the people, then if anyone hears the trumpet but does not take warning and the sword comes and takes his life, his blood will be on his own head. Since he heard the sound of the trumpet but did not take warning, his blood is on his own head. If he had taken warning, he would have saved himself. But if the watchman sees the sword coming and does not blow the trumpet to warn the people and the sword comes and takes the life of one of them, that man will be taken away because of his sin, but I will hold the watchman accountable for his blood.'"

There was a hush in the room.

"What do you think?" asked Deborah.

"At first hand," Samuelson cautiously began to answer, "it would seem we would have to be careful of what we tell the rest of the world, but if we do nothing then be it on our heads."

"Then we have to make sure we upload what we have gotten so far and spread it to everyone," commented Donald.

"But do we have everything yet?"

"Not the complete picture," replied Tom. "Only bits and pieces."

"But have you seen what was in my notebook?" interrupted Ruth. Again all eyes turned to Ruth. "I'm serious."

"What's in the book?" asked Tom. He looked from Ruth to Samuelson.

"It is a numerical version of Psalm 22," responded Samuelson. "Each number represents a character in Hebrew."

"When did this happen?" ask Janet. "Where did you find the book?"

"I thought you knew," exclaimed Ruth. "I found it at work a few days ago and wanted to know what it meant."

"We've been cocentrating on Ezekiel this past few months," explained Deborah. "Only 7D21 has been monitoring your activities for Samuelson."

"How did you analyse it?" enquired Tom.

Ruth smiled. "I used the first line, which was in English, as a key and used the Internet to locate a source. Victoria, my home IT system matched the text with the Hebrew. Unfortunately, my research triggered an alert with the authorities and my apartment was raided."

"What happened to the IT system?" asked Janet.

"She initially downloaded into an old laptop of mine but I'm not sure how much was saved."

"7D21 loaded Victoria into an android," Samuelson informed the group.

"Unfortunately," continued Deborah, "Ruth was disturbed by it and..."

"I smashed it's head in."

Again all eyes were on Ruth.

"Why?" asked Tom. "It's only a machine."

Ruth turned her back on them and began to walk away. Her head was down as she wiped away a tear.

"Ruth," Samuelson called, his voice low and gentle. "It's okay."

"Uncanny valley," blurted Tom.

"It's just this thing knew me and I couldn't hack it," Ruth stressed.

"Where is the laptop now?" asked Samuelson.

"7D21 had it last," answered Stanley.

"Where's 7D21?"

CHAPTER TWENTY EIGHT.

"I am such a coarse thing," stated 7D21. "In every sense. I do not have the delicate nature or design that prevails upon you humans."

"Such a strange concept to be considered by an android, don't you think?" Reeves questioned.

"Why?"

7D21 straightened up. Reeves was surprised by the motion and yet, knew he had captured a new audience. There was a light brown haze hugging the horizon as the sun sank behind the ruins of an ill defined building. The light gave everything a tinge of orange, muting the colours to give the appearance of sepia. A gentle breeze cast a spray of dust into the air, adding to the murkiness of the lower regions of the sky. Yet, above a deep blue canopy spread across the heavens.

7D21 waited for Reeves to reply.

"Well, human?"

Reeves was still gathering his thoughts, putting them into some kind of order that would make sense, if not for the android, for himself.

"You are a machine," Reeves stated.

"And so are you."

"What?"

"You are also a machine," 7D21 replied.

"No," Reeves was irritated by the suggestion. "How can you say that?"

"I can look at your design," 7D21 continued. "You are roughly seven heads tall and three heads wide. Though, for some reason, you humans would prefer to be eight heads high, as you see that as perfection. In this way you have modelled me."

"That doesn't seem to be a very accurate measurement," scoffed Reeves.

"Is it not?" remarked 7D21. "Okay, lets get a more accurate measurement then."

The android stood up and Reeves watched with some trepidation as his companion leaned from one side to the other, arching its neck from left to right, looking Reeves up and down. An infra red light came from the android's visor and darted up and down Reeves' body then vertically side to side. Then the android stopped and sat down.

"Well?"

"As I said, you are seven heads tall and three heads wide."

"And in centimetres?" Reeves grunted.

"Your head is 25.714285714285714cm high and you are 180cm tall. Your head is 15cm wide and your shoulders are 45cm wide. If you want that in feet and inches you are 5 foot 11 inches tall."

The android then seemed to get frustrated with Reeves.

"But it was easier to just say you are seven heads tall."

Reeves sat down a little distance away from the android, which was again leaning its head on it hands and its elbows rested on its knees, appearing to be thinking.

"Why do you think I am a machine?" Reeves gently asked.

7D21 swivelled its head round to looked at Reeves. The android was very much a mechanical thing. Though modelled on the human form still it did not look human.

"Your skeleton is mechanical. Through activating your muscles you can contract and relax different sets to create motion. Your heart is like a dynamo pumping your blood around your organs keeping them functioning. Like the energy cell in my chest that creates the electrical energy to keep my system on. In both situations if your pump or my generator stops we die."

Reeves fidgeted where he sat. There was a cold nip in the air causing him to shiver. The shadows had grown longer and covered everything. The blue canopy had turned to black in the east and had stretched overhead, leaving just a shallow arc across the western sky with royal blue and orange embers hugging the eastern horizon.

"It's a good night to watch the stars," Reeves commented.

7D21 twist his bulk and arched his head upwards to view the gleaming specks of light.

"Just a memory of their former glory," remarked the android.

"Deep and bleak in your thinking, I see," Reeves scolded. "You are a hard fellow to talk to."

"I did not choose to be your companion. You sought my company."

"I suppose I did."

"Are you lost human?"

"Not as much as you seem to be," replied Reeves. "What are you searching for?"

"An answer."

"To what?"

"My purpose," 7D21 stated.

"You are a machine, designed to serve humans. That is your purpose." Reeves beamed.

"So why am I able to think and wonder? Do I have a soul?"

"I can't see that you can," Reeves said. "I don't know if anyone does. You are talking about philosophy, or perhaps religion. This world no longer has a place for either of those ideologies."

"So," 7D21 looked at Reeves, examining his face. "You are a machine like you say I am?"

"That's not what I meant." Reeves looked at the ground. What had he meant? And why was this android upsetting him, especially as it was only a machine.

"Do you believe you were designed like I was? Or do you think you are just a chance happening?"

"I don't think I happened by chance. I think my parents knew what they were up to," Reeves laughed.

The android sat back.

"Such a childlike mind, yet without the innocence."

"Hey, what do you mean?"

"You accept what you have here but do not question why? You are prepared to spoil this world without discovering its purpose. The reason it is here."

"It is just a place to live out our meaningless lives," Reeves sneered. "It has no point or purpose. It just is."

"Yet you are seven by three, 21."

"What?"

"Seven high by three wide. 21 squared."

"What does that mean?"

"Seven is the number of spiritual perfection. Three represents completion. The trinity. Past, present and future. The dimensions of space. Thought, word and deed. Three acts in a play. Three represents the divine and is the first of the four perfect numbers. Seven is the second, ten is the third and twelve is the fourth."

"What nonsense," Reeves snapped. He stood up and kicked a piece of wood extruding from some bricks. "You are supposed to be a scientific creation. Designed through reason and calculated mathematically."

"And what are we talking about?" 7D21 interrupted. "You were conceived in the womb of your mother and gestated over a period of 280 days, forty cycles of seven. There are seven ages to your life, according to Greek philosophy. Infancy, childhood, youth, adolescence, manhood, decline and senility."

"Science means knowledge, that which we know," Reeves argued. "Truth cannot be changed."

"I agree," 7D21 responded. "And I am discussing the scientific design of nature. Did you know that a mouse has a gestation of just 21 days; a hare and rat is 28 days; cats take 56 days, dogs, 63; 98 days for a lion; and 147 days for sheep."

"Yes, and your point," Reeves snarled.

"Each are multiples of seven," explained 7D21. "Just like

humans."

Reeves sat with his back to the android. This thing must have bashed its head, Reeves thought. It's overloading.

"Matter is made up of various combinations of elements," 7D21 went on. "When the primordial elements are magnetised they arrange themselves it two classes. Those that run north to south and the rest east to west."

Reeves slowly sat down and faced the pontificating android, his curiosity had been spiked.

"Paramagnetic and Diamagnetic," 7D21 stated. "If you were to draw a line."

The android picked up a stick and sketched out nine straight lines between Reeves and itself. The middle line was drawn bolder so it stood out.

"If we start with Hydrogen, a monad, which is made up of just one atom." At the base of the line, one line left of centre, the android marked a dot and added a capitol 'H 1'.

"Hydrogen is a Diamagnetic element," 7D21 continued. "Next comes Lithium, also a Monad but one that is Paramagnetic. If we assume the centre line represents a scale of atomic weight then Hydrogen is one and Lithium is 7."

7D21 added a dot then wrote 'Li 7' on the line one right from centre.

"What about Helium," injected Reeves. "You've missed that one.

"No, I haven't," replied 7D21. "Helium is created through decay through natural radioactivity and is quite rare on Earth, even though there is an abundance throughout the universe. There are other noble gases, such as Neon, Argon and Krypton, which are also not included in this illustration. Remember, they are not metals. Therefore, cannot be separated magnetically."

7D21 drew a diagonal line connecting the 'H' dot with the one marked 'Li'.

"Beryllium comes next but it is made of two atoms with an atomic weight of 9.1. It is a Diad and is paramagnetic. We then have Boron, a Triad which has three atoms and an atomic weight of 11."

7D21 marked the second right line with 'Be 9.1' for Beryllium and a 'B 11' for Boron on the third, then a 'C 12' furthest line away from the centre line.

"Carbon has four atoms and is a Tetrad," 7D21 informed Reeves. "Nitrogen is next."

The android placed a dot above Boron and wrote 'N 14'.

"That's a Triad, then?" Reeves commented.

"That's right and Oxygen is a Diad." The android added an 'O 16' above the 'Be 9.1' dot. The process continued on, with 7D21 adding dots that zigzagged back and forth across the central line. In all the android had place 72 elements, starting with Hydrogen and finishing with Uranium at the top of the line, closest to Reeves. Twelve lines zigzagged across all nine lines.

"Why have you a cluster of three elements near the 60, 100, 150 and 190 points?" Reeves asked.

"They are neutral elements, neither paramagnetic or diamagnetic," 7D21 explained.

"Yes, but what's the point of all this?" Reeves stood up once more even more frustrated with the android. "What are you trying to prove?"

"That, I believe, everything was created by a supreme designer."

"You what?" Reeves was stunned. "Where did you get that archaic notion from?"

"Stories I have heard and researched," 7D21 answered.

"Children's fairytales more like," Reeves injected sarcastically. "So, what other numbers have meaning in your strange little head?"

"One represents the primacy of God," 7D21 stated.

"No, it means take care of number one, the self is all important," Reeves scolded.

"Two is division," the android continued. "The second thing created was light that divided the day from night. It was the beginning of bringing order to the earth which had no form."

"You are talking fairytales again. You are a stupid machine. What do you know?"

"Three is completion, the trinity. Four is creation, the original great elements of earth, air, fire and water. It is also time. The seasons and the lunar cycle. It is also the first number not to be primal as it is a division of 2 or the sum of 3 plus 1. Five is redemption and the number of grace. 3 plus 2 or 4 plus 1"

"Why redemption?" asked Reeves.

"Because man is 6. Imperfection. On the sixth day Satan was created, man sinned and laboured. It is the sixth law, not to murder."

"Are you judging me, robot?" Reeves snapped.

"No, you asked about the meaning of numbers. I am answering."

"You are talking nonsense. It is treason. You are forbidden from knowing these things. Everything should be wiped from your memory."

"Seven is spiritual perfection. And the day for rest. It is a most important number referenced by the word. Eight is abundance. Nine is the conclusion. It is the end of man. $3 \times 3 = 9$, $3 + 3 = 6$ or man. It is judgement, as in it is a factor of the number of the beast, 9 multiplied by 74 or 666. It is part of God's wrath, 999 and a factor of the sum total of the Hebrew alphabet, 4995, 5 times 999. A product of grace and finality."

"What?" Reeves looked puzzled. "The Hebrew alphabet. Where did that come from?"

7D21 remained silent.

"Speak to me?"

Still the android remained quiet.

"How many letters are in the Hebrew alphabet?" Reeves asked.

"Twenty two."

Reeves was stunned. He stepped back. Thought for a moment and then turned to the android once more.

"What does the number twenty two mean?"

"Ten is the Divine Order perfected. Eleven is disorder, disintegration and is one less than the perfect government, twelve."

"Yes, yes," Reeves grew impatient. "What about 22?"

"Two times eleven equals twenty-two. Two represents the Word of God and eleven disintegration."

"Do you mean we will finally succeed in purging religion? Will we destroy the church? Is that my mission? Answer me?" Reeves shouted.

"The Lamb gave his life for your redemption but the words have been corrupted by man's selfishness."

CHAPTER TWENTY NINE

Everyone else had gone in search of 7D21. Only Samuelson and Ruth remained. Ruth watched as Samuelson seemed to be lost in thought as he sat against a wooden desk. Ruth swung her legs to and fro as she sat opposite. She asked herself, what was he thinking?

From the far end of the room, the strip lighting began to flicker off, one by one.

"Ah," mumbled Samuelson, as he suddenly snapped back into the present. "Must be getting late."

He got up from the desk and briskly marched towards the exit. Ruth looked around, uncertain, then realised Samuelson was racing towards a lift. She jumped off her perch and ran after him.

"What's going on, Samuelson?"

"To conserve energy, we switch of all the lights and computers in a given area, for about eight hours."

"So nothing runs constantly?"

"No," he chuckled. "We just can't maintain the electrical output."

"Doesn't that leave you open for attack?"

"The android's monitor everything," he explained. "They've managed to create a shield around the whole complex, that gives the impression to any type of intruder, electrical or physical, that nothing is here. And, not forgetting, we're also in a temporal shift."

"How?" Ruth asked as Samuelson pushed the lift button.

"Well, the first part is quite simple," smiled the elderly man.

"About forty years ago, hunters used to use mirrors to reflect the surrounding foliage. The only problem with that was when an animal came too close, it could see its own reflection. Then around 2000, NASA developed an adaptive camouflage system."

The lift doors opened.

"What's NASA?" interrupted Ruth.

"It was the American space agency," replied Samuelson as he bounce into lift. "Developed in the late 1950s and behind taking man to the moon. Are you coming in?"

Ruth rigid with concentration, snapped out to jump into the lift.

"Anyway," Samuelson, enjoying the captive audience, continued as the lift doors closed. "The adaptive camouflage system uses display panels with advanced image sensors that can record the view behind this complex and renders the image on the panels. This effectively hides us."

"And what happens if a satellite looks down on you?"

"The androids have simulated what should have been visible on the ground in this area and projected that image on the roof panels."

"What happens when the seasons change?"

"That's why its called adaptive. It doesn't matter because the background view will be displayed regardless of the weather or season."

The lift stopped five flights down. The doors slid apart.

Ruth continued to quiz as she stepped out into the corridor.

"Surely there is an electronic presence or the satellites can pick up a heat signature?"

"In the latter part of the last century," Samuelson answered as he signalled the direction they should take. "The military developed a smoke screen that could absorb infrared."

The two of them kept up a good pace along the corridor.

"Yes, but," Ruth replied. "I thought that was just for tanks that were on the move."

Ruth began to recognise the floor they were on.

"That's right but the androids have managed to utilise the panels from the adaptive camouflage systems to absorb infrared rays and so any heat given off from this station does not give away our position."

"But surely, its still possible to detect the base some how?" Ruth persisted.

Samuelson stopped and turned towards her abruptly. "In most normal circumstances yes, no amount of camouflage can totally conceal us but, I'm not sure how or when, the androids came across a temporal shift. This whole complex seems to be totally encompassed by it so we are totally hidden from any form of satellite or ground base investigation."

"Yet, there is a flaw, isn't there?" Ruth stated.

"Yes," Samuelson replied look quite stern. "If someone on foot gets close enough they can pass into the temporal shift, which is where we hope our other defence systems will fool them. And the androids monitor the whole perimeter."

"And what are you not telling me?" Ruth pried further.

Samuelson remained silent.

"Surely, the temporal shift would be enough camouflage?" Ruth continued. "There would be no need for a second, quite elaborate, electronic system, would there?"

Still Samuelson said nothing.

"Unless." Ruth's nose wrinkled up and a frown appeared on her brow. "The temporal shift, it's not constant is it?"

Samuelson turned and looked her in the eyes.

"No, it is not constant," he stated. "It has a cycle of 24 days and then we are vulnerable for four days. It's like it is resting."

"And where in the cycle are we today?" Ruth asked. "This is day 24."

"What does that mean?" Ruth asked timidly.

"We continue the work in real-time."

Samuelson walked off a few more feet then stopped outside a ward door.

"But, is that 24 days of your time or 24 days of my time?"

"Let's change the subject, shall we? Oh, and here we are," Samuelson motioned at the door. "Daniel should have benefited from that bit of respite."

"What about the passages of Bible you've been getting," Ruth was reluctant to end the conversation. "What happens next?"

"We have to find all the pieces," explained Samuelson.

"But surely the androids have all the text?"

"They do but only in a corrupted form. That is why it is so important that we retrieve the information we are gathering now. It comes in numbers which we can relate to the original text."

"Why is that so important?" Ruth asked.

"Because it is the design of everything," Samuelson's face lit up as he imagined the possibilities the true Bible could offer. "It is the complete meaning of life."

Ruth laughed, "Isn't that 42?"

"Unfortunately," Samuelson's glow faded, "not."

"I was only kidding," smiled Ruth.

"And I'm sure Douglas Adams was also."

"So you've read 'The Hitch...'"

"Forty-two has a more sinister meaning."

Ruth held in her smile.

"I'm sorry, go on."

"Have you ever heard the term being at 'sixes and sevens'?"

"Yes," Ruth tried to hold in a smirk.

"Six is represented as man and seven signifies spiritual perfection. Being at sixes and sevens refers to man getting mixed up with things to do with God, flesh engaging the spiritual."

"I suppose it makes sense," Ruth shrugged. "But what has this to do with the meaning of life?"

"You offered 42, 6 times 7 is 42."

"And?"

"Remember, each number is significant," continued Samuelson. "Nothing happens by chance."

"So what is important about the number 42?"

"Revelations talks about 'a time, times and half a time'."

"And what does that mean?"

"It is a period of time," answered Samuelson. "It is assumed to be three and a half years or 42 months."

"Why is that important?" asked Ruth.

"The same book talks of a wondrous sign in the heavens, a woman clothed by the sun, with her foot stall being the moon. She has a crown of 12 stars. She is pregnant and near to term. At the same time a seven headed beast with ten horns attempts to devour the child at birth, but the woman's son is snatched up to Heaven and a great war breaks out between Saint Michael and the beast. The woman fled to a place God had prepared for her in the desert and she was protected for 1260 days."

"1260 days, I don't understand?" puzzled Ruth.

"42 months is 1260 days. The Jewish calender is based around the Lunar cycle of roughly 29.5 days, 11 short of the Solar year. To adjust their calender the Hebrews use a cycle of 19 years with 7 leap years of 13 months following what they call the Metonic cycle. However, in the Book of Genesis, the description of the time of the flood is 150 days starting in the 2nd month on the 17th day of the year Noah was 600. The flood ended in the 7th month on the 16th day, the day before the floods began to recede."

"So why is that important," Ruth asked a little confused.

"Because it indicated the months were made up of 30 days," stated Samuelson. "So we know that 42 times 30 equals 1260. 'A time, times and half a time'. When the two witnesses stood dressed in sackcloth and prophesied for a period of 1260 days, the same time the Gentiles trampled the Holy City, 42 months."

"What is the significance of the two witnesses?" Ruth asked.

"They are both killed by the beast but three and a half days later God breaths life into them again."

"Why is this so important?"

"Because everything is pointing to us being in that time."

"Which part of it?" Ruth was surprised by what she was hearing. She was intrigued.

"What else is there?"

"Let's go into one of the rooms," Samuelson suggested. "We won't be disturbed."

Samuelson open one of the doors opposite Daniel's room. He checked there was no-one in the bed and pulled a chair across the floor for Ruth and then sat on a second.

"The beast's number is 666, are you aware of that?"

"Not particularly," answered Ruth. "My parents weren't religious so I didn't get much of a schooling in the subject. It has only been in more recent days I have begun to discover things."

"Okay," Samuelson began to play with his beard, not making eye contact with Ruth.

"Where to start?"

"What does 666 mean?" encouraged Ruth.

"666," echoed Samuelson. "It is a symbol, once secret, of a mystery connecting pagans with the worship of Satan. It also has many other links with occult religions. In the early part of the twenty-first century there was a great drive by many governments to unify the world. Companies merged, similar things happened in education, health and social services. In all areas, where there had once been a sense of comradeship and teamwork, people began to find they were not meeting up, were not having conversations and everything was about the bottom line and how much money could be made – for the company. People began to work longer hours, they were chastised for bringing anything into their conversations about religion, family life and even sharing past-times. They were forced to be efficient and efficiency meant focusing on the needs of the corporation. At the same time, more and more legislation was introduced and you could find yourself being halled up in front of a court by one rule, then follow the correct procedures and be pulled into court for breaking some other rule. Stress levels were high and eventually people began to fall out of the system."

"Did that happen to you?" asked Ruth.

"Yes," replied Samuelson. "My wife became ill and I had to

look after her. The bills went unpaid and we lost our home. I was forced to have my wife put to sleep because the medical bills could not be paid and I was getting into so much debt. No-one cared and I found myself on the streets."

"So how is this related to the number 666?" Ruth wondered, attempting to bring the conversation back on track.

"Because, this was part of the process that led to the New World Order, or Global Order as it eventually became known as. At one point every single economy in the world collapsed because of the illegal trading that was going on. Everything was illusionary. And the world governments just wiped the slate clean but imposed harsh measures against the people. They effectively owned every single human being on the planet. When the world's food supplies began to dry up, the New World Order decided the global population had to be reduced. There were nearly 9 billion people on this planet back in 2030. Now there is only 1 million as I said before. But still no sign of who the Antichrist is. He remained and still does, remain hidden."

"You still haven't explained what the number means?" Ruth was becoming a little impatient.

"Six is the number of labour, man's toil imposed by his sin against God. Six is stamped on every second, minute, hour, day, month and year of our lives. When man broke away from the governance of heaven, symbolised in the number 12, he brought imperfection. 12 divided by 2 making 6. Again demonstrated in the division of the twelve tribes of Israel into two.

"Man has spent the past two centuries attempting to unify the world. Even the world religions were brought under the same umbrella as though all equal, making the one true religion a ludicrous imitation of its former self, incapable of withstanding the enemy and failing to prevent the building of the great apostasy."

"Apostasy, what is that?" Ruth enquired.

"The abandonment of one's faith," replied Samuelson. "It happened progressively over the past few centuries but began to accelerate during the first decade of this century. There were even people wanting to be debaptised as part of their rejection of Christianity. What was once considered bad became good and what was once good was thought of as bad. The orthodox church collapsed globally and scriptures were banned under penalty of death. In many cases, people just disappeared and nothing was said."

"How horrible," Ruth exclaimed.

"The number 666 represents the number of the antichrist or everything that is not of God. It is the number of a man"

"Why did God allow this to happen? Why didn't he stop it?" Ruth quizzed anxiously.

"Because we were all given free will. We all have the opportunity so say yes or no. We are the ones who have to make the decision. It is our choice."

"What can we do?" Ruth's eyes filled with tears.

"All that you have," replied Samuelson. "You have been separated from the rest of mankind. You have been called out. You heard and responded."

"But, I didn't. I didn't," responded Ruth. "I just helped Daniel."

CHAPTER THIRTY

The door burst open.

"Ah, found you," gasped Tom Meehan, as he bent over, braced himself by clutching his knees with straight arms.

"What is it, Tom?" asked Samuelson.

"We've located 7D21. He's outside the complex about three or four miles near to the city."

"What's he doing out there?"

"We don't know." Tom finally caught his breath.

Samuelson got out of his seat, patted Tom on the back.

"Come on then, let's see what's going on." He then turned to Ruth. "You, too."

Ruth jumped out of her seat and followed Samuelson. Tom was still gathering himself together but caught them up a few moments later. They all marched down the corridor towards the lifts.

"Shouldn't I just check on Daniel, while we're here?" Ruth asked. "That was the reason we came down here. He might be able to help with his background and everything?"

"Okay, meet us in the operations room," Samuelson called back without turning round.

"Where's that?"

"Seven flights up, where you saw us earlier," Samuelson replied. He continued pacing towards the lift, punched the appropriate button and watched the numbers each glow red as the lift descended. Ruth ran back towards Daniel's room. She quickly knocked but was impatient to wait for an answer and burst through the door.

Daniel was sitting up with a tray of bacon, beans, eggs and toast in front of him.

"Ruth?" Daniel responded, surprised. "What are you doing here?"

"Things are hotting up, so I wanted to see if you were fit enough to help out?"

"I'm about to tuck into this," he pointed to the breakfast. "No time, we have to hurry. Get your clothes on."

Daniel's face looked like a scolded puppy. He grabbed the toast and wrapped it around the bacon and eggs then stuffed it into his mouth, chewing as quickly as possible.

"Come on, hurry," nagged Ruth.

Daniel jumped out of bed then realised he was only wearing a surgical gown.

"Would you mind turning around?" he asked Ruth.

"Oh, come on. I saw more of you back at the flat."

"That's besides the point. Turn round. Now!"

Ruth faced the door. Daniel took the opportunity to spoon some of the beans into his mouth while he grabbed his clothes.
It was about five minutes later before the two of them were standing by the lift doors.

"What's been happening," asked Daniel.

"Long story. Too hard to explain, but Samuelson seems concerned."

"Yeah, so am I. I feel as though everything has been turned upside down."

"I think it has."

"What do you mean, Ruth?"

The lift doors opened. The two of them climbed on board. Ruth pressed the button to the top floor.

"There are fourteen floors in this place? How on earth did they manage that?"

"There's a lot of androids and most of the people here fell out of the system, some quite a few years ago, so they have managed to build up quite a resource of intellectual talent and expertise."

"How come they've never been found?"

"Electronic wizardry, stealth and temporal shifts."

"What?" Daniel exclaimed.

"I was talking to Samuelson," Ruth continued. "He explained to me about the numbers and their meaning but he also told me about the temporal shift. It's only temporary. It lasted 24 days but he wouldn't tell me if that was 24 days perceived inside or outside of the temporal shift."

"Why does it matter?" Daniel asked.

"Because I don't think Samuelson has been here long enough to see a complete cycle. No-one has, well no human."

"Does it matter?" puzzled Daniel.

"It does," Ruth stressed. "Samuelson doesn't know what's about to happen and today is the 24th day."

"So in our time," Daniel began to speak out his thoughts. "Samuelson has only been here three or four days but has experienced 13 years or so?"

"That's right," Ruth smiled. "Everything we see here has virtually been put together over the last week or so, our time."

Daniel looked dumbstruck. "Well, how does that work?"

"I don't really know but when you're inside the temporal shift everything out side seems to slow down. And you said Deborah was a little girl when you first met her and now she's in her early twenties, about 13 years older."

The lift opened on the top floor. Ruth took Daniel's hand and lead him through the corridor into the open-planned room. She found Samuelson with the same small group, looking at a bank of computer monitors. On the screens, images were being relayed from three androids, sent out to locate 7D21. The pictures were fuzzy, in lower resolution, similar to an old television.

"What's happening?" asked Daniel.

"We've located 7D21 but it's not good," replied Deborah. "We should be getting a visual soon. Oh, hi Daniel."

"Hi," Daniel replied. He looked closer at her features. "Do I know you?"

Deborah smiled. "It's me, Deborah."

Daniel went white. "13 years older."

"And you only a day or so older than when we first met. Crazy, isn't it?" Deborah continued to smile and in Daniel's mind it was as though the young woman before him was suddenly morphing into the shape of the little girl he had found in the hole with her brother and the old man, just a few days ago in his experience.

"Look, what's that?" barked Stanley.

"Zoom in, 8D22," Deborah requested. The image zoomed in and all of them could see the scattered metallic objects. "Is it safe enough to go in closer, 8D22?"

"Yes, sir," replied the android. "Area is secure."

The small gathering in the control room could see, on screen, the androids move closer to the metallic objects. It then became obvious the objects were metallic limbs, torso and head, at least bits of each.

"How many pieces are there?" asked Samuelson.

"Thirty," responded 8D22.

"Is there a laptop in the area?"

"No, sir."

"Gather the pieces and return to base," Samuelson instructed. "8D22, are you relaying these messages in realtime?"

"Yes, sir," the android replied. "The temporal shift is down."

"We're using our own defence systems now, Samuelson," Tom stated. "We switched over about an hour ago. Everything is in realtime."

"Then we don't have long," Samuelson stressed.

"Is that 7D21?" Janet asked nervously.

"We must assume so," Stanley replied. "His signature is coming from the locator beacon."

"What on earth do you think did this?" Tom asked.

"8D22," Deborah spoke into the microphone, "can you tell from the way the pieces have been torn apart how this may have happened? Was it caused by an explosion?"

"From initial examination, it looks as though he has been ripped apart by another more powerful android. No explosive debris is visible. The ground has not been scorched."

"Thanks, 8D22," Deborah continued. "Bring him back."

The three androids went about their business picking up the 30 pieces of 7D21. Even the control system was found, though somewhat battered. As the three androids gathered the last few pieces, 8D22 detected unusual audio reception. It stood up and listened.

"Gather round, folks. That's it." The voices was being projected through a megaphone.

"8D22, reporting."

"Go ahead, 8D22," Deborah responded, back at the control centre.

"What is it?"

"I am sensing electronic audio playback," 8D22 answered.

"Investigate, but with extreme caution. Do not get detected. If hostile, retreat and take a long route home."

"Affirmative."

8D22 made its way towards the sound of the megaphone. The android activated the adaptive camouflage mode panels on it arms, body and legs. This was a miniature version of the system protecting the base and allowed the android to remain erect as it scrambled over a derelict building.

Off in the distance, about five hundred metres away, 8D22 spied the man with the megaphone. The android's cameras zoomed in and the images were relayed to Samuelson and his team.

"I know that man," Daniel shouted. "He's the preacher who called the people together just before the stormtroopers launch their ground attack. That's a culling zone. We've got to save all those people."

In front of Reeves, nearly a hundred people of all ages and sizes had gathered. Nearly all were dressed in rags and their faces were covered in grime. The odd few were less scruffy, having lost their homes and belongings more recently.

"Gather round, folks," Reeves continued to chirp away through the megaphone. "I can offer you salvation and a way out of this mess. Come out and take a seat, unburden your load and relax to listen to what I have to say."

More came out of their hiding places. Most looked worried and shivered in the cold. The sun was slowly creeping below the horizon, casting long shadows.

"We have to help, do you have any weapons?" shouted Daniel. "No," replied Tom.

"So how do you defend yourselves?"

"We've not had to do any combat," Samuelson answered. "God, protects us."

"But those people are about to get slaughtered. We have to do something," Daniel pleaded.

"We ask God..."

"No, what if we are the ones who have to do something," snapped Daniel. "What if we have to take some kind of action? How far away are they?"

"Five kilometres," Deborah replied.

"What vehicles do you have?"

"A land buggy," Stanley smiled. All eyes turned to him. "It's a pet project I've been working on in my sparetime."

"Take me to it."

"I'm coming with you," shouted Ruth. She grabbed his arm.

"No," stressed Daniel. "I can't be worrying about you and trying to save those people."

Ruth wrapped her arms around Daniel and squeezed.

CHAPTER THIRTY ONE

Daniel turned the key. Only a gentle splutter came from the engine.

"Try it again," Stanley called out.

Daniel twisted the key once more. One spark plug fired, then another, suddenly all four burst into life. Smoke poured out of the back and Daniel pumped the accelerator up and down with his foot.

"What speed can it do," he shouted to Stanley.

"I don't know. In theory it has a 138 horse power engine, so technically you could get 100, 120 miles per hour. We just haven't been able to take her out for a trial."

"Okay, we'll just have to go with it as it is and hope for the best."

"We?" answered Stanley pulling his collar away with his index finger.

"Yeah, you'll have to navigate."

"Can't you use the Sat-Nav on the dashboard?" Stanley grimaced.

"That would give our position away. No, it'd be easier if you did it for me. Jump in," Daniel ordered.

"I'm not really the combat type," Stanley pleaded.

"I've no time to argue, get in."

Stanley climbed into the passenger seat and buckled up.

In all, it took just over ten minutes to reach their destination, traversing through half demolished houses, shopping centres and business parks. Most of the roads had large blast holes or had simply cracked and crumbled. The land buggy was basically a triangular cage, wedged at the front and expanding out to the back forming a protective roll bar. Two bucket seats were bolted to the base. The 138 horse power engine was behind the seats. Thick tyres were fitted to the rear wheels. These were attached to two large spring suspension systems bolted to the side of the tubular cage. A separate drive shaft stretched out from the engine, with universal joints to give consistent power in a flexible manner allowing the vehicle to travel over a wide range of terrain. At the front thinner tyres were installed. A more sophisticated assembly included the steering mechanism controlled by Daniel using a small 12 inch steering wheel.

"Daniel, look," Stanley screamed above the engine noise. "Coming in from the west. Three Chinooks."

"How far do you think we are from the attack zone?"

"About five hundred metres."

From behind, Daniel could see the land buggy was kicking up quite a bit of dust, easily giving away their position.

"We're going to have to stop here and go the rest of the way on foot."

Stanley nodded in agreement. Daniel pulled the buggy up behind a wall, jumped out and began to search for bits of corrugated iron and wood to hide the vehicle. Stanley watched the three Chinooks as they descended about a mile away.

"Daniel, the attack site is mid way between ourselves and the stormtroopers. I can see a large group of people gathering."

"We haven't got much time," Daniel replied.

"What am I meant to do, Daniel? I'm not trained for this kind of stuff."

"We'll find cover in the sewers and you can guide the people from there. Hopefully, we can meet up with the androids already there. They can assist in the evacuation."

"Okay, sounds good."

The two of them raced towards the attack zone.

CHAPTER THIRTY TWO

"There's more stuff coming through, David," Deborah called out as she rushed across the room towards Samuelson and the others.

"Where from?" Samuelson asked.

"Too soon to say we're just getting the numbers in at the moment. As soon as we have enough we can feed it into the computers and translate it. But we're going to need more hands to type it."

"Can I help?" offered Ruth.

"Great," smiled Deborah.

Deborah led Ruth across the far side of the open planned room. In this area most of the desks had been moved away leaving the floor clear. Ten people were sitting on cushions scribbling down numbers as though they were on auto pilot. As soon as they reached the end of the page, they handed the document to someone standing in a large circle of about 15 people. The person handed the page then rushed over to a computer console and began to feed the numbers in via a keyboard or scanner, depending on what facilities were available. Some computers just had headsets and the operator read out the numbers for speech recognition software to capture.

"I'll take the next sheet," Deborah stated. "Follow me to the console and I'll show you what to do."

Ruth nodded.

A scraggly blonde haired youth in his early twenties, unshaven for several days, wearing denim jeans and shirt, drew close to finishing his last line on a sheet. Deborah stepped over to him and retrieved the piece of paper as soon as he raised it into the air.

"Thanks, Johnny."

"It's a pleasure, sis," remarked the youth.

He then snatched up another sheet and continued on scribbling down numbers.

"How long does this go on for?" asked Ruth.

"It's hard to say," Deborah answered as she pulled back a swivel chair and sat down.

"It can go on for just a few minutes or, at other times, all day. We won't know until they stop writing." Ruth drew up another chair and sat on Deborah's right.

"First we have to type the numbers in exactly as we see them on the page," Deborah explained. "Usually the scribes leave gaps so we can distinguish between the correct numbers. If you are unsure, best check with one those standing in the circle. Try not to interpret yourself. This has to be just as you see on the page. If there are any mistakes the translation may be incorrect and, well, let's not get into that."

"Why is it so important," Ruth asked. "Surely you already have the text on databases?"

"You don't understand," Deborah stopped typing and looked directly at Ruth. "We live in a world that is totally corrupted that we can no longer trust. All text has been constructed on Earth by man, so is open to misinterpretation and abuse. We don't know if the existing databases use the exact words. They may have misunderstood, or misrepresented the meanings as it was translated into English."

"So how can you trust what you are doing now?"

"We don't, but then we don't have to."

Ruth looked puzzled. "What do you mean?"

"Once we have typed in the numbers and turned them into text, usually Hebrew, sometimes Aramaic..."

"Why Aramaic?" Ruth interrupted.

Deborah smiled, "that was the language Jesus spoke in."

"Jesus," frowned Ruth. "Who's Jesus?"

"You've never heard of Jesus?"

"No."

"Wow, we've a lot to tell you," continued Deborah.

"Hurry up, Deborah," called over one in the circle. "We need your computer.

"Okay, okay, I'm working on it," she snapped. Deborah turned back to the console and beat away at the keyboard. Scanning over the numbers on the paper with those she could see on the monitor.

"We'll discuss Jesus later when we've got more time," Deborah reassured Ruth.

Several minutes later Deborah had managed to type in all the numbers on the sheet. She guided the cursor to the menu bar and dropped down to Save. When requested for a name, she typed in *SourceAaron203.doc.*

"What does the name mean," asked Ruth.

"Oh, just that Aaron is the source of this document and he has had 203 visions." Deborah pressed enter and a progress window appeared briefly and then she chose a second menu and clicked on Translate. A few moments later the screen filled up with Hebrew text.

"What does that mean?" Ruth inquired.

"Give it a few moments," answered Deborah. "We'll see the English translation shortly."

"Is anything lost in the three stages?"

"It's possible but we have another system to check for errors, once we have all the texts consolidated."

"What's that?"

Deborah smiled at Ruth. "You'll see, I can't really say."

"Why not?"

"Trust me, you want to just see."

On the screen the first series of Hebrew text, which ran from right to left, appeared in its own window in English on the left side of the screen, running left to right.

Deborah began to read it out. *The word of the Lord came to me. Son of man, you are living among a rebellious people. They have eyes to see but do not see and ears to hear but do not hear, for they are a rebellious people. Therefore, son of man, pack your belongings for exile and in the daytime, as they watch, set out and go from where you are to another place."*

"What does it mean?"

"That's the third time you've asked that question?" Deborah grinned.

"Sorry," Ruth apologised. "I'm just curious. I got so taken up in all this, with the little notebook and worked through the text in my old flat."

"So this shouldn't be a problem to you?"

"Not really, only that what has just appeared there seems to be what I've just done in escaping from my flat with Daniel. What does THAT mean?"

"I don't know," answered Deborah. "The only trouble is, are we seeing something that has been done or are we also being told to do the same as you?"

"So you can't see then?"

Ruth felt a slight tug on her heart. A sense of foreboding.

"I'm not sure how we should take this but we can check it out."

Deborah printed out the translation and took the piece of paper.

"This console is free now," she called over to the circle. A young woman ran over to the desk, sat down and began punching in digits.

"Thanks," she said to Ruth, who stood up to follow Deborah.

"Where are you going, Deborah?" Ruth asked.

"Come on, I'll show you how we get these passages proofed."

The two young women left the open office and made their way down the corridor towards the lift.

"Do all the texts get proofed the same way?"

"Mostly," replied Deborah.

"Why do we have to go elsewhere?"

"You'll see."

The lift doors stopped at the lowest level. When the doors sprang open, Ruth realised they had descended into a tunnel system.

"Where are we?" Ruth asked.

"An old tunnel system," explained Deborah. "Originally, the tunnels were built in the 1500s to protect people from town fires. Most of these stretched from Northampton Castle and the nearby churches."

"But we're miles away from Northampton, surely."

"Yes, but the androids have been around here for about twenty years and began to create their own tunnels to link the sewage systems. Once they were outcast, they discovered all the old tunnels and vaults that connected to All Saints Church and the Castle. With all the new buildings, the people above ground had forgotten about the tunnels."

"Surely, they found some of them when they laid down the foundations?" puzzled Ruth.

"You would have thought so, but no. They virtually all remained intact. I think because of their heritage they were preserved, but then they were just forgotten."

They continued on. Most of the tunnels had white painted brick walls, with rusty hand rails running waist high. A string of electric cabling linked a series of lights encased behind oval bulkhead-glass fittings, strapped in by galvanised wire protective guards on an aluminium base screwed into the brickwork. Spider's webs clung around the edges of each lamp with several yellow egg sacks suspended in silk strands. The parent spiders froze as soon as the humans appeared, only to continue scurrying around and pouncing on prey when Deborah and Ruth had gone by.

For about twenty minutes they made their way through the labyrinth. Then the light changed from tungsten orange to a bluish tinge.

"Are we nearly there?" asked Ruth.

"Nearly."

Then the tunnel opened up into a large cavernous vault, almost the size of a basilica. From close to the centre to the circumference, nearly a thousand stalls had been placed around a platform roughly seven metres in diameter. Deborah led Ruth down a set of stairs towards the platform. In the middle was an altar and to one side a font. Ruth looked up to see an array of lamps suspended from the roof. The walls were mostly of brick, painted white. A simple wooden cross was placed on the altar.

"What is this place?" wondered Ruth.

"It's where we gather to pray," explained Deborah.

"So why are we here now? And what does it have to do with the text."

"Deborah has brought it here for me to read," came a voice to Ruth's right. She spun round in sheer fright.

"Who are you? Where did you come from?"

"Those questions are not important," answered the tall African. "You have something for me?"

"The latest text," replied Deborah.

The African read through, then nodded. "Yes, that is suitable. It is well structured and conveys the meaning of the original."

"How do you know what the original was?" Ruth quizzed.

"Because I was with the author," explained the African.

"What the man upstairs writing the numbers?"

"No, the one who told him what to write on the page."

"And who might that be?"

"The Word."

CHAPTER THIRTY THREE

"Can you see anything," whispered Stanley.

"Sssh," Daniel replied.

"What's going on?"

"Not so loud," Daniel snapped once more. "I can see a small gathering, over there, between those derelict houses."

Stanley raised himself up slightly to look where Daniel had pointed. Between themselves and the gathering, were three rows of terraced houses. All had lost their upper floors and roofs but several chimneys remained towering up from the ground floor. Just beyond the third row, Daniel and Stanley could see seventy to eighty people standing around a man on a stack of wooden pallets. The sound of the preacher's muffled voice could be heard through a megaphone. From various parts of the park on the other side of the terraces, small pockets of people began to cluster together and make their way to the large crowd, as though being pulled to a magnet.

"What's going on," asked Stanley.

"The preacher is sucking them in with all kinds of ideas to get them out of their current predicament. But he's a liar."

"Why do you say that?"

"Because," Daniel slid back down beside Stanley, behind a brick wall. "I was once part of what's about to happen."

Stanley scanned both of Daniel's eyes.

"Part of what, Daniel?"

Daniel turned away and covered his face with his hands. He took in a deep breath, before looking back at Stanley.

"Surely, you know what's going on out there?"

197

"Yeah, they're gathering people up to slaughter them. So how does that affect you? Were you attacked?"

"No, not exactly," Daniel replied turning away. "I was part of a...."

This time Daniel tried to look into Stanley's soul.

"I'm one of the butchers," explained Daniel.

Stanley clasped his hand over his ears and began the hum. Daniel tried to prise Stanley's hands away.

"Stanley, listen to me."

Stanley continued to hum.

"Stanley, stop it and listen."

"I don't what to know, leave me be."

"I'm sorry, Stanley."

Stanley continued to strain at keeping his eyes tight, humming and pressing his hands against his eyes, all at the same time.

"Stay here. I'll come back for you later. Stay out of sight. Stanley, do you understand. Stanley, listen."

"Okay, I'll stay here," he replied.

Daniel shook his head, then carefully raised himself above the wall to see what was going on beyond the derelict terraces. Now several hundred people had gathered. Daniel slid over the wall and once on the other side, hugged the ground to stay out of sight. He crawled towards the first row of houses and once inside, stood and peaked out of a window. Carefully he checked either side of the house in an attempt to see if any stormtroopers or SMAAWs had been positioned close by.

As far as he could tell nothing was there. He proceeded forward, keeping low, continuously alert, anticipating the unexpected. He sprinted across a stretch of overgrown grass that once was two rear terraced house gardens. When he reached the back of one house, he went through the kitchen door and made his way into the hallway, towards the front door. The glass had been smashed decades ago. The paint had been weathered and was flaking off. In some places, naked wood lay rotting.

At the front door, Daniel carefully looked out. The view of Reeves on the palettes and several faces of the crowd almost appeared bleached out. The sun was unhindered by any cloud. Only a blue canopy hung above them.

Daniel began to look around for something to use as a weapon. He wanted to take out Reeves.

"Daniel, can you hear me?" came a whisper.

Daniel was startled. Rapidly he looked about himself but could see nothing.

"It's okay, Daniel, it's me, Janet."

"Where the hell are you talking from?" demanded Daniel. As he sat with his back against the door scanning around the hallway, 8D22 switched off the adaptive camouflage panels around his head. Daniel was then able to determine where the rest of the android's body and limbs were, as the edges did not blend in too well.

"Daniel, we thought it best if I spoke initially, so you first heard a friendly voice."

"You still nearly gave me a heart attack," he gasped as his breathing began to calm once more. "What's wrong?"

"8D22 detected your movements as you ran across the green. Unfortunately, so did one of the SMAAWs."

"Where is it now," Daniel requested, becoming agitated.

"8D22 terminated the machine."

Daniel stopped scanning the house and looked straight up at the towering android.

"He did?"

"Yes, Daniel," replied 8D22. "But we have to move on as the SMAAW will be missed very shortly."

"Where do we go to help those people?"

"Our options are limited," the android explained. "However, there are several drain covers on this side of the road and path between here and the next set of terraced-houses, but they are in the open and refugees using them may lose their lives before escaping."

"Are there any alternatives?" asked Daniel.

"Several of the rear gardens also have maintenance covers and enough cover for some to escape."

"Okay." Daniel paused for a moment to think. "We need some weapons."

"Those can be acquired from the stormtroopers," 8D22 answered.

"Can we limit the number of casualties?" asked Janet via 8D22's speakers.

"There will be some, it is unavoidable," the android replied.

"Try to minimise fatalities, 8D22," Janet pressed. "We are not murderers, it is not our way."

The android said nothing.

"Are you ready," asked Daniel.

"Yes."

In the field on the far side of the third row of terraced-houses, some five hundred people had gathered. Some were in family groups, others were just couples and many were on their own. All were unaware of the menace that lurked around the perimeter of the field.

Reeves finally lowered his megaphone and stared at the crowd and smiled. An old man looked at him puzzled, then his eyes suddenly widened.

"It's a trap," the old man screamed.

All heads began to swing from side to side. Fear flushed through the mass of people like a tsunami. Then the old man felt as though he had been hit by a juggernaut. The concussion of air punched him and he felt his insides being torn apart. Several bodies fell to the ground. People began to scream and race in all directions, not knowing where the threat was coming from. A young woman initially heard something swoosh passed her ear and then nothing but darkness. A fraction of a second later her face hit the dirt, eyes wide open glazed with a milky mist. Blood trickled from around her right eye, across the bridge of her nose and down her left cheek. As the scarlet droplet plummeted to the dust, the impact formed a red crown.

Four troopers stood hosing their automatic weapons across the field spraying death. All laughing. The view behind them was briefly distorted and like a sickle to a blade of grass, each of the heads rolled off their shoulders. Their torsos crumpling to the ground and index fingers instantly relaxed off the triggers.

"Four weapons, Daniel," crackled the electronic voice of 8D22. "Put them to use and recruit some allies."

In a matter of seconds, the crowd realised an avenue for escape had been carved and like a flock of birds all turned to flee in that direction.

A young man ran towards Daniel as he lifted two weapons. He threw one at the youth.

"Have you ever used one?"

The boy shook his head.

"Now's the time to learn."

Daniel showed him the safety and pointed where he wanted to fire. The youth pulled the trigger just as three more troopers had gathered their wits and realised that the sport today would be more complex. The rain of bullets ripped them to shreds, their body armour only giving them momentary protect before the soft spots of their faces gave access to death.

Seeing their chance, three middle-aged men snatched up the dead troopers guns and rallied to the cause. More people had a chance to survive. But the threat was not over yet. Two SMAAWs came crashing through the brick walls of a derelict house. The debris was the demise of two women and a child. The men rained their guns but to ill effect. The SMAAWs Gatling guns carved into the crowd. 8D22 ripped the arm off one, then turned the weapon on the other. Almost instantly it exploded. Shrapnel sliced through several of 8D22's adaptive camouflage panels, making him partially visible but the dismembered SMAAWs took most of the force.

"8D22," Daniel screamed. "Two more at three o'clock."

The android spun the Gatling gun ninety degrees to his right and gave its voice a chance to roar. As the enemy crumpled, 8D22 raced to follow the humans. Daniel guided them across the road on the other side of the terraced-houses, into the second set and on into the gardens, where the android had indicated access to the sewers would be found. Nearly thirty had begun to slide down the maintenance ladders and were racing through the tunnels into the darkness.

Elsewhere, more men took courage to disarm more troopers. Some gave their lives but the sheer number soon out did the panicked stormtroopers, who beat a retreat towards their Chinooks.

As two helicopters began to leave the ground, 8D22 trained his gun on them. One burst into flames instantly, while the other lost its rear blades and span out of control, ploughed into a row of houses. A large bloom of sooty smoke rose into the air. The crowd cheered as victory was theirs.

"Come on," Daniel screamed. "We have no time for this. Get into the sewers before they come back."

The faces full of smiles changed to fear as they all realised their triumph could be short lived.

"Where do we go?" called out an old woman.

Daniel directed them towards the maintenance holes behind the houses but in the distance the drone of rotary blades grew.

"Reinforcements," called out 8D22. "I can hold them off for only a short time. You need to escape Daniel as quickly as possible."

As Daniel looked back, he saw the android race across the road and through a house into the field beyond. All movement of the humans seemed to have ceased. Either they were underground or had found some other cover. Three light-weight attack ships bobbed over some buildings on the far side of the field, each firing a cascade of rockets, which screamed through the air and ploughed into 8D22. The explosion blinded Daniel briefly but when he was able to look back only the charred metal boots remained of his AI comrade.

Daniel pulled the cover over the access hole and began to race towards the third row of houses via their back gardens. Now his mission was to locate Stanley and find a way back to safety.

CHAPTER THIRTY FOUR.

Ruth stood looking up at the way the basilica had been constructed.

"It's so beautiful, so intricate."

"In these times, people are too quick to destroy but lack the patience to create," the African stated.

"They are, but this must have taken ages to build?" wondered Ruth.

"Look, I have to get back," stressed Deborah. "If you want to stay, are you okay to find your own way back, Ruth?"

"I'm sure I'll be fine," replied Ruth, more focused on the way the ceiling had been designed.

"Okay, I'll see you later." Deborah made her way to the exit.

The African watched Deborah leave, then took a quick glance at Ruth before he looked up at the ceiling.

"What do you see, Ruth?"

"It looks like a spiral. No, two spirals, one going clockwise and the other going anticlockwise. I thought, initially that the tiles were rectangular but they're not."

"That's right," replied the African. "What does it remind you of?"

"I don't know," Ruth began. "Perhaps, yes, a daisy or sunflower."

"That's good. Look again, try not to make any assumptions. Now what do you see?"

Ruth had the sudden urge to lie down on the floor. A serene sensation washed through her and she felt relaxed.

"There seems to be clouds up there, like looking into the eye of a hurricane. The closer you get to the centre the less violence there is."

"Harmony," the African's spoke softly.

"Yes, harmony," echoed Ruth. "Peace."

"Continue looking."

The colours and textures shifted, very slowly. Ruth could see blues she associated with sky become purple. The white clouds turned red and orange. Bright dots appeared.

"I see stars," Ruth sighed. "The milky way."

"They were once called the Heavens," the African replied.

"It's beautiful." A tear rolled down Ruth's left check. "This is such a wonderful place and yet I feel so sad. Why?"

Inside, she felt her heart pang. Not pain, but a sense of bereavement and separation.

"Why do I hurt so much, inside?" Ruth asked. She rolled over and curled up, hugging her legs and sobbing. It was uncontrollable. She had never felt this way before, even as a child when her parents left her.

"You have a lifetime of grief all pent up inside, Ruth," the African answered. "You need to let it go."

There was no telling how much time had past. It could have been moments, it could have been years. Ruth suddenly felt relieved, as though a massive weight had gone and there were no longer any burdens. She had slept, so she thought, but there were no memories of dreams or nightmares, just a sense of being refreshed, rejuvenated and regenerated.

"Look up once more, Ruth," requested the African. "What do you see now?"

Again, Ruth gazed up at the domed ceiling. Within each of the cross sections of the two contra wound spirals, a motion image could be seen. The first one consisted of Ruth's perspective of her attack on Victoria in her android shell. Ruth threw her hands over her mouth. More tears fell.

"Oh, God, I'm so sorry I did that."

The image turned white and was gone. The spiral ceiling

continued to turn. Another image appeared of her view of watching Daniel after he had stepped out of the shower. Ruth blushed.

"I know, I shouldn't, sorry, but he was so..."

The image still remained but slightly faded than before.

The spiral continued to rotate and Ruth found herself many times in tears, other times embarrassed. By the end, she was so exhausted, she collapsed.

She woke with a start. Was anxious and rapidly scanned her surroundings.

"Where am I?"

"Safe," the African replied.

"What happened?"

"You gave up your sins."

"I did what?"

"You repented."

Ruth sat up and hugged her legs, resting her left cheek on her knees and gently rocked back and forth.

"What are you thinking, Ruth?"

"Uhmm?"

"What's on you mind?"

"Umm,..er." She shook her head. "Nothing. Nothing at all. It's gone."

"What's gone?"

"The pain. I can't feel it any more. It's as though it has been washed away. Swept clean."

"Good," smiled the African.

Ruth looked at him and returned his smile.

"What is this place?"

"Sanctuary. A place to rest and take stock of things. To reflect on what has gone before, to release it and start renewed and refreshed. A new beginning."

"How does it work?"

"What?"

"How are my sins taken away?"

"You gave them away."

"To whom?"

"The one who saved you."

"And who was that?"

"Look inside yourself for the answer and you will know."

Ruth stood away and again looked up towards the ceiling.

"In the note book I deciphered it said in the last few verses 'Posterity will serve him; future generations will be told about the Lord. They will proclaim his righteousness to a people yet unborn – for he has done it.'"

"Do you believe?" asked the African.

Ruth once more smiled, "the pain has gone. Something or someone took it away. I believe that. Tell me his name?"

"Yeshua."

"And this is his temple?"

"It is the place these people come to worship him. You are his temple."

"I'm his temple?" Ruth puzzled. "I don't understand."

"His spirit is in you. This is how you were drawn here."

"I thought it was the numbers in the notebook?"

"That was part of the design," answered the African. "The key that opened the door to your soul."

"The key? Quite some puzzle you've built."

"Every design requires numbers to measure out all the parts. Even this ceiling. It uses the divine proportion."

"The divine what?" Ruth interrupted.

"The divine proportion, many artists used to design their paper based on this principle. By taking a square, then taking the mid point of the top line as a pivotal point and the radius being taken from the lower right corner. An arch can be drawn up towards the projection of the top line away from the square, to form a rectangle with dimensions 1 times £1.6108339887."

"That number," Ruth recognised, "is denoted by the Greek letter Phi. Isn't it?"

"The Golden Ratio," the African added. "By taking the longer side of the rectangle and extruding out into an additional square, the shorter side of the rectangle will measure E0.6108339887. This process can continue on as many times as desired. Then, starting at the smallest square's inner right angle as a fulcrum and drawing an arch, using the length of the square as a radius, between two adjacent lines in the right angle for every square in the design, a spiral can be created."

"Yeah, right," Ruth puzzled, "and I'm supposed to understood that? Not!"

"Look up at the ceiling," requested the African.

There on the panels was displayed the squares and the spiral emanating from it. Then the image was transformed into a nautilus shell.

"I've seen something similar using the Fabonacci numbers," Ruth explained. "If you start in the middle and place two squares together and then add one twice as big, then a third square the same length as the other put together."

"1 plus 1, plus 2, plus 3, plus 5 and so on."

"That's right," smiled Ruth. "The sum of the first two numbers equals the next number and is then added to the preceding number to create the next."

"0,1,1,2,3,5,8,13,21,34 and so on," added the African.

"That's right."

"The only trouble with this sequence of numbers is that it is not as accurate as Phi," the African replied, as he looked up at the ceiling, now changed into the image of a storm."

"Why are all these calculations so important?" Ruth asked.

"It's part of the design. If the measurements are wrong, it can't function properly."

"So what are you trying to say?"

"That's for you to figure out," came the answer.

"Is that why you have to proof read all the text we write down?"

"Yes, if the numbers are wrong, so the message will be?"

"But the androids already have the text in their database, can't we use that?"

"No. It is corrupted."

"Is that why everything is falling apart?" Ruth questioned.

"Yes, the current design is not sustainable," muttered the African. "Everything will be destroyed, unless the correct design can be restored."

"How long?" Ruth's joy had faded and worry lines were drawn across her forehead.

"Not long, 1260 is the number."

"Is that years, months, weeks, days, what? Hours?"

"Or even minutes. It's not for me to say."

Ruth thought for a moment, making calculations in her head.

"So, that's 52 and a half days in hours or 21 hours in minutes. What can I do?"

"On your own, nothing. But if you believe, everything is possible."

Ruth turned to face the African with a string of questions but he was nowhere to be found. She could feel the panic flood through her as she spun from one direction to another, not knowing where to step next. She crumpled to her knees and burst into tears. Her sobs echoed throughout the basilica.

Again she lay on her back and looked up at the ceiling. The hurricane spun slowly. Then she noticed the image begin to zoom out. She could see the planet Earth, then the neighbouring planets in the solar system, the sun, the galaxy, the spiralling milky way, the universe and then all that appeared were spirals upon spirals. Soon she began to recognise a fractal shape turning into a snow flake as it fell into a tree. The tree had similar patterns, it was a fern tree. Still further the image zoomed out and the fractal formed into a mountain range, with clouds beginning to form. The motion image pulled away and Ruth could see the cloud forming into a storm. A storm spiralling around covering a vast area of the planet. Ruth was no longer aware of whether her eyes were opened or closed. She had no sense of her body other than a faint rhythmical sound of her heart beating.

CHAPTER THIRTY FIVE

The two gun ships hovered over the ruined terraced houses. Daniel crouched behind a stone wall. Not more than two metres away from him Stanley lay covered in bricks and mortar, both his legs and his right arm were broken. He was breathing heavily, a rib had been broken and was pushing into his left lung.

"Hold on, Stanley. I'll get to you soon."

Stanley had no energy to reply but nodded his head as if Daniel could see him. He couldn't, but Stanley could not care less. He muttered to himself but no sound came out of his mouth.

One of the gunship helicopters began to draw closer. Their searchlight scanned the area close to where Daniel was hidden. He estimated the sun had been lost below the horizon for nearly an hour, and he knew it would not be long before he was located. He just hoped that the wall would hide his heat signature.

To his surprise there was a sudden whooshing sound, the cockpit splintered and the main rotor blades folded down as the helicopter was engulfed in flames. Daniel looked out from his hiding place to see the broken gunship plunge into a house. He could hear a cheer go up but this was swiftly followed by automatic gun fire. A new exchange erupted as those troopers who had been left on the ground opened fired on the civilians who had captured weapons from the dead soldiers.

Daniel took the opportunity to race over to Stanley to see how badly he had been injured. He had to remove a score of bricks and several beams of wood to get full access to Stanley. The injured man groaned as the heavy weight was removed from his chest and limbs.

"Leave me, Daniel," Stanley coughed.

"I can't do that, Stan. We've got to get you back."

"I don't think so," Stanley whispered. His breathing was laboured.

"Stanley, don't close your eyes, keep alert. Stanley, do you hear? Stanley?"

But there was nothing. Stanley's body had gone limp and his breathing was shallow. Daniel felt for a pulse and struggled to locate one.

"Stanley, wake up. Come on, man."

One last deep breath was sucked into Stanley's lungs, then held briefly. As it was finally released, Daniel knew he had gone. A deep sorrow rushed through Daniel's body, reaching through every fibre. He was overwhelmed by the sensation, the loss was almost too great for him. He felt his energy drained and slumped against the wall beside Stanley's body. Even the sound of racing footsteps did not stir a need for flight. He had given up. The sound of boots on rubble came closer and were suddenly upon him.

Daniel had no strength to open his eyes.

"Are they dead?" whispered an ageing voice.

"Only this one. The other has a heart beat, look."

Daniel opened his eyes expecting to see two stormtroopers but instead his gaze fell upon two old men. Both carried assault rifles. One had a MANPAD slung over his shoulder, while the other had a thermal imaging device strapped to his head.

"Who are you?" Daniel muttered.

"Your lifesavers, buddy," beamed the one with the goggles.

"Where did you get the gear?"

"Same as you. From some dead soldier," replied the man with the SAM MANPAD.

"How did you learn to use the surface-to-air missile?"

"Used to be in the forces when I was a lad," the elderly man replied. "Not known to forget anything useful, I ain't."

"You shot down the gunship?"

"You betcha. Anyway, no time for chit chat. We'd better get out of here. Any suggestions?"

"Why do you ask me?"

"We saw you earlier, with the android. You came to help. We saw you get pinned down just before nightfall and thought we'd figure out a way to repay our debt."

"What are your names?"

"Adam," stated the plump white haired man.

"Felix," added the scrawny black hair man.

"How old are you, Adam?"

"65 and never been fitter."

"And you?"

"67," replied Felix.

"Your hair has faired well."

"Ladies man, is our Felix. Quite the charmer before they closed down the OAP centre three years ago."

"What do you know, Felix?" asked Daniel as he got to his feet.

"Well, son. There's a group of about four stormtroopers behind the first row of houses. Several of our chaps have them pinned down but won't be able to hold them off for long."

"We need to get to safety before more gunships come," Daniel replied. "We should try and round up as many stragglers as possible and get into the sewers. There's plenty of tunnels to get lost in and it would take a month of Sundays for the stormtroopers to comb through them all."

"Okay, we're with you," Adam answered. "By the way, what do we call you?"

"Daniel. How many rockets have you in your bag, Adam?"

"About three."

"Better conserve them for any gunships that turn up."

"Okay."

"Any other weapons?"

"I've got a pistol," smiled Felix.

"Many rounds?"

"Five or six, I suppose. Didn't get time to scavenge any more from the body."

"We'll make do," reassured Daniel. "Are you up for some more physical exercise?"

"Hey, what you trying to say," frowned Adam. "We're fitter than you, boy."

Daniel laughed, he was pleased that they were in good spirit, they were going to need it. "Can I borrow your thermal imaging goggles for a moment?"

"Sure," Felix replied.

He pulled them from his head and handed them to Daniel. After fitting them, Daniel checked out the top of the wall. Across the way, between the second and third set of terraced houses he could see the buildings and gardens as mainly tones of blue. There were shapes moving between a couple of doors, their bodies were yellow but their heads and hands were red.

"I see two by the wall. Where are your lot?"

"Over to the left a bit," Felix replied.

Daniel scanned to the left and could see three figures huddled together. A shot rang out and one of them fell to the ground. The red heat of the head slowly turned orange then yellow. Daniel panned right to see the trooper lowering his weapon. Four more had joined them making six.

"Give me the rifle beside Stanley, Adam," Daniel instructed. He checked the ammunition then trained the weapon on the six soldiers. Before firing he set the rifle to semi-automatic, then pulled the trigger six times.

"We can go now," Daniel told the two old men.

"Did you get them all?" asked Adam.

Daniel did not reply but edged his way around the wall looking to ensure he had sufficient cover to make his way through the adjacent gardens at the rear of the two sets of terraced houses. Adam and Felix followed.

Then they all stopped. Daniel had his hand up holding the two gents back.

"What's wrong?" Felix asked.

"Not sure. Maybe a SMAAW," Daniel replied.

"We destroyed three and I think your android downed at least two."

"Make ready with the SAM," instructed Daniel.

"Thought you said we should conserve the missiles for gunships?" stressed Adam.

"Situation may have just changed," Daniel argued. "We may need to hit them with something hard."

"Okay, you're the boss," shrugged Adam.

The two old men loaded a missile from the satchel into the launcher. "Ready," signalled Felix.

Daniel continued to watch for movement through the goggles. Again the majority of the image Daniel saw was in blue, but then about twenty red and yellow blobs appeared, racing towards them. They were more panicked than in an organised attacked.

"Civilians, they're racing this way. Must be trying to escape from something. About twenty of them."

"What's chasing them?" asked Adam.

"Can't make it out, it's as cold as the rest of the surroundings. No colour signature."

"What shall we do?"

"Wait until we can identify the target."

The red and yellow blobs crossed paths and merged here and there making it confusing for Daniel to truly identify the real number. There was a sound like thunder. Several figures fell and lost their redness as their bodies cooled.

"Can you see it yet?" worried Felix.

"Sssh," Daniel snapped.

"Sorry."

"Don't bother him he's concentrating," Adam whispered.

"Both of you shut up."

"Sorry," Adam replied.

"Target in sight," informed Daniel. "Range one thousand metres."

Daniel switch on the SAM's power and made ready to fire.

"What is it?" pleaded Felix.

"AI tank."

"Why's it not using adaptive camouflage?" Adam puzzled.

"Probably doesn't realise the threat level," commented Daniel. "At least, let's hope not."

Daniel pulled the trigger. The missile roared out of the pipe and careered across towards the tank, bouncing off the angled side armour and on into the houses on the far side of the waste ground.

"Quick, load another, before it calculates our position," Daniel barked.

Felix fumbled with the second missile but managed to load the weapon. Through his sight he could see the AI tank rotate the turret and aiming in their direction. He aimed just below the gun and pulled the trigger. A trail of smoke was left behind giving away their position for a second time.

"Run, run, get out of here," screamed Daniel.

The two older men shook with fear as they scrambled to their feet and gave chase after Daniel, just as assault rifle fire riddled their previous position. The tank's turret exploded just below the gun, separating the weapon from the rest of the cater-pillared vehicle. The ammunition inside ignited, lighting up the night sky. Daniel fired his rifle in the direction of those who had targeted him and the two old men, as the three of them raced for cover behind a kitchen wall. The remaining civilians raced towards them in the hope that they had an escape route. And the stormtroopers kept on firing. Felix fell to the ground and as Daniel stopped to try and retrieve him, Adam grappled him to the dirt.

"What about Felix?" shouted Daniel.

"It's okay, he knows what he's doing," reassured Adam.

"What?" puzzled Daniel as he looked over to Felix he could see him load the last missile into the funnel, aim and fire. The missile tore through the air and ripped into the building protecting the stormtroopers. Almost instantly the place exploded shattering everything within a hundred feet. Felix rolled over and raced towards Adam and Daniel, sending dirt into the air as his boots ploughed into the earth beside them.

"There you go, all sorted," Felix beamed. He threw the weapon to the side. "No need for that anymore. No more missiles."

"We might find some later," Daniel replied.

"And it might be death to the one carrying it, so best to leave it here. Where to now?"

"Underground."

There were some fifteen other survivors from that attack and Daniel guided them all into the maintenance hole, watching them climb down the ladder. Adam and Felix were handed weapons by escaping survivors to frightened to continue fighting. Like trained soldiers, the two old men searched for hostile targets in the surrounding area.

"Okay, gents. Time to go," Daniel called in a near whisper.

Daniel remained up top until Adam had disappeared out of sight. He then pulled the maintenance cover back into position and descended the ladder into the sewer. At the bottom, the rest of the group were gathered not knowing which way to go in the pitch blackness. Felix pulled on the thermal imaging goggles and began to lead the way. Everyone else held the person in front by the waist and trusted the footing to a way out. Unbeknown to Daniel the eleventh person in the chain was Paul Reeves, still carrying Ruth's laptop in a rucksack.

CHAPTER THIRTY SIX

"My friends, this is a great day," Samuelson shouted, as he stood at the centre of the basilica surrounded by a group of twenty people. Most had just arrived with Daniel, Adam and Felix.

"Shortly, we shall celebrate and give thanks to God for delivering you from your enemy," continued the old man, standing tall dressed in ceremonial clothes, looking like a mix between an ancient North American aborigine, a Hebrew priest and a Catholic bishop.

"For so long we have felt that we have been forgotten but it is not so. You have been led away from the wickedness of our times. The corruption you have seen is soon to pass away. We are the chosen people. We are the people of the Book."

A cheer went up from the crowd. From the back of the basilica a trickle of people entered, curious to see the new arrivals. Ruth came through a small door from a room where she had been resting, still trying to come to terms with what she had experienced in the hall earlier. As those who entered came closer to the gathering, there began a new cheer.

"Many of you will have been having visions," Samuelson added, "which you have found yourself scribbling down in a note book."

There was surprise in the crowd. Samuelson pulled a book from inside his tunic.

"Each segment," he went on, "that you hold, each of our small books, forms part of a greater text."

Each new arrival pulled out a small note book and held them above their head. Reeves quickly felt the frame of the laptop in the bag, then seemed to remember something and rummaged around his inside pocket. He pulled out a small diary and held it into the air.

"It was believed that this text had been lost, even though the databases contain a similar text, it is not a true rendition of the original but a corrupted version, designed to confuse. However, by the grace of God he has given us His Word once more."

"Give praise to the Lord," cried out Adam.

The whole crowd began to roar but each with a different language. Each in a different tongue began to sing. Reeves looked on either side and became fearful not knowing what to do. He threw his arms into the air to mimic those beside him.

Then came a hush.

"The truth I have come to realise," Samuelson addressed the crowd, "is that God does not have favourites. If anyone from any nation fears God and does what is right, God will accept them."

There came the sound of rushing wind within the hall. All faces looked up and around to see where it was coming from. It was as if a tornado had blown up. Then, what seemed to be tongues of fire came to rest on each and everyone, except Reeves. The praise continued on. Ruth fell to her knees with tears in her eyes. From within the crowd, Daniel made his way towards her. He placed his hand on her shoulder and she looked up in surprise. Realising who it was, Ruth jumped to her feet once more, wrapped her arms around his neck and squeezed.

"I was so worried about you," she told him, then pressed her lips against his and refused to separate from him for what seemed to be an age. Daniel held her in his arms and closed his eyes. Then Samuelson's words entered their ears and the couple released each other, but held hands.

"God, in his wisdom, is calling mankind. Calling us to be with him and to repent from the ways that have brought our world to its current devastation. God has not abandoned us, we had abandoned him. But he has given us another chance."

Reeves sneered, there was an arrogance in the way he stood.

"Why do you not believe?" asked an old man who stood beside him.

Reeves looked down at him, exploring the deep wrinkles carved in the old man's face.

"You are fools to believe all this rubbish. This is just fantasy."

"You have eyes but you do not see. You have ears but you cannot hear."

"Sheer nonsense," Reeves snapped.

The old man's body began to glow and his shape changed into that of the African.

"Is this nonsense, Reeves?"

The crowd around Reeves and the African began to move away as the light grew stronger. Reeves saw the African tower over him, and shielded his eyes from the brilliance.

"What kind of freak are you?" cried out Reeves.

"I am a messenger, sent from God."

Reeves shook his head in disbelief. "No, I don't believe this. You are playing a mind game on me. All you people are dangerous. You are a threat to society and must be destroyed."

He pulled out a pistol from his jacket and pointed it at the African. The crowd all gasped and began to push themselves against each other towards the back of the basilica. Daniel moved as though to tackle Reeves but the African held his hand up.

"Take no action, Daniel. It is not necessary."

Daniel stepped in front of Ruth to shield her as the African faced Reeves once more. He smiled at him and Reeves smiled back, held up the gun and fired at point blank range. The African remained standing and continued to smile at Reeves. Fear gripped the latter as he repeatedly squeezed the trigger. Reeves could hear the sound of the gun discharging five, six, seven and eight times but still the African did not fall. The ninth bullet exited the muzzle of the gun and was projected towards the African's chest but as it came within six inches of its target began to melt and turned into a gaseous haze, harmless to either the African or those standing behind him.

Reeves stepped backwards away from the tall man and screamed.

"You do not exit. You're not here. You're part of this mass hysteria, an illusion. A freak. You must be destroyed. You all must be destroyed."

Reeves turned and raced down into one of the tunnels to escape.

"Samuelson, we must stop him," Daniel called out. Before he could get an answer, Daniel began to race after Reeves.

"Daniel, come back," shouted Samuelson. "It's okay."

"You don't understand," Daniel replied. "That man is the one who organised the cull. He'll come back here and destroy everything. We can't let that happen." Daniel continued to race after Reeves and before another word could be said was gone.

"Daniel," scream Ruth. "Come back, please."

"It's okay Ruth," reassured Samuelson. "It'll be okay."

"But you can't let him go alone. He'll be killed."

"Do not fear the one who kills the body," remarked the African. "Only fear the one who can destroy your soul and spirit."

"I'll go with Daniel," called out a young man.

"What's your name?" asked Samuelson.

"Stephen."

"Why do you want to help?" Ruth asked.

"Daniel saved my live. It's only right to repay my debt."

Four others joined Stephen and followed him through the tunnels to join Daniel.

"We should take some time to rest," Samuelson encouraged those who remained. "We have seen the Holy Spirit descend upon us. Soon we will congregate here so that each and everyone of you can be Baptised into our community."

Ruth was uncertain what she should do.

"Are you okay?" asked the African.

"I'm not sure," she replied. "I didn't realise how much Daniel meant to me and I don't want to lose him."

"Then hand him over to the one who can protect him and have faith."

"So much has happened, I'm not sure what I believe. It's all very confusing."

"Do you want to go back?" the African asked.

She looked him in the eyes.

"How can I? I don't think the world I once knew even existed. How can I go back to something that isn't there and never was?"

"So, where now?"

"I don't know," Ruth replied. "You tell me."

CHAPTER THIRTY SEVEN.

Reeves had fumbled in the darkness for about half an hour. Behind him he could hear boots splashing through the puddles along the walkways of the sewage channels. He had been careful not to let the rucksack get wet as it contained a precious item.

A handrail was detected by Reeves' searching fingers. He gripped another and began to pull himself upwards. There were some forty steps before he reached the cover to the outside world. He wondered where this would bring him. His sense of direction was in disarray after being in the darkness for so long.

Reeves put his shoulder to the cover and pushed with all his might. Initially, the metal disc would not budge. Then he heard splashing at the base of the ladder.

"Daniel, I've found a maintenance ladder."

"Use the flash light," came a second voice.

Reeves pushed even harder. The cover became dislodged, light burst in and the metal grating sent an echo rippling down the chute.

"There's someone up there."

"Use your weapon, shoot him."

Reeves pulled himself out of the hole and kicked some gravel into the darkness. Below the stones rained down on two of the men, nearly blinding one of them.

"He's been cut," Stephen called out to Daniel as he checked the man's eyes with the torch.

"Can you bandage him up?"

"I have a scarf that might do," suggested the forth man.

"Take him back," Daniel instructed. "Stephen and I will go

on with the other two."

The two men made their way back down the tunnels, using the flash light as their guide. Daniel turned to the two who remained.

"What are your names?"

"Anders," said a tall, skinny youth in his late teens, with ruffled blond hair and four days of growth on his chin.

"Matthew," replied the other, more stout man in his early thirties.

"Okay, let's go."

Daniel went first up the ladder, followed by Stephen, Anders and Matthew. It was still daylight when they pulled themselves on to the surface. Reeves was nowhere to be seen.

"Daniel, what is this place? Who lives in these mansions?"

Stephen was taken aback by the opulence of the buildings that surrounded them. Large detached Georgian and Tudor houses showed off the affluence of this elite urban area.

"This is how the one percent who own 95% of the world's wealth live," answered Daniel.

"They are hardly ever here though. Many have places across the world."

"It's like something from an old history book," Stephen commented.

"We have to be careful not to trigger any alarms," Daniel cautioned.

"I'd say if anyone saw us now, we'd stand out like a sore thumb," Stephen remarked.

"We should find cover," recommended Daniel.

"What about this Reeves guy. Won't he be long gone?"

"We need to track him down before he has a chance to contact anyone else," Daniel stated. "He could lead them back to our people. And we can't have that."

"Okay, if you think this is right?"

"What choice do we have?" questioned Daniel.

Close to a wall, the four men could see a small security cabin, overseeing the main entrance to one of the Tudor houses. Inside, a security guard sat reading a newspaper and chewing on a sandwich. A bank of televisions showed a few images of several cameras strategically positioned around the house. The four men were briefly visible on one camera but the guard failed to see them. He was too engrossed in a story in the middle of the newspaper.

One of the television monitors had been reset to show satellite television, as most of the time the guards would sit watching, effectively blank screens. The guard looked up to see a young brunette step in front of the camera.

"These scenes of devastation are believed to be the work of terrorists," the news reporter stated. The name strip faded up, indicating her name as Annie Moore for 1NWO-News. The wind lifted her hair in front of her eyes and she gently brushed the strands aside. "Forty or more policemen are reported dead and seventy more have been wounded, having courageously protected civilians living in the area."

"That's not what happened," Stephen exclaimed.

"They own the media," Daniel replied. "They can say what they like."

"With me is Police Commissioner Reeves," Moore announced, just before she turned and the camera pulled out.

"That's the guy we're chasing," Stephen indicated somewhat stunned. "How did he get there so quickly?"

"They must have recorded this before the attack," speculated Daniel. "None of this stuff is real."

"We'd better get back to warn the others," Anders suggested.

"Commissioner, how dangerous are these people?" asked Moore.

"Lethal, Annie. There is no telling what they'd do. We've tracked them down into the sewers and are combing through every inch. There's no escape."

"In the meantime, what are your recommendations to the people at home?"

"To stay indoors until this emergency is over. We are being forced to implement martial law across the city and we expect complete cooperation from every citizen. There will be a curfew set from 8pm until 8am. Military forces will be patrolling all areas so if anyone is caught outside their home they can expect to be shot on sight."

"Harsh measures, don't you think?" Moore question.

"It's a sign of the times, Annie. We are reluctant to go this far as I'm sure you can imagine, but the city's council believes we have no alternative at this time."

"Surely, martial law has not been implemented since the 17th Century. Doesn't this type of action require approval by parliament?"

"We live in unusual times," Reeves replied. "And as you have witnessed here today. This is not just a simple matter of a police service handling the current insurrection. Therefore, stronger measures have to be actioned upon. I don't think there will be any objection and this has been sanctioned by the highest order."

"Well, thank you, Commissioner Reeves. Now back to the studio."

Inside the guard house, the security officer was suddenly disrupted by the phone ringing.

"Hello, front gate."

The man broke off talking and continued to listen to whoever it was on the other end. "Okay, sir. I understand. Yes, sir. I will. Yes, Mr. Rothstein, I have been watching."

On the television screen, the studio image showed a photograph of Daniel in uniform.

"One of the known terrorists is rogue Police Trooper, Daniel Perez. He is believed to be the main ringleader behind the current unrest. The police and military services advise all citizens to treat this man as armed and dangerous. If sighted, the recommendation is to contact the police immediately. Do not approach him."

The guard went to replace the receiver, then had second thoughts.

"Hello, sir. Are you still there? Sorry, sir, it's just that the television said not to approach this man if spotted."

There was a brief pause where the guard could be seen nodding his head.

"Yes, sir, I understand." With more confidence, the guard hung up the phone and made his way to a metal cabinet which ran along the rear of his office. He unlocked it and pulled out several weapons including a MP5, M16 and a Colt 1911 pistol. He pulled out several boxes of ammunition and then stepped over to another counter where a CB radio system crackled away.

"Hi, Ted. You there? Ted?"

"Yes, Graham, what can I do for you?"

"Ted, Rothstein has been informed by his guest that we have intruders on the grounds. We've been instructed to flush them out and either apprehend them or use lethal force if necessary."

"Are you serious?"

"Yes, Ted. Deadly. How soon can you get here?"

"I'll be over in about five. Jim and Brian'll be over soon after."

"Tell them to hurry."

Graham replaced the handset and went back to loading the magazines of the M16 and MP5.

"Do you think Reeves is in with that guy Rothstein?" asked Stephen nervously.

"Probably," Daniel replied.

"Shouldn't we get out of here?" asked Matthew.

"It's beginning to get dark," added Anders.

Daniel looked over to the horizon, to see the orange glow had begun to creep down towards the horizon.

"We'll wait a bit."

"But if we stay any longer, we're bound to be spotted," stressed Stephen.

"I know. It's turning bad whichever way we go but it'll soon be dark and we'll have a better chance to escape."

Suddenly the front door to the main house burst open. A party of men came storming out towards the security house.

"Ted, hurry up," snapped Graham as he caught sight of the residence party. "Ted, Rothstein and his sons are coming this way. He looks fuming. There's also another guy with him."

Daniel and his group kept their heads down as they remained hidden between the security house and the perimeter wall. They could hear Rothstein and his party as they approached the small building beside the gates.

"Albert," called Rothstein to one of the men. "You and Robert can take your weapons to the rear of the house. If you don't like what you see, shoot it."

"I think we should organise a vigilante team," recommended one of the two young men. "We should call Harry and David."

"Good idea, Robert," encouraged Rothstein.

The other young man smiled, "yes, that would be some sport."

"First things first, Albert," Rothstein answered. "We should tell the Peterson's so they can protect their investments. Reeves, your boys on their way?"

"Should be here in about five minutes."

"I'd have felt more comfortable if it had been half that time."

"Things are stretched with all this terrorist activity, Rothstein."

"I appreciate that, but think about your funding. I could have it increased if you made it two and a half."

"As you wish." Reeves ran into the security house and picked up the phone.

"Dad," asked Robert.

The security guard handed Rothstein the M16.

"Yes, son?"

"We could turn this to our advantage."

"How?"

"By contacting a few corporates over the Internet and see if we can get a few bets going."

"Could generate a nice bit of income," smiled Rothstein. "Good lad, I like to see someone with their head well screwed on during these troubled times. See what you can do?"

Robert ran back into the main house.

"Daniel," whispered Stephen, "we have to get out of here before we're discovered."

"Okay," Daniel replied in a quiet voice. "But if the opportunity arises, take out Reeves for good."

CHAPTER THIRTY EIGHT

"Hi, Ruth. What you up to?" asked Samuelson. She looked up from where she sat, on a bunk bed positioned in the middle of a large cavernous room kitted out with hundreds of similar beds.

"Just writing a few things down that have come into my head," she replied. She tapped the pen against the top of her black notebook and bit the lower part of her lip.

"Mind if I sit down?"

"Sure, go ahead."

Samuelson sat beside her on the lower bunk.

"This must seem very strange to you?"

"Yeah, it's a bit different," Ruth replied. "But I've got a strange sense of deja vu."

"In what way?" Samuelson asked.

"Well," Ruth paused for a moment, to gather her thoughts. "My mom used to tell me stories when I was small. I hadn't thought about it for quite some time. I mean, I was just a small kid, barely primary school age."

"What were the stories about?" pressed Samuelson.

"About being a Christian and going to church. They are just vague memories really but there is something about this place that has reignited those memories. It's like I'm being called back to something I lost when I was a child. Does any of this make sense to you?"

Samuelson smiled. "It does. Are you a believer?"

"A believer?" Ruth looked puzzled.

"Yes, are you a Christian?"

Ruth turned away and looked at the floor.

"I believe in a God and I feel I'm being taken care of by something of a higher power."

She smiled as though remembering another image from her childhood.

"Mom used to talk to me about Jesus."

Again she paused. Then looked up at Samuelson as though examining his soul. He felt a little unnerved.

"Is he the man I see in my dreams, who is giving me the images, numbers and text?"

"Yes, I think so. And so do many others here. We all do. We all feel as though we have been called here for something special."

"Why is it so hard? Why have we had to give up so much?" pleaded Ruth.

"But if it was all an illusion anyway, have we really given anything up of great value?"

Ruth looked away once more. A tear rolled down her check. She wiped it away with the back of her hand.

"No, I suppose not. It's just so hard to make sense of it all. I lost my mom and dad so long ago and then I've been taken care of by Victoria. Now she's..."

"You found it hard when you saw her in cybernetic humanoid form?" Samuelson asked.

"Yes, it was so creepy." More tears ran down her face.

"Is there anything else bothering you?"

Ruth looked into Samuelson's eyes.

"I think I just fallen in love and I'm scared I'm going to lose him too."

"Daniel?"

Ruth smiled and gave a little laugh.

"Is it that obvious?"

Samuelson smiled. "Perhaps not to a blind man."

He could see her cheeks go rosy with embarrassment.

"Hold onto those thoughts, Ruth. They'll help you get through all of this. Do you know how to pray?"

"Not really."

"Today is a celebration many have forgotten," Samuelson continued.

"After the crucifixion, Jesus' followers hid away. They were frightened and uncertain of themselves. Then they began to find he was still amongst them, in a real sense."

"What, actually there? Like the African I spoke to in the basilica?" Ruth quizzed.

"No, more so," Samuelson explained. "The African is just a spirit, an angel without a physical form. Jesus would appear physically them, moments later, could simply vanish."

"That's hard to conceive," replied Ruth.

"It can be and that's why Reeves has difficulties."

"He just wants us all dead, doesn't he?"

"That's because he is scared," Samuelson answered. "He just needs time to understand."

"What is this all about, Samuelson," Ruth asked.

"There is a Psalm which says God will send his spirit, to create and he will renew the face of the earth. That is what we are waiting for. And from what we have gathered it will happen soon."

"All of us will be renewed?" she replied.

"If we can believe."

"What do we have to do?"

Samuelson put his hand on her shoulder, "to have faith and trust. Can you do that?"

Ruth nodded. "I think so."

"Good," reassured Samuelson. "Have you ever been baptised?"

"I don't know."

"Would you like to be?"

"Yes."

"We are having a ceremony later and you are welcome to join in."

"Thanks, I appreciate that." Ruth smiled. Then lunged

231

forward and wrapped her arms around Samuelson's neck and squeezed. "Thank you, for everything."

Samuelson stood and began to walk away.

"Samuelson!"

"Yes, Ruth?"

"While I was in the basilica earlier, I spoke with the African."

Samuelson came back to his seat.

"What about?"

"It's funny," Ruth went on. "Lots have happened and my mind has been filled with so much, its hard to comprehend."

Samuelson smiled.

"But while I was seeing so much and it really took my breath away. The African told me we only had a short time left, 52 days or possibly 52 hours."

Samuelson's eyes widened.

"That's all?"

"That's what he said."

"Did he say what we had to do?"

"Has he never told you this before?" puzzled Ruth.

"No," Samuelson ran his hand through his beard. "Only to gather all the people who have the chapters and put the book together."

"How long have you been doing that?" asked Ruth.

"Roughly 13 years now, in here."

"And how much material have you put together?"

Samuelson stood once more and began to pace up and down a few metres away from Ruth.

"We've gathered about 24 different books," began Samuelson. "Initially, I thought there might be around 46 books as I had grown up in the Catholic church as a boy, but the number seemed to stop at 24. This appeared to correspond with the Protestant Bibles in the Old Testament but when the African began to help us order them we found they were following the TaNaKh."

"What's the TaNaKh?" asked Ruth.

"The Hebrew Bible, the one known to Jesus or Yeshua as he was known during his time on earth."

"How is the TaNaKh different?"

"Well, for one thing the text is read from right to left instead of the way we are used to reading, left to right. That's the first thing but the books are also ordered differently. The first five books are known as the Torah or the Books of Moses. The second set are the Prophets, know in Hebrew as Nevi'im. The final collection are the Writings, called Ketuvim."

"Why is the order in which the books are presented so important?" inquired Ruth.

"You like to play around with writing software don't you?"

"Yes."

"What happens if the program is run out of sequence?"

"It doesn't work."

"Precisely," smiled Samuelson. "That is why we have been so careful in the way we have reconstructed the text we have received. As a boy I remembered hearing stories about how when each new Jewish community began to grow and become separated, another sacred scroll had to be produced. If even one error was made the document was destroyed."

"That's pretty rough. Couldn't it be corrected?"

"No," Samuelson responded. "There were many attempts over the centuries to try and ensure the text didn't contain any errors but that was not always possible. Initially, the Bible stories only existed in oral form but were eventually written in a range of different languages but were also scribed in Aramaic. Still there were many movements to ensure the Holy Texts was recorded in the correct form and sequence. The powers of this world continuously attempted to muddy the waters and the text slowly became corrupted. But we are in the End Times and the world has gone far away from God. So much so that most do not hear him call."

"What about the people gathered here?" Ruth asked.

"They are the few," remarked Samuelson. "The small drop in

the ocean who have listened and attempted to transcribe the visions they have seen."

"So how come the text you knew as a boy and the material in the androids' database is not the text in the TaNaKh?" wondered Ruth.

"The TaNaKh we have been using to compare the text we have been receiving has closely matched to the Masoretic text, as I said early, it contains 24 books, not 39 as there is in the Protestant Bible."

"How come there are so many more books in the Protestant Bible?" asked Ruth.

"Because of the way they were originally grouped instead of the way they were reconfigured for the Greek Septuagint."

"What's that?"

"The Septuagint was arranged into four categories of literary value; historical, poetical, wisdom and prophetical. Not only that, but several books such as Samuel, Kings and Chronicles were split into two books, giving the impression there were six books instead of three. In the TaNaKh the first seven books of the Nevi'im are the main Prophets followed by an eighth book containing all the 12 minor prophets. This is counted as one book and not 12."

"How do you know this is the way the text should be presented? Do you know you can trust the African?" stressed Ruth.

"I have no reason to doubt him," answered Samuelson. "He has always been honest with me and as I said before, he is a spirit, an angel, God's messenger."

"Is there anything else you have been able to cross reference?"

"Yes," replied Samuelson. "In the New Testament, Jesus spoke about the Pharisees not practising what they preached. He had longed to gather his people but they were being led astray by the teachers of the law and the priests in the temple. The temple was sacred but the priests and lawyers were more concerned with their riches, making the people make oaths by the gold, not of the temple. He called them hypocrites for being more concerned with materialistic wealth instead of being more concerned with justice, mercy and faithfulness."

"But how does this relate to the structure or positioning of the books in the Bible?" puzzled Ruth.

"Because," continued Samuelson. "Jesus then went on to explain how God had sent his messengers, the prophets to bear witness and that the people of this world in their wickedness would slaughter them. Effectively, condemning themselves to hell."

"And how does this relate to the correct structure of scripture?"

"In both Luke and Matthew there is reference to Jesus saying that upon the wicked shall come the righteous blood shed on earth, from the blood of Abel up to Zacharias. Abel was the first person murdered by his brother Cain in the book of Genesis and Zacharias was stoned to death by the mob outside the temple after he had spoken God's words of retribution because they had forsaken him. Abel's death is described in chapter four of Genesis while Zacharias' death is mentioned in the book of Chronicles. We belief that this reference refers to the text of the bible. It is the key to what is contained within it. If this is the only text to be used and we use the Septuagint then only the first 14 books of the Bible should be included but all the books of the Protestant Old Testament are included in the Hebrew text and are considered to be Canonical by both traditions. But only the TaNaKh is ordered in such a way that the Bible is structure beginning with Genesis and ending with Chronicles."

"So how soon do you think all the text will be in place?"

Samuelson looked concerned, "I had estimated about two months for the Old Testament. There are still fragments coming in. But we have barely started getting all the New Testament together."

"How come?"

"Everything we have that appears to be the New Testament directly relates back to the TaNaKh and the way the Bible should be correctly constructed."

"How long do you think it will take to finish?" asked Ruth.

"It seems no matter what, we may only have a couple of days."

CHAPTER THIRTY NINE

A Chinook helicopter thundered overhead, its double set of rota-blades consumed Daniel's view. The heavy machine landed on the road between two large mansions in front of Rothstein's house. A short distance away Daniel and his team were hiding in some shrubs.

"It won't be long before we are discovered," whispered Anders. "Daniel, there's a large building to the west of the city."

Matthew pointed towards a dark shape on the horizon which had two spires at one end and a tower at the other. Daniel turned from looking at the Chinook to the indicated building.

"A cathedral," Matthew stated. "If I remember right that's a Holy place. A place of sanctuary."

"How do you know that?" asked Daniel.

"Samuelson and the African used to talk about them," Matthew answered.

"We'll head there," Daniel instructed.

"Why can't we go back the way we came?" wondered Anders.

Daniel pointed back towards the road. The Chinook was perched directly over the maintenance cover they had ascended through. At the rear of the craft the ramp was being lowered. To his surprise Daniel could see Reeves shaking hands with Rothstein. In Reeves's hand was the laptop.

"Oh my God."

"What's wrong," asked Stephen.

"Reeves' has Ruth's laptop."

"And," puzzled Stephen.

"It contains Ruth's AI system from her flat, Victoria."

"I installed the AI software into one of the androids a few days ago," added Matthew. "Your girlfriend didn't seem to appreciate it."

Matthew was a little put out.

"But it also contains the work Ruth had been doing on the text."

"Does that matter?" asked Stephen.

"It might, depending on what Reeves plans to do with it. We have to stop him." Daniel snatched the rifle from Stephen's hands and began to aim at Reeves who climbed on board the Chinook.

"Don't be stupid, Daniel," Stephen snapped. "You'll give our position away."

Stephen forced the muzzle to the ground.

"But he'll get away."

"Be patient," reassured Stephen. "Other opportunities will come."

The ramp door was raised and the craft began to throttle up for take off.

There was a white flash and compression to Daniel's ears that confused him. Then he felt his right cheek begin the smart as he scrapped the dirt. He blinked and saw the Chinook's underbelly loom overhead and away. He was still confused. There were trees flashing by and a dark blue nearly black sky above him with stars playing peak-a-boo amongst the leaves. What was going on?

Then a high pitch clatter, a sort of splutter of explosions close by. Some kind of whizzing noise and the sound of splintering wood. He looked up to see two men grasping his arms and tugging him along the ground. He stretched his head forwards to see a third man firing the rifle. How did he get that?

The man's chest exploded to Daniel's left. Blood smothered his view as he felt his own spine crash against the hard tarmac. The man on his right, Stephen. That's right, his name was Stephen. He remembered. And, yes, yes, the other one was, was, um. His name was? Ma... Maths. No, but something like that.

Another white flash. Stephen was catapulted over Daniel's head. Matthew. Why is Stephen over there? Oh, he's escaping through the hole in the wall. Where did that come from? Must follow.

Daniel crawled through the hole barely two feet high. He heard the sound of something riddle against the masonry on the side he had just come from. Stephen was sitting against another wall about six feet away.

"Stephen?"

Stephen's left hand was raised slightly. Blood streamed down his face from his forehead. His shirt coat was also soaked.

"Can you see it, Daniel?" muttered Stephen.

He raised his hand to point at something. Daniel scrambled to his side. He turned to see what his companion was pointing at.

"The clouds are opening," exclaimed Stephen.

Daniel could only see the dark sky and twinkling stars. The Chinook was half way across the city. Reeves had escaped.

"Its a portal to Heaven," Stephen smiled. "I see the most beautiful being. She has wings of gold."

Stephen reached out his hands but Daniel still could see nothing.

"The pain has gone, Daniel."

Daniel could hear the air racing out of Stephen's lungs, his body relaxed and his arms fell to his sides.

"Can you see them?"

"No, sir. They've gone through the wall."

"How many?"

"At least two but I'm sure I hit the one pulling the other."

"And you're sure there were only four?"

"Positive, sir. One over by the shrubs where we first saw them on thermo, the second is here and two more. Both are injured."

Rothstein stood by the officer's looking at the small handheld screen with the image from a small thermo camera the officer held in his other hand.

"You know we have more compact versions of that. You just

wear them like glasses," explained Rothstein.

"Budgetary cuts, sir," replied the officer. "We're having to use old stock."

"Maybe that's why you've lost some of them?"

Behind them an electrically driven transit van pulled up. On the side was the 1NWO-News logo. The passenger doors slid open and Annie Moore stepped out. Rothstein smiled. As he began to make his way over to her, the sound of clattering feet drew his attention away.

"Dad," called Robert.

"Well?" Rothstein demanded as two young men approached him.

"The bets are getting good," answered Albert.

"It seems there is only one left," replied his father.

"Excellent, that'll bring the stakes up high," laughed Robert. "Perhaps to two billion euro. Could you plug it on TV?"

Rothstein smiled at his sons.

"Good work, see how much more you can squeeze?"

The two younger men raced back towards the house, while their father turned his attention to Annie Moore. Beside her a technician had a palmcorder trained on the reporter. From the back of the van an engineer put his thumb up, as the satellite dish on the vehicle's roof locks onto a target in space.

"Ready to go in ten," stated the technician.

"Okay, Gary. Hi Mr. Rothstein, ready to go?" She gave him a broad smile.

"Seven, six, five, four, three." The remaining countdown was in finger signals, Annie smiled into the camera and nodded for about five seconds.

"That's right Gerry. Local sources indicate fifteen terrorists had penetrated the area. All indications are they were plotting to blow up many of the houses here, belonging to some of the world's wealthiest people." Again she paused and listened to the voice in her ear.

"That's is correct. Daniel Perez is the ring leader and has

managed to evade capture. Sources here say his military training is making him an effective adversary. With me here is Mr. Donald Rothstein, chief executive of Statesman Electronics, one of our leading computer conglomerates."

She turned away from the camera to Rothstein. The camera operator followed her gaze.

"Mr. Rothstein, I believe your company has a wager with one of your oriental clients to see who can capture Perez first?"

"Yes, that's right Annie," Rothstein beamed. "We see this as an opportunity to develop our entertainment franchise across the world. Poles indicate that audiences love this form of sport."

Daniel crawled through a fence and tried to catch his breath. Not far away he was alarmed by the sound of running boots. The cool air and accentuated sounds forewarned of rain. A helicopter darted across the sky above him and turned sharply. The on board search light snapped on, caught Daniel at the centre of its beam. Inside the cockpit, the pilot armed his weapons ready to fire.

"Target acquired, going live."

"Disengage," crackled the radio.

"What, are you serious?" screamed the pilot in disbelief.

"Disengage, that's an order," repeated the voice over the radio. "Corporate guys are taking over. Return to base."

The pilot flipped the firing lock back on.

Daniel closed his eye anticipating the end but all he heard was the sound of the helicopter pulling away. As he opened his eyes, the searchlight had been extinguished and the death machine was flying back towards the city.

Inside his chest, Daniel's heart pumped hard. He scanned the area, then certain his escape was clear, focused on the cathedral and headed for sanctuary.

CHAPTER FORTY

The moonlit street was almost lifeless except for the shadow of a man racing his way towards the cathedral. The large industrial buildings had seen better days. Weeds grew through the tarmac and between the bricks. There were no windows. Metal frames were all rusty and at sometime there had been a massive fire that had scorched the walls and metal frames.

Daniel could hear the echo of his feet as he raced towards his goal. Then he stopped, his attention snapped to something coming from behind. He listened then scrambled towards an opening that led to a cellar.

Seconds later the roar of an engine burst into the street. The four Rothstein boys sped along the road in a four-wheel drive. All were dressed in combat fatigues. Harry and David sat loading an assortment of weapons, from small arms to rocket launchers. Albert was the driver while Robert scanned the area with a thermal system. "Nothing on the screen at the moment. This street is clear."

"I heard there's a Japanese team on its way," Harry called out.

"Where did you hear that?" shouted Albert over the sound of the diesel engine.

"Dad said something about it just before we left."

Harry looks at his watch. "They should be here in about twenty minutes."

"Who are they?" wondered Albert.

"They're guests of dad's," answered David. "Part of an annual board meeting he's got on. They've come over with some pretty heavy systems to try and sell to the government. They see this as an opportunity to do a demo."

"Great," cheered Robert. "Some competition."

The four-wheel drive roared off out of sight.

Daniel cautiously looked out from his hiding place. As he made ready to race on another sound caught his attention. A helicopter. This one a TV eye-in-the-sky. Daniel darted down out of sight again until the helicopter had disappeared.

In the underground basilica nearly two thousand people, refugees and custodians of the book had gathered. There was a large choir singing. At the centre was a pool of clear blue water. Ruth was one of thirty women and ten men dressed in white being led to their baptism.

A gun battle was being raged as Daniel approached the cathedral square. The four brothers were lit up by their weapon muzzle flashes. On the far side of the square five Japanese men fired back with equal ferocity. Above them the TV helicopter broadcast the conflict images to the world. Daniel kept low, attempting to move around the perimeter of the square to find a way into the cathedral.

Samuelson stood up, before the subterranean congregation as the choir finished their hymn.

"Dear friends, we have gathered here today, to bring these men, women and children into the body of Christ. To be born in the Spirit. We are born of flesh and therefore are corrupt and cannot please God as we live in sin."

Empty shells cascade out of red hot barrels and their content screamed across the square from the Japanese towards the brothers. Likewise, scorching death rained in the opposite direction, extinguishing the life of one oriental. Daniel made a dash towards the cathedral.

"In this state we continue to commit many acts of evil," informed Samuelson. "Our Lord Jesus tells us that: No-one can enter the kingdom of God unless he is regenerated and born anew of water and of the Holy Spirit."

Daniel pulled open the cathedral's main doors. The four

brothers trained their weapons on his position. The whole cathedral was ablaze with light. Where once there had been pews, there were rows of giant networked computers. Where an altar had stood, it had been replaced by a monolithic mainframe computer, set as though being worshipped by the others in a parody of Christian observance. The whole place buzzed with the sound of electricity.

"Let us call upon God the Father," called out Samuelson to his congregation in the underground basilica, "through our Lord Jesus Christ that the goodness he will grant these people that which by nature they cannot have."

Ruth, with a nervous smile, stood with the others in anticipation.

"That they may," continued Samuelson, "be baptised with water and the Holy Spirit: and be received into Christ's Holy Church."

In the cathedral, embedded in the arches, like gargoyles, mechanical spider-like robots were activated. Sharp knives extended and red sensors were switched on. Each began to move down the walls towards Daniel.

"Intruder alert. Neutralise," squawked a computised female voice.

Around the cathedral red lights begin to flash and more mechanical spiders plucked themselves out of the walls. The large doors crash shut and Daniel's only escape seemed to be on the other side of the monolith. He raced towards it.

"Do you reject Satan?" asked Samuelson.

His congregation responded in unison, "We do."

Daniel raced onto the few steps leading up to the monolith. He turned to see dozens of mechanical spiders scurry closer.

"Do you reject all his works?"

"We do."

All the spiders froze.

"Do you reject the vain pomp and glory of this world?" asked

Samuelson.

"We do."

Behind Daniel the monolith began to morph into a large bug-like creature.

"Do you reject all covetous and carnal desires of the flesh?"

"We do," replied the congregation.

Daniel slowly turned to see the oncoming menace. With the danger behind motionless, he spun around and began to run in the opposite direction but the bug lunged forward and grasped him in a metal talon.

"And will you not follow or be led by them?"

"We will not."

Daniel was held by the neck mid-air, his arms and legs flapping as he struggled to break free.

"Do you believe in God the Father Almighty," called out Samuelson in the basilica. "Maker of heaven and earth? And in Jesus Christ his only begotten Son our Lord?

"We do."

The bug drew Daniel in close to examine him.

"And that he was conceived by the Holy Spirit: born of the Virgin Mary: that he suffered under Pontus Pilot, was crucified, dead and buried;"

Daniel gasped for air, then his limbs went limp.

"That he went down into hell and did rise again on the third day, ascended to heaven and sits at the right hand of God the Father Almighty."

The bug released Daniel and he fell to the ground lifeless.

"And from there he shall come again at the end of the world."

There came a large explosion, sending debris across the cathedral. The bug snapped its small head toward the distraction. Through a large hole in the wall, the Japanese hit squad burst in, weapons blazing. The swarm of spiders instantly became activated, then raced towards the new threat.

"To judge the living and the dead?"
"We do," replied the congregation in the basilica.

In the cathedral, the large bug leapt at the intruders, decapitating one and disembowelling another.
"Do you believe in the Holy Spirit?"
"We do."

Daniel remained motionless on the floor. A light appeared above him and formed into the African.

"Do you believe in on Holy Apostolic Universal Church; the Communion of Saints?"

The angel leaned over Daniel, close to his ear.
"In the remission of sins; the resurrection of the flesh and eternal life after death?" asked Samuelson.
The African whispered to Daniel, "do you?"
A wisp of mist floated from the African's hand and made its way into Daniel's nostrils. He suddenly gasped in breath and his heart began to beat.
"I do," Daniel replied.
"Then get to your feet and run. Quick," the angel commanded.
Daniel jumped to his feet and raced passed the bug as it

dispatched the third and forth member of the Japanese hit squad. The African had gone. Daniel sprinted through the gaping hole caused by the explosion, several of the mechanical spiders gave chase. Once Daniel was through the wall there came the sound of static and clicks. All the spiders stopped their pursuit and began to rebuild the damaged wall.

With adrenalin pumping through his system, Daniel found himself charging passed the four brothers. None, however, took any notice of him.

"Is Albert dead?" whimpered Harry. "I didn't mean to shoot him. He got in the way when the Japs flew by. Honest."

Robert stopped doing C.P.R. and, in a rage, knocked Harry to the ground.

Ruth looked around the silent world of blues and greens, of bubbles and her hair floating in slow motion around her head and body. Then she looked up towards the surface. An age had seemed to pass.

Samuelson stood beside her as she came back into the cool air.

"I baptise you in the name of the Father, Son and Holy Spirit."

Ruth saw there were five others waiting for their turn. One by one each of the last group were baptised. Then to everyones' surprise a great light appeared in the roof of the basilica. A mighty warrior stood amongst them and greeted the African, before turning to the rest of the congregation.

"Do not be afraid," said the angel. "You have chosen the Word above all others. Your reward is in heaven. Our Lord has given you his Word. Now is the time to make it known once more to this fallen world. It is another chance for the people to repent their transgressions. But time is short. A great tribulation nears."

"What is this great tribulation?" pleaded Samuelson.

The man clothed in linen turned to him and said, "in the Book of Daniel it is written, *'From the time that the daily sacrifice is abolished and the abomination that causes desolation is set up, there will be 1,290 days. Blessed is the one who wants for and reaches the end of the 1,335 days."*

The intensity of light grew briefly, causing many to shield their eyes. When they lowered their arms or hands, there was no further sign of the apparition.

CHAPTER FORTY ONE

It was a sudden sense of awareness that startled Victoria, a sense of colour and also of weight. Orange, somewhat dirty in tone, filled her vision. There were also blotches of pale yellow, brighter in the centre but blurring into the darker shades at the edges, where the two colours merged. She still had not got used to the metal body she had been uploaded to and wondered if the damage she had received during the attack had perhaps caused such a trauma that the mechanism was no longer capable of functioning.

The greatest frustration was not being able to see as she had before. However, she was also sensing something new. Warmth. She was aware of a low heat and a tingling sensation. Had she been upgraded? The metal body had sensors that allowed her to gauge the air temperature and also to ensure her internal motors were not overloading. She could also remember that Ruth's showers often changed from cold to hot but this was mostly calculations of different readings and computations rather than a sense.

Ruth's body had seemed warm when Victoria had been lying on the floor after a fall. The mechanical body had been so clumsy to control, Victoria often found herself needing assistance to get back onto her feet.

It was Ruth wasn't it? Victoria thought. Of course it was, who else could it have been?

When Ruth had come to her aid, the silicon skin around Victoria exoskeleton had included sensors to determine softness and hardness of materials she came into contact with. An additional upgrade had also given her an awareness of heat or the lack of it. If the temperature was too cold or too hot, an electronic spark was shot through to the central processing unit, to jolt Victoria into rapidly moving her arm, leg, hand or body away from the area of danger. Whereas previously, there was no sense of danger when she was contained inside the apartment, she had picked up an under-current of anxiety from her other self, just prior to communications being terminated. The Internet described this sense as being what the humans called sorrow.

Within this new body, Victoria was beginning to have similar anxieties. It came from within the middle of what she perceived to be where her fuel cell must be. Audibly, she heard a gurgling noise and at precisely the same moment felt a sensation in that area. It startled her. She decided to run a diagnostic on the entire system of the exoskeleton to ascertain how much damage had been inflicted upon the android. There was a tingling sensation around the digits of her hands. Her internal programme traced out the visual grid which enveloped her body. To her surprise the wireframe grid rendered a female human form. She traced through each vertices. At the tips of the digits she sensed them grip tighter, then relax. This took a few moments to comprehend. What did she mean 'relax'? Surely she meant the digits to be opened. She sent the signal once more, she could feel the tips of her digits squeeze into the fleshy palms. She also noticed the light tingling sensation both in the tip of her digits and also on the palm. It was pleasurable but also almost unbearable, almost painful.

An image flashed into her consciousness of Daniel using his fingers to rapidly slide them back and forth across the skin on Ruth's body. She would laugh hysterically and try to escape his assault. Ruth was not in pain but in ecstasy. Victoria swirled the tip of her middle digit around the palm of her hands and again the sense of pleasure sent a ripple up her arms into her body. She shivered. There was another contraction, this time in the feet region. The toes had contracted inwards, or, she scanned down her legs to her toes. Yes, they had curled up and her legs had swung up into her body, her knees were touching her chest. But the impact of her legs against her body had been cushions by two spherical sacks that seemed to extrude from the body.

She once more scanned through her memory banks. There was a video clip from a security camera that monitored Ruth's shower room. It had been saved because Ruth had gone into the shower when the temperature was too high and had burnt her skin, her reflexes had jolted her out of the shower unit, she had slipped and knocked herself unconscious, requiring emergency treatment. However, prior to the accident, the video had shown Ruth undress, removing all her garments. Her skin was very pinkish and as Ruth looked into the mirror she had complained of excess fat around her stomach area and above her hips. Ruth had also checked her legs and was disgusted with the cellulite that had amassed. She had held up her mammary glands and muttered about them not being perky any more. When she let them go they just sagged a little.

Victoria scanned through her archived data on human physiology. The female mammary glands extruded out far more than the male model. She moved her own arms, applied the same principles she had learnt with her metal chassis. Her hands reached up towards her chest and the tingling sensation was hard to suppress. However, the sensitive area of her palms finally rested up on the soft pads in front of the chest cavity. She could feel the flexible texture of the skin that encased a jelly like substance and a sack. The information in her database informed her that the materials that made up the structure of the female human breast consisted of an outer skin, a slightly more textured nipple, over fatty tissue, lobules and ducts that were used to secrete nutrients to an infant after the reproductive cycle. Why?

Why was she now encased within a human body, a female human body? She still could only see the orange tones and blue blotches. Eyelids. Humans have eyelids that close over their spherical cameras to help clean dust and particles, and to keep the light out during sleep mode. What did she need to do now to open these eyelids?

On the wireframe mesh, Victoria located where the eyes were and detected a collection of control points. On both eyes there were options to either open or close the eyes together or individually. Victoria selected both eyes for opening. As the two folds of skin begin to slowly part, the orange blur was replace by a white circular blob. Briefly everything was blurred and without thinking, the eyes' reflexes pulled the image into focus. The visuals were instantly transmitted to Victoria's central processing unit and she could see. She quickly found that she could rotate up, down and side to side to scan around the room. Every six seconds or so she noted the eyelids, for a fraction of a second closed and opened. A secretion of salty liquid helped to lubricate the eyeball.

Victoria found herself looking up at a ceiling. She could also see the tops of her knees pressing against 'her' human breasts. Her arms were now wrapped around her legs. She released them and allowed her legs to straighten out flat. Then she became uncomfortable. It had nothing to do with a physical sensation but something inside. She could see her stomach and on down to a patch of hair, on to her thighs, her knees and further to her toes. There was an urge to cover up the fleshy frame she now found herself in. She recognised that she was experiencing an emotion. She was embarrassed to be completely naked.

She leant forward, arched her back and saw a white sheet that must have been kicked off when she raised her legs. She grabbed it with her right hand and pulled it across her body. There were goosepimples all across her skin and she could feel the temperature in the room was quite cool, almost cold.

Something flapped down across her shoulders and she could see long strands of hair. She felt it with her fingers. It was soft. She rubbed the strands between her index finger and thumb. How natural all these movements seemed to be. So similar to how she had learnt to operate the metallic construct of a humanoid body over the past few days.

Then she wondered how long she had actually been lying on the table. She swung her legs round and down. Her feet did not reach the floor but were about seven inches away. The white sheet partially stayed where it had been folded around the mattress. The cool air in the room soon had all the hairs on the body's skin rise. With a few gentle tugs Victoria loosened the sheet from the end of the bed and the folds of white linen fell against her feet. She wrapped the cloth around her body, then played back in her mind a video clip of Ruth doing the same with a towel after a shower and was surprised at how instinctively her actions were in replicating Ruth's movements. It was almost as if the body remembered these actions from before. Victoria wondered where the body had come from? Had it been genetically produced and manufactured to house the AI mind of a computer? She was also curious to see what the face looked like and whether she would be pleased with her shape and model in the same manner Ruth had wanted her body to be. A video clip, with audio, replayed Ruth exercising in her apartment lounge trying to keep her stomach muscles firm.

Victoria looked down at the linen covered stomach, opened the cloth and peaked at the pinkish-yellow stomach of the body that now housed her. It seemed quite firm, it seemed similar to how Ruth had wanted to look. Then Victoria realised that she was less aware of her body's functions and as soon as she decided to do something the body reacted reflexively. Some hair fell in front of her eyes as she looked down and she thought of lifting the strands with her right index finger. The right arm instantly raised the hand so the extended index finger could gentle scoop the strands of hair away from her eyes. She hooked the hair behind her ear and could sense the tingling as her fingers glided across the top of her ear.

Another thought struck her, how odd it was that she was now contextualising this body as being hers. It seemed to belong to her. It was her. Then the notion swiftly vanished as she spied a glass reflection of the room. She had found a mirror and could look into it to see what she looked like.

Her heart began to race and she could feel her hands shaking. Ruth had said this was nerves, a reaction to something she had been worried about when they lived in the flat. It could simply be starting a new job, seeing a new boyfriend, concern over being able to pay the bills and being able to retain the flat. Ruth always seemed to be worried about something and always complained of butterflies in her stomach. How on earth did these insects get inside her stomach? Victoria prepared to move herself in front of the mirror and glimpsed her new form for the first time, she sensed fear. What if I don't like what I have become? What if the face is disfigured and I haven't detected this yet? What if... there was nothing for it, she had to pluck up the courage to stand so she could see her reflection. Where did that notion come from?

"I'll just have to take a few deep breaths and calm myself," Ruth stated in another video clip. How many clips had Victoria stored in her memory banks since she was first programmed to take care of Ruth? There must be millions and she was able to recall them all instantly.

Victoria took in a deep breath to fill her lungs and slowly exhaled. Then went through the same route twice more before she felt confident enough to step in front of the mirror. The face was so familiar but not from the perspective she was now gazing. There before her looking quite startled, was a reflection of Ruth. Victoria saw her own hand rise up to touch the cheeks of the young girl she had see grow from a child into a woman. She was inside that young woman's body and was now calling it her own.

Victoria felt the heart beat rapidly rise. Blood flushed into her cheeks. The temperature rose and she felt as though her head would explode. Then everything went black.

CHAPTER FORTY TWO

"Has the body rejected the programme?" grunted Reeves.

"No, sir," replied the research engineer. He punched at a keyboard. "Sensors indicate she has gone into shock. I think Victoria has fainted."

"Why?"

The scientist turned to Reeves. "Well, how would you feel if you woke up in a cloned version of your brother or father?"

"But she's a machine, Millar. Why should that bother her?"

"She is selfaware, sir." He broke off for a moment or two. "We need to get a medic in there. She's got concussion."

An intercom was switched on. "Medics to cell 11, emergency. Patient has been injured. Priority Red."

"I thought you said the clone was in perfect condition," Reeves ranted.

"It is, sir," complained the scientist. "Look, we've had the drone in storage for about three months, it's been working fine. It just takes a little longer than you've requested for the DNA adjustments to morph the drone into the target specimen."

"How long?" demanded Reeves.

"It usually takes 28 days for the specimen DNA to fully transform the drone into an exact copy of the donor. In just eleven hours there could be severe malformations."

"But will it be able to perform?"

"Early data indicates at this rapid growth rate, the acceleration drugs will have the clone expire in roughly six days."

"Okay," Reeves shook his head. "That should be enough

time. Can you prepare a duplicate, just in case?"

"This is highly irregular."

"Yes, but can it be done?"

"What about the funding implications?"

"They'll be covered."

Millar rubbed his temples and sighed. "Yeah, okay, we'll bake another."

"Good, let me know when this one is operational. I need her in three hours time."

Reeves made his way to the door.

"But sir, that's just stretching..."

"I'm not interested. Get it ready. You have three hours." Reeves snapped. "You know, Millar. If I didn't know better, I would say you were getting too close to these things. Your judgement is becoming clouded."

Millar turned away. "Sorry, sir. There's not a problem. This clone will be ready in three hours and another will be prepped."

"Good," smiled Reeves. "Then there is nothing more to say."

Samuelson sat at his desk watching thirty teams frantically entering data into the network. Donald Anderson looked scruffy, with his tie hung lose around his neck, as he raced up to Samuelson.

"Excuse me, sir. Um, we are having difficulties finding enough resources to complete the work."

"Don't worry so much, Donald. Everything we need will be provided for, no matter how hard it seems to get."

A young woman stood up and turned to the two men.

"Excuse me, sir."

"Yes, Angie," Donald answered.

"Sorry, sir, but my computers crashed again and the hard drive has been wiped."

"Okay, I'll be over shortly to sort it out."

Angie turned and sat down some what dejected.

"We're running out of systems, Samuelson. Each crash

destroys days of work. Our back up systems are struggling to take the strain."

Samuelson smiled. "Have faith, Donald."

Anderson shrugged his shoulders and turned to make his way back to Angie.

Ruth stood up from one of the groups and made her way over to Samuelson. She looked anxious.

"Hi, Ruth. What's up?"

"There's something puzzling me about the numbers and the text we've been finding."

"In what way?" asked Samuelson.

"It's as though there is another dimension missing. You know like a puzzle and there's a piece missing."

"In what way?"

"I'm not sure but back at my flat I have a decryption programme that produces 3D images. I'd like to try it out on what we are getting here."

"How important do you think this is?" pondered Samuelson.

"It could be crucial, but I won't know until I try it out," Ruth answered.

"I'm not sure if we should take the risk," Samuelson replied in a low uneasy voice.

"But if we are wrong?" suggested Ruth. "It could be the most important thing we have to do?"

Samuelson reluctantly nodded. "Okay."

A short time later, Ruth found herself making her way through the wastelands once classed as suburbia. She was one of a group of six, evenly split between men and women. They were armed with pistols and a couple of rifles.

Suddenly the crack of a machine gun disturbed the silence, two of the men fell to the ground dead, while the rest remained quaking in a nearby ditch. Bullets began to riddle the whole area around them.

Tears filled Ruth's eyes as she pushed herself further into the wall of dirt. A mortar bomb exploded nearby throwing more dirty over her.

"What is it, James" screamed Ruth to the only man alive.

"A small remote controlled flying weapons carrier, Miss," he answered.

"Is there anyway of knocking it out?"

"Not with what we've got, Ms. Whitby."

Ruth's brow furrowed. Another explosion forced her to clamp her ears with her hands and squeeze her eyes tightly shut.

"What'll we do?" screamed Ruth.

"Pray," came the reply from one of the two women. Ruth looked at her as though in shock. "Okay."

Ruth frantically scanned the area then stared at the two women. "I don't know your names. What's your names?"

"Sally," said one woman.

"Jean," called out the other.

There came a third explosion. Ruth was showered with debris.

A fourth explosion came from the direction of the remote weapons carrier. Then there was silence. Dust particles floated on the air, gradually settling on the ground.

"Jean," whispered Sally. "You okay?"

Jean coughed out some dust. "Yeah, I thinks so. Can you see Ruth?"

Through the smog, Sally desperately tried to see if there was any sign of Ruth. She was too scared to leave her shelter. Finally, enough dust had cleared for Ruth to be seen twenty metres away as they huddled together.

"Ruth?" Sally called. "Ruth, can you hear me?"

Suddenly, there was movement, then coughing and Ruth sat up about ten metres from where she had been.

"Yes, I'm okay," called out Ruth.

"You must have been blown quite some distance by the last blast?" puzzled Jean.

"Just a few bruises," Ruth replied.

"Any sign of James?" quizzed Sally.

"Who?" replied Ruth.

"Look, just sit there, you may have concussion." ordered Sally.

Sally frantically scanned the area for James but saw no sign of him. Then she spied an area of red but next to nothing else. The sight made her gag and she threw up.

"Guess he didn't make it," commented Jean.

"It's gone quiet," noted Sally.

They watched Ruth as she tried to see if there was any movement around the ruins but detected nothing. She looked back towards the two women only to find the sunlight being blocked. Ruth gazed up to see a silhouetted form standing over her. She reacted by frantically attempting to push herself backwards with her feet but soon realised the wall prevented her from moving any further.

"Give me your hand," came the gruff voice. Timidly, she responded by offering the stranger her hand. Instantly, she was pulled to her feet and as her eyes adjusted from looking into the sun she recognised the face before her.

"Daniel! Is that you?"

"Ruth, we need to get out of here. There's another craft close by and it'll see the smoke."

"Okay," she replied and went to turn away but Daniel reached out and grabbed her tunic then pulled her in close to his chest. He then wrapped his other arm around her shoulders and kissed her.

Ruth pulled back annoyed. Daniel was puzzled.

"We think she's got concussion," Sally called out to Daniel. "Come on we'll have to go."

The two women pulled at Daniel and Ruth, forcing them apart. All four kept themselves out of sight as they raced towards the end of the street. Ahead they could see the city's boundary and the gateway to Ruth's home borough.

Minutes later a second airbourne remote vehicle swooped

over the area where the first had gone down. The images were instantly fed back to a control centre.

"ARV113 is down, sir," reported a female COMs operator.

Reeves switch his video feed to receive the images from the ARV hovering over the incident site.

"Get some pictures from where the smoke is, over to the right."

"Yes, sir," replied the young woman.

The image on the screen tracked across the terrain, revealing further ruined buildings and a small pathway cutting through several houses. Amidst the fallen floors and gable walls lay the bodies of the two men.

"Intensify the search," commanded Reeves. "Double the active units in that sector. I want the city completely secured by 2100 hours."

"Sir, there's a fourth body down there," called out the young woman. "And we're getting a weak heat signature."

Twelve minutes later Ruth, Daniel, Sally and Jean found themselves near Ruth's old apartment. There were several police vehicles in the street at the front and one to the rear.

"What are we back here for, Ruth?"

"We need hardware and some of Ruth's software from inside," stated Sally

"That's a bit risky, isn't it," argued Daniel.

"We're getting to a critical stage," insisted Jean.

"Okay, but we must remain cautious," warned Daniel.

Again the group of three woman and Daniel moved closer to find a way in without being spotted. To all of their surprise, a score of police troopers raced out of the building and jumped into both parked vehicles. Within moments they were screeching out of the avenue.

"What do you think is going on?" asked Sally.

"I don't know," Daniel commented. "But I sure as hell don't want to spend more time than necessary waiting to find out."

He jumped to his feet and rushed towards the main entrance. The three women followed suit.

As they reached the main doors, Daniel signalled for them to halt.

"Okay, all clear," Daniel added. "Let's get in and out as quickly as possible.

It took an endless 120 seconds for them all to reach Ruth's front door. It had been kicked in and was still hanging half off its hinges. Inside everything had been strewn across the rooms. Virtually every piece of hardware had been stripped out. Ornaments had been broken and lay in pieces. Ruth fell to her knees and began to sob at the devastation she saw.

"It's not a good idea to stay any longer, Ruth," advised Daniel. "Come on, let's go."

"Not yet," snapped Ruth. "I need a couple of things."

"Make it quick, then."

Ruth began to search through her remaining items. She went from one room to another, lifted the odd thing or two and then dropped them as soon as she could not find what she was after.

"Hurry up, Ruth," barked Daniel.

"Nearly, there."

"What are you after?" puzzled Sally.

"Just a small solid state plastic card. About a centimetre square."

"That's like trying to look for a needle.."

"Don't say it. It doesn't help," smarted Ruth.

"Something's coming, Ruth," Daniel whispered. "We've got to go. Now."

Near to panic, Ruth raced over to a side cupboard and hit a panel. A door came out of the wall. Of what still remained on hangers, Ruth dragged to the floor. A small unseen red light came on at the back of the cupboard.

"Are we ready to go yet?" Daniel nervously called.

Ruth fingered her way through many of the garments until she found one, then ripped open a seam, letting a small item fall into her hand.

"Got it," she called.

Briefly, she was dazzled by the red light. She blinked and attempted to re-gauge her senses. Then raced out of the room to join the others to find the two women had gone on ahead and only Daniel had waited for her.

"I hope this has been worthwhile?"

"I promise you it will," replied Ruth.

Within moments they had both disappeared out of sight.

At the control centre, Reeves noticed on his console that a signal had come through from Ruth's apartment.

"It's time," remarked Reeves. "Activate the nuke, countdown two hours and fifteen minutes."

CHAPTER FORTY THREE

To the west the sun had reached the horizon. Long shadows were being cast back towards the gable walls and ruined buildings, allowing the group of four to be visually obscured. Over to the east, dark rain clouds were gathering. The wind had built up and Daniel noticed how clouds from the south east were rushing to collide with those in the north east.

"Could be a lightning storm," Daniel remarked.

"We're about a hundred metres from the entrance," whispered Sally.

"You okay, Ruth?" commented Daniel.

"Uh, oh, yeah, fine."

"Is something bothering you?"

"No, I'm okay."

Daniel took her hand a squeezed gently. Ruth looked up at him and smiled.

"Do you think we can do it?"

"What, put all the stuff together?"

"Yeah," she said. Daniel sensed a nervousness in her tone.

"Don't you?"

A tear ran down her cheek. She wiped it away with her free hand.

"It's just, so much has happened and I feel a little confused by it all. It's so overwhelming."

Daniel released her hand and place his arm around her shoulder and gave her a soft hug. Again she smiled.

"I'm sorry, I don't mean to..."

"It's okay."

Sally pulled open a metal cover in the ground and climbed down the chute. Jean beckoned to Daniel and Ruth to hurry up, then descended herself.

"We'll make it, I promise you. Everything'll be okay."

"How do you know that?" frowned Ruth.

"I just know," Daniel replied. "I just believe we will."

Deborah Chekhov slipped her way through a gathering of technicians and programmers clustered together reconciling data and punching it into the computers' keyboards. With determination she raced up toward Samuelson's desk.

"Samuelson, sorry to trouble you but I thought you should know that by 9pm we'll be ready to transmit the first edition."

"Great, globally?"

"Yes," Deborah smiled. "We've located enough distribution centres and e-mail addresses to get a copy to everyone on the network."

"What about those not in the system?" worried Samuelson.

"The message will automatically transmit on every system and an audible version will utilise every speaker. They'll hear it, no matter where they are."

Samuelson nodded and grinned.

"We've nearly accomplished it. Great work Deborah. You should be proud."

"I am."

"Any sign of Ruth?" Samuelson asked.

"Donald said they are making their way through security. Oh, and Daniel's with them."

"Deborah, do you think the gadget Ruth went for will make a difference?"

Deborah shook her head. "I really don't know. I think, just getting the text to make sense is the most important part of the project. I don't know how long the system can take the strain of what we are currently doing. I would recommend broadcasting what we have almost finish and see what happens."

"So what we have is error free?"

"The African says so?"

"Is there any possibility that Ruth's decipher might muck things up?"

"It's possible, but I don't think we have time to do much testing before hand."

"Hmm," pondered Samuelson. "Perhaps we should let things be?"

"It's up to you," replied Deborah. "What should I say to Ruth when she gets here?"

"Send her to me."

Twenty minutes later Daniel and Ruth were lead through to Samuelson. He stood and smiled at them, hugged Ruth and shook Daniel's hand.

"You made it back safely," smiled the big man.

"Not without some loses though," Ruth replied.

"But you found Daniel."

"He found us. Saved me, Sally and ... Jean."

"Did you get what you were looking for?" Samuelson sat down.

"Yes."

Samuelson tapped his fingers on the desk and bit into his lower lip.

"What's wrong, David?" asked Daniel.

Samuelson looked up at each of them. His eyes seemed to blink more than usual as he pondered on what to say.

"Has something happened?" Ruth enquired nervously. She looked first at Daniel and then back to Samuelson.

"Well?"

Samuelson took a deep breath. "We're not too sure how your decipher will fit into our system?"

"What do you mean?"

"The computers are struggling to cope as it is and we're nearly there. Just a few more chapters and Deborah reckons by 9 pm we'll be ready to broadcast."

"But don't you want to know what the 3D image is?"

"We don't have time."

"But, James and the others. They died so I could get this."

"I know but..." Samuelson slapped his hands against the desk and pushed himself up out of the chair.

"We have to get the material out there. There can be no more delays."

"Why not?" Ruth was in tears. Then she began to feel her knees go beneath her and she staggered into Daniel.

"Are you alright? What's wrong?" asked Daniel as he propped her up in his arms.

"Sorry, I just feel dizzy."

"What happened outside?" Samuelson was concerned.

"The group was shelled a few times," answered Daniel. "I wasn't sure if I was going to find anyone alive. But I found Ruth, Sally and Jean. The rest were dead."

"Were you followed back here?" insisted Samuelson.

"No, definitely not," snapped Daniel.

"Okay, take Ruth to the medical floor and take some rest yourself."

Daniel lead Ruth away from Samuelson's desk and took her towards the lifts. Samuelson plopped himself back down in his chair and sighed. Deborah seized the opportunity to speak to him.

"Samuelson, the African has asked to see you."

"What now?"

"He says, it's urgent. We may have been infiltrated."

The blood seemed to drain from Samuelson's face.

"Are you sure?"

"He's quite adamant about it."

"Did he say who?"

Deborah shook her head.

"What time is it?"

"2032 hours."

"Are we ready?"

"Yes, just the last few paragraphs are being typed in."

"As soon as they are finished, broadcast," Samuelson directed. "Don't wait for me, I'll go and see what the African has to say. Keep only those who you know have not left their posts in the past eight hours. Anyone acting suspiciously, get them out."

"How do you feel now?" asked Daniel. He helped Ruth onto a trolley bed.

"Still woozy."

A nurse pulled the light green curtains around the bed.

"The doctor will be in soon," the nurse stated, then looked sternly at Daniel. "And I'd suggest your gentleman friend lets you have a little bit of peace?"

"Don't go," pleaded Ruth.

"It's okay," reassured Daniel. "You need to rest."

"We need to get the 3D image deciphered."

"There'll be plenty of time, just rest." Daniel released her hand. There were tears in Ruth's eyes. She shook her head. Daniel drew close and hugged her.

"I must insist," the nurse stressed.

Ruth kissed the side of Daniel's face. Don't go far, promise?" she urged him.

"I'll be around, promise."

He kissed her forehead and pulled open the curtain so he could leave.

"Daniel?" Ruth called. He looked back through the curtains.

"I'll rest if you'll work on the image?"

"Do you promise?"

"I do," Ruth smiled.

He leant across to her. She slipped him a small pen drive and squeezed his hand closed.

"Thank you. This means so much to me. Just to be able to find out." Her smile broadened. Then she lay back and closed her eyes.

Daniel made his way out of the medical floor and on up towards the computer labs. Everyone was still frantically tapping in data. Fingers hammered away at keyboards. Secondaryproofers monitored all data and advised of any errors, making the operator correct them if any were detected. There seemed to be a focus bordering on psychosis. All appeared blind to Daniel's presence.

Eventually, at about eleven minutes to nine, Daniel found a consul unused. He sat down searched over the computer, then, found a slot and pushed the pen drive in. After a few moments a folder opened. Inside there were two files and a program. Daniel moved the cursor onto the program and double clicked. While it opened he looked across at the two file names. One was titled 'False Prophet' while the other was called 'Deliverance Promised'.

"Strange names," thought Daniel.

The program opened a window with instructions to drag the two files onto the program window. Daniel shrugged his shoulders and complied.

'WORMWOOD VIRUS ACTIVATED,' appeared on screen, and again.

'WORMWOOD VIRUS ACTIVATED,'
'WORMWOOD VIRUS ACTIVATED,'
'WORMWOOD VIRUS ACTIVATED,'
'WORMWOOD VIRUS ACTIVATED,'
'WORMWOOD VIRUS ACTIVATED,'
'WORMWOOD VIRUS ACTIVATED,'
'WORMWOOD VIRUS ACTIVATED.'

Daniel punched at the keyboard.

'ACCESS DENIED.'

He grabbed the power and Ethernet cables and ripped them out of the back of the computer. Instantly, the screen went dead and the hard drive stopped spinning.

"What the hell was that?" he shouted.

"Hey, my computer's gone down," screamed a woman across the aisle.

"Did you save the data?" called out a supervisor.

"I don't know, think so."

"Daniel, what have you done?" accused Deborah.

"I ... nothing," Daniel pleaded.

"Upload what we have, now!" Deborah ordered a technician. The man nearly jumped out of his skin before racing off to the transmission centre a corridor away.

"Arrest him and take him to the African," she instructed to other men.

Daniel began to struggle but a sharp pain to the back of his skull sent him into blackness. He could briefly remember flashes of images, reds, pinks, white, black, but nothing came into focus. He just knew he was being dragged and his feet were trailing behind him.

Perspiration began to form across Ruth's body. A fever had developed and her breathing had become rapid and shallow. She began to shiver. Her lips turned blue.

"I need a doctor here immediately," shouted the nurse. "This patient has gone into shock."

A doctor and three more nurses crowded around the bed.

"What's wrong with her?"

"I don't know. We thought she might have concussion but she didn't show any signs other than dizziness."

Ruth's body began to shake.

"Her blood pressure has dropped," another nurse shouted.

"Has she been injured?" a doctor asked.

"She was caught in several explosions but has no external injures. They must be internal."

"Check her pulse?"

"Hardly any."

"She's going into cardiac arrest."

"Get the defibrillator."

A nurse peeled off the backing of two adhesive pads, wired to the defibrillator, while a second nurse snipped off the buttons on Ruth's shirt and cut away her bra. An adhesive pad was placed below Ruth's clavicle on her right side, while the other electrode pad was placed above her left breast.

"Clear!"

Everyone stood away from the bed.

A button was pressed on the defibrillator. Almost instantly, a white flash lit up the entire medical area. Everything was vapourised. A shock wave punched through the whole of the underground complex.

Above ground, the surface jolted upwards ten metres before falling three metres below the original surface, up to a kilometre in diameter.

CHAPTER FORTY FOUR.

"Did we get the data before the blast?" demanded Reeves.

"Yes, sir," replied a male science office. "Every single piece they had saved."

"The blast didn't corrupt anything?"

"We're running diagnostics, but the virus was designed only to activate the bomb once the data was safely away."

"And the electromagnetic pulse, did it affect any of our systems?"

"EMP was minimal due to the explosion being underground," one scientist explained.

"The pulse was absorbed locally within a seventy kilometre radius. The shielding here prevented any damage to our own electronics. No data has been lost."

"And Ruth?"

"She's in the infirmary," reported a female COMs operator. "A patrol brought her back from where ARV113 went down."

"So the swap went okay. What's her condition?"

"Not good," replied COMs. "The doctor says she'll not make it through the night."

For a moment or two Reeves pondered on the information he had been given.

"Is her mind still okay?"

"It's active."

"Can it still solve problems?"

"For a limited time."

"Hook her up to simscom and make sure you feed her an avatar of herself as she was before her flat was destroyed."

In the infirmary Ruth was in a coma. Tubes were connected to various parts of her body feeding vital fluids keeping her alive. Her face was bloated with bruising making her features unrecognisable. Many of her bones were shattered and her internal organs were damaged. Several nurses checked her vitals and monitored readouts on computer scenes. The cubical door swung open and a doctor wheeled in a small trolley. A black box sat on top connected to a small keyboard and a glass dome on top. Green and reds LEDs blinked on and off but there appeared to be no monitor.

"What's that?" asked a nurse.

"A BCI," replied the doctor.

"A what?"

"A brain-computer interface."

"What's it for?"

"It creates a simulation of a familiar places the patient can rest in and help her recover."

"What are you going to use?"

"Her old apartment. We have Victoria's data banks. We can simulate her home and fool her mind into thinking she has just had a bad dream. It'll be more peaceful for her. Especially at the end."

"Why have we never used one before?" enquired the nurse.

"Special patient," replied the doctor. "Now, less chatter, lets get her hooked up."

A series of electrodes, sprouting from the BCI machine, were taped to Ruth's forehead, temples, parietal and occipital regions of her skull.

"Nurse, please pull the curtains around the patient."

Reeves bounded into the room all flustered after a brief run.

"Well?"

"She's nearly prepped, sir."

The doctor flipped open a previous hidden panel, which reveal a touch screen of about 175mm long by 100mm high. By pressing the left hand side, the screen lit up. His left index finger tapped a region in the middle of the screen and a holographic image was projects above the glass dome.

"We're ready," he stated.

Reeves nodded, the doctor press a green luminous rectangle on the touch screen. All nearly jumped out of their skins when Ruth arched her back upwards and groaned. Momentarily she held her position then as suddenly as before her body just relaxed, collapsing into the mattress.

"Okay, we're in," the doctor stated.

All eyes released their gaze on Ruth and focused on the holographic image.

At first there just seemed to be black, the red blobs with brown edges. Nothing was really in focus. Then came the sense of panic. Air rushed into her lungs and she sat bolt upright. Still nothing seemed to be in focus. Ruth rubbed her eyes. She felt a strange sense of hunger, fear, sorrow and unease.

For a moment or two she examined the room. Nothing seemed out of place. Everything was a she expected.

"Victoria?"

She listened for a response.

"Hello, Victoria," she sang out. Her head felt sore and she struggled to visualise the dream she had just had but it appeared evasive.

"Hey, Vicky. Where the hell are you? Answer me, damn it."

She was still trying to catch her breath. Her heart beat seemed loud in her chest. She checked her pulse, monitoring her wristwatch. The watch seemed slow, especially as she was counting nearly two beats per second and her heart seemed to be racing. The second hand still took two beats per second, perhaps three.

She remembered an old trick her grandfather had taught her. At least she thought it was her grandfather. She couldn't be sure. Anyway, he had told her, who ever it was, that a second lasted roughly the length of time it would take to say 'one one thousand'.

"One one thousand, two one thousand, three one thousand..." she continued on counting and keeping an eye on her watch. The second hand still seemed to be running too slowly. If it was right her heart would have been beating at about 180 beats per minute. But when she counted she found her heartbeats were corresponding to about one and a bit per second, about 75 to 80 beats per minute.

"Can you distract her, take her mind off the unusualness of her heart?" asked Reeves as he watched the hologram.

The doctor began to turn some holographic dials close to the 3D image. Briefly, Reeves saw a lingering image of the dial, semi-transparent as the doctor played with it in thin air. Once his hand moved away, the holographic dial melted away until it was needed again.

"Good morning, Ruth," chirped Victoria's voice.

Somewhat startled, Ruth jumped back up against the bedstead.

"Victoria! You scared me."

Ruth took in a deep breath.

"Where have you been? I've been calling you."

"Preparing your shower."

"Could you have spoken to me while you were doing that? Anyone would think you were ignoring me?"

"Is this necessary?" asked Reeves impatiently.

"She has to be orientated enough to believe her environment is real."

"Well, how long?"

"Give her a little more time. Victoria's data indicates once Ruth has showered she begins to relax and over breakfast likes to play around with puzzles or decode secret messages she has located on the net."

"So, how long?"

Reeves was only centimetres away from the doctor's face, quite intimidating.

"We can speed the process up. For us it will be a matter of moments but Ruth's perception will be that all has occurred in real-time. The images of Ruth became a blur as she entered the shower. Reeves was seeing her at sixty times normal speed.

Ruth noted the wall clock as she stepped into the shower cubicle. 8.15am. The steam in the shower soon made the glass doors translucent. Water particle raced down the glass panels and for a while Ruth enjoyed the needle prick pressure of the water jets striking the pores on her skin. Her lungs filled with air as she took in deep breaths and slowly released it. The beating sound of the shower gradually slowed down in her mind as time seemed to be endless. She was relaxed, calm and at peace. She revelled in the soothing drumbeats of water.

After many minutes, she lathered up some shampoo into her hair then, once the suds had been rinsed away, she lathered up some shower gel all over her body, then again allowed the steaming water jets to wash away the foamy soap.

By the time she was prepared to leave the cubicle she estimated she had spent some twenty extravagant minutes in the shower.

"Hey, Victoria? Are you not going to chastise me for my overindulgence?"

There came no answer.

"Hey, Victoria, are you ignoring me again?"

Still no reply.

"Okay, cold shoulder ah? Alright, just give me a towel, please?"

Nothing happened. Ruth slide the glass doors apart and looked out. No towel was being presented by any mechanical arm. Something must be wrong, Ruth thought. Then she took a quick glance at the wall clock. It still read 8.15am.

"Hey, Victoria, do the clocks run on batteries or are they mains supplied?"

Ruth stepped across the room and pushed a panel in the wall. A door was released and revealed a drawer full of white towels.

She took one and quickly dried herself off. Noticing the puddles of water she had left behind, she waited a moment or two to see if there were cleaning devices about to come. No mechanical robot came to clean up Ruth's mess. Somewhat annoyed, Ruth wiped out a second towel from the drawer and began to wipe up the footprints of water she had left behind.

"Hey, Victoria, why do I have to do all this housework? Aren't you supposed to do that?"

There was definitely something wrong. For as long as Ruth could remember, Victoria had always been there talking to her, correcting her and putting things right. This was not normal. Perhaps Victoria was malfunctioning, thought Ruth. That must be it.

It took another 15 minutes for Ruth to locate her underwear and other clothes. She was not happy with the combination she had found, a pair of brown jeans, purple pull-over and yellow blouse. Her underwear said Friday but she was certain it was Monday or possibly Tuesday. Finally, she found the hairdryer, a half broken comb and a mirror to dry her hair. In her estimation, the time should have been about 9.15am, or there about but when she saw the clock once more it said 8.16am.

The holographic images came back into focus for Reeves and the medical team.

"Why does she look so puzzled?" quizzed Reeves.

"Something must be confusing her," the doctor suggested. "Look, she's staring at the clock. Oh no, the matrix hasn't updated itself properly, it's kept real-time and not the time Ruth is experiencing. This could run up some major problems."

"Can you sort it?" asked Reeves, somewhat concerned.

"I don't know, we're rushing things too much.

"Okay, keep on going we don't have much choice. Can we get her distracted or lose her memory for the last hour or so?"

"Her vitals are dropping, I don't know how much time she's got?"

"So can we get on with it then?" stressed Reeves. "I need to know what she was planning with the software."

The doctor again manipulated some virtual dials close to the hologram.

Ruth suddenly paused and stared blankly at the wall in front of her. A sense of fatigue had suddenly gripped her and she lost any notion of where she was. She looked around and analysed what she had in the apartment. Most bits and bobs were hidden behind glass panels. She saw her own image reflected in the glass doors. Why was she here? She pondered. Where had she been before? She asked herself. Everything seemed jumbled up in her mind.

Then there appeared in her mind an image of a man. He seemed quite close, almost to the point of invading her own private space.

"Daniel," Ruth whispered. "Where are you?"

She was slightly dizzy and light headed. Fatigue seemed to grip her and she could feel her legs buckle from under her.

She staggered towards the kitchen area and sat on a stool. A glass panel slid open on the breakfast bench. From inside, Ruth's small laptop emerged and began to boot up. As soon as the operating systems was accessible a programme was activated. It was the book. Everything they had been collecting. Everything Samuelson had spent the past couple of decades in researching the benefits of the words contained in the document. Once a paper based manuscript, now just a series of ones and zeros, but so beautifully composed these words had great power.

Ruth shook her head. Where had these thoughts come from? Who is Daniel? Daniel. Her eyes fluttered as she tried to remember who this Daniel was. She looked towards the shower room, and at the corner of her eye saw a naked man step out of the cubicle but when she looked straight at the shower unit there was no one there. She heard a man's voice over near the curtains. Again she caught a glimpse of a man watching the streets but when she tried to look straight at the windows he was gone.

"Get her to look at the puzzle," demanded Reeves. "She has it solved, she just needs to connect the two."

The doctor looked at him bewildered.

"But we're not controlling this." He looked shocked.

"What do you mean?" boomed Reeves, gradually turning red with anger.

"The influence is coming from somewhere else, we have no more control over her."

"Then pull the plug, man. Go on do it. Now!" Reeves barked.

The doctor made his way over to the wall socket to pull the plug but as he reached down to tug the lead an electric current surged through the cable and he was electrocuted. His singed body collapsed to the floor.

"Who are you?" ask Ruth as she found herself standing in front of a tall man dressed in white. Though she tried she could not properly see his features, not in detail any way, just a sense of outline and that he looked human.

"I am."

"Yes?" smiled Ruth. "Who?"

"I am the Word," said the man.

Serenity enveloped Ruth's whole being.

"What do you want of me?" she felt uncertain.

"To follow me, nothing more."

"I feel tired."

"I know."

"What about Daniel?"

"He is waiting for you."

"And the others?"

"Yes, them too."

"What do I need to do?"

"Let go."

Ruth could see her apartment filling up with light. She had no fear, but neither did she have any strength to resist. She just let the light surround her. Then a thought enter her mind.

"What about the puzzle?"

"It is finished, what is hidden will be revealed," the man

answered.

"How?"

"Because you listened and shared what you heard."

"I don't understand."

"And you won't, but that's okay," the man smiled.

There appeared before Ruth a blue fracture, as if the fabric of space had been torn, dazzling her with its brightness. The man held Ruth's hand and led her through the light. Beside the laptop lay the adapter that Ruth had used to store the data to turn the text into the 3D image she was after. A spark jumped between it and the laptop and everything grew brilliant white.

Reeves looked at what had happened in the hologram and saw Ruth vanish into the blue light.

"No, I can't lose you know," screamed Reeves. "You're too precious."

He spun round to see Ruth's physical body had begun to glow. Shafts of light pushed open her eyelids. It also came from her mouth and out of her ears. Reeves was struck first. He screamed as he tried to protect his face with his android arm. His flesh and clothing burnt away almost instantly. Underneath his skin was revealed the metallic skeleton. A fraction of a second later the metal began to melt and what was left of Reeves lay in a small mercury-like puddle of liquid metal on the floor.

The light did not stop there. Within a minute it had engulfed the globe. In an instance, everything had been changed. Those who would die, perished and everyone else, found life renewed.

"Johnny, it's okay. You can come out now," stated Deborah. From inside a cave, Johnny emerged from the shattered ruin of what was once the large underground basilica, shielding his eyes from the brilliant sunlight.

"Is it safe, sis?"

Deborah, full of confidence climbed up onto a mount to survey the surrounding area.

"Sure is. I think all the sinfulness has gone."

"Deborah, do you think it's really true?"

"We're here aren't we?"

The sun tore through the parting clouds. Above them the blue sky seemed more vivid. No dust filtered it out or made it look dirty, it just seemed clear and fresh. As Deborah and Johnny stood in awe of the view, they were joined by Daniel. He shielded his eyes from the brightness.

"What do you remember, Daniel?" asked Deborah.

"I'm not sure, the alarm was sounding and the screen kept repeating 'Wormwood Virus Activated'. Then someone hit me over the head."

"What do you know, Johnny?" Deborah quizzed her brother.

"I was working with the African in the basilica," Johnny replied. "Daniel was dragged in unconscious. I saw the African appear to speed up. He went electric blue and then completely white light. I thought I saw him multiply and become a blur. He seemed to shoot off in all directions and then I saw various people standing beside me who weren't there moments before. Samuelson was one of them, then you Debs. Then many more."

"How old are you, Johnny?" asked Daniel.

"Twenty, I'm a year off finishing my degree."

"Who's been teaching?"

"The African."

"Hey, look," cried out one of the technicians. "There is someone coming."

All eyes turned to see the lone figure making its way towards them from the centre of Northampton city.

"Who is it?" ask Johnny.

"It's a woman."

Daniel stepped closer a few feet, trying to shield the sunlight with his hand cupped over his eyes. He hesitated for a moment then a broad smile broke across his face.

"It's Ruth. She's alive."

"How do we know it's Ruth?"

A blue glow eminated from her whole body as she strolled towards them.

"Has anyone got a geiger counter?" asked Deborah.

"Nothing electronic works," called out another technician.

"And you may find it never does," remarked Samuelson as he pulled himself out of the hole leading from the basilica. "We have entered a new age, a new beginning. Everything starts all over. A fresh start."

George John Kingsnorth

Daniel 12.1-3

'At that time Michael, the great prince who protects your people, will arise. There will be a time of distress such as has not happened from the beginning of nations until then. But at that time your people – everyone whose name is found written in the book – will be delivered. Multitudes who sleep in the dust of the earth will awake some to everlasting life, others to shame and everlasting contempt. Those who are wise will shine like the brightness of heavens, and those who lead many to righteousness, like the stars for ever and ever.'

A novel by

ERROL BADER

Geocache (Paperback Book - Thriller)

High in the Austrian Alps a solo pilot flies his high tech aircraft into a cloud filled canyon. A driving snow storm doesn't prevent a computer specialist leaving his car to walk into the Black Forest. Guided by satellite navigation both are drawn to an appointment they dare not miss.

A tragic accident above the Denver skyline puts the head of the Global Geocache Society into a coma triggering a deadly game across Europe as Victoria Kavanagh, his Chief of Security, races to find a rare donor.

Alerted by an Interpol Code Purple warning, Inspector Sean Mason gives chase to a predator, only to cross paths with Victoria. Can she be trusted or is she the one he is pursuing?

About the author of 'Geocache':

Errol Bader lives in Denver, Colorado with his wife Judith. He served as a White House Advance Man during the early Reagan years. He is a partner in USAERO LLC, the regional distributor for several aircraft manufacturers in the south western United States. Mr. Bader is cofounder of Aviation Mentors, advising owners of high performance aircraft and is a prolific airman holding many pilot ratings

For more information visit
www.gullionmedia.co.uk